REPULSE
MONKEY

ALSO BY DICK CLUSTER

Return to Sender

REPULSE MONKEY

DICK CLUSTER

Dick Cluster

to Betty, personally,

Dick Cluster

E. P. DUTTON
NEW YORK

Publisher's Note: This novel is a work of fiction.
Names, characters, places, and incidents either are the product
of the author's imagination or are used fictitiously,
and any resemblance to actual persons, living or dead,
events, or locales is entirely coincidental.

Published in the United States by E. P. Dutton,
a division of Penguin Books USA Inc.,
2 Park Avenue, New York, N.Y. 10016.

Published simultaneously in Canada by Fitzhenry and Whiteside,
Limited, Toronto.

Library of Congress Cataloging-in-Publication Data
Cluster, Dick, 1947-
Repulse monkey / Dick Cluster. — 1st ed.
p.   cm.
ISBN 0-525-24811-0
I. Title.
PS3553.L88R46   1989
813'.54—dc19   89-1287
CIP

ISBN: 0-525-24811-0

Designed by Rocco Piscatello

1   3   5   7   9   10   8   6   4   2

First Edition

The two stanzas on p. 43 are from "Into the Twilight" by
W. B. Yeats and are from The Collected Poems of W. B. Yeats.
Reprinted by permission of A. P. Watt Ltd. on behalf of
Michael B. Yeats and Macmillan London Ltd.

Steve Halpern, given to meditation in motion in many forms, long ago introduced me to both cross-country skiing and tai chi chuan. For my knowledge of tai chi I am also grateful to Arthur Goodridge, Linda Harrington, John McMahon, and the writing of Master T. T. Liang. They are not responsible for any distortions of that art in this book. I am grateful to my students at the University of Massachusetts at Boston for sharing their spirit and their thoughts. For timely, constructive, and mutual criticism, it has been a pleasure to be a member of a writers' group with Candice Cason, Frances Lang, Lucy Marx, Barbara Neely, and Kate White.

REPULSE MONKEY

PROLOGUE

The winter twilight made everything fuzzy. It smoothed the hard edges left by the passage of the big plow. It rendered physical details, which might recur with frightening intensity, mercifully indistinct. In this twilight the driver did not switch on his headlamps. He knew the road. He knew what would be on it. He did not want to illuminate the enormity of what he was going to do. It was bad enough in his imagination: the brute, machine-powered mangling of flesh and bone.

What would happen reminded him of the slaughterhouse that girl had described. It reminded him of bits and pieces Paul had coughed up about Vietnam. He accelerated around the curve, the car an extension of his hands, his feet, his will. Except his will wasn't his own. That was what was worst about it. He felt he was not so much driving as being driven over the edge of a cliff, being hurled off a high cornice of snow. He didn't think it was going to work. He doubted there was much of a future for him after this.

He didn't know how right he was.

1

MOTION IN STILLNESS

"...too many changes at once," Alex was saying. He recognized this for a rationalization, and an old, barnacle-encrusted one to boot. He wondered how many other times it had been enunciated, sotto voce, over this same slippery table, by men or women whose fingertips traced, as his did, circles of diluted bourbon on the black Formica top. He envied the piano player, whose dry fingers glided brilliantly over shiny keys.

The pianist, Meredith had said, was playing a song cycle by Franz Peter Schubert. Alex hadn't been able to identify the composer, though he could have said it was a European who worked after Bach and before Stravinsky. He did happen to know one surprising fact about Schubert—at least it had been surprising to him—which was that he had died even younger than Mozart, at the age of thirty-one. "Hey, listen," Alex had said more than once since coming upon this fact, "I've already outlived Schubert by nine years, and Che Guevara by one."

Tonight Alex had expected jazz piano, not classical. And why not, when he had watched the pianist amble in from his break: a dapper man, rimless glasses and well-shaped mustache, a sort of older Herbie Hancock, though then Alex had realized that Herbie Hancock himself wasn't so young anymore. The musician had sat down, flexed his long brown fingers, and conjured these august Germanic rhythms out of the machine.

It was okay, though, finding classical rather than jazz tunes in the piano bar tonight. This was a night of celebration, during which Alex was not inclined to be critical of things. Besides, this was a town whose ear had always been more attuned to Europe than to Africa or New Orleans. This was Cambridge, Massachusetts, after all.

Meredith, Alex thought, ought to be happy about the music.

3

She had been brought up to play the classics on a spinet for the amusement of visitors, but she enjoyed them nonetheless. He stopped drawing circles and let his hand rest on hers, smoothing his fingertips over her knuckles, feeling for barnacles there. The pair of them had come to this dark and spacious piano bar to celebrate a one-year milestone. They were happy in this, though the words *Happy Anniversary* were not going to be formed by either partner's once-married lips.

"Rubbish," Meredith said as Alex's hand played its exploratory tune. "If you don't want us to live together, you wouldn't be bringing it up. You're afraid to take the plunge, that's all."

"And you're not?"

"I'm afraid of not taking it."

"I know," Alex said. "You want to be able to invite the faculty to a housewarming while all my faculties are intact." He squeezed her hand to show that any meanness in this bad but spontaneous joke was his. He knew that Meredith respected his effort. For all her skill with words, she did not play with them very well. "So. By this time next year. How about that?"

"Yes," Meredith answered. A smile split her long, lightly freckled face and dimpled her otherwise sharp chin. "Isn't that what you've had in mind all evening to say? I wonder what else you've already decided in the privacy of your head."

"A piano. I'd like a piano in the parlor and a pool table in the conservatory. You can teach Maria to tinkle one kind of ivories and I'll teach her to shoot the others."

Since his marriage, Alex had been through a number of more or less serious relationships. None of them had involved giving up his and his daughter's separate address. So he mocked the idea of living with Meredith, even as he admitted he was ready to give the nuclear family a second, if different, try. "Do you know anything about player pianos?" he added. "Terry asked me if I'd take a look at what's wrong with his."

Meredith shook her head but smiled. Alex squeezed her hand once more and then brought his up to rummage in his beard. "I told him maybe it was waiting. Motion in stillness, stillness in motion." Alex's tai chi teacher was the only authority figure, other than his doctor, whom he had admitted into his effort to survive a cancer and thus keep living longer than Schubert, longer than Che. Still, Alex found he could bear the master-student business with Sifu Terry Newcombe—and the solemnity

4

of the Chinese ritual itself—only by cracking enough jokes to keep it at bay. "He said it would be worth a month's tuition for me to open the thing up."

"I remember one that worked," Meredith said. "They're... air-driven, aren't they?"

Alex nodded. He imagined the small, pink, and very British Reverend Phillips delivering a lecture on air-driven machinery to his red-haired, green-eyed, watchful daughter. Meredith would have returned a level stare to her father, but she would have taken in the content and made it her own. Alex thought it would be nice to sit here with her and not talk much more, to hold hands and listen to the sounds the pianist's skillful muscles made as they worked out on the keys. Although it would be nice, too, to go home before they were too tired to want to make love. They should want to—not have to—on the evening that celebrated the end of their first year. But Alex had no desire to go out and face the icy streets—and there was always the morning, and anyway by now there was more than one way of making love. He felt in his pocket for a dime so he could call the new sitter to make sure that a while past midnight would be okay. "Let's stay longer," he said hopefully. "I'll call Suzanne."

The phone was next to the smoking section, so as Alex dialed he waved the heavy cloud from his nose and eyes. Speaking of milestones, he thought, finding sitters would soon be behind him. Maria was more and more willing and able to take care of herself. It was a matter of coming up with just one or two more sitters, to get through one or two more years. Meredith's student Suzanne Lutrello seemed like a perfect if expensive discovery. A sitter over twenty was justified in charging five dollars an hour, Alex thought. Shit, he charged twenty-five to take apart and put together inanimate objects, cars. But then, she shouldn't be asleep in front of the tube like one of those thirteen-year-olds. Why was the phone ringing for such a long, disturbing time?

Maybe, despite instructions about bedtime, Suzanne and Maria were deep in conversation. He should feel flattered that a college student considered his daughter better entertainment than a book or TV. Or maybe Maria was long since in bed, and Suzanne was in the bathroom and would soon pick up the damn phone. Across the darkened lounge he could see Meredith unconcerned, watching the fingers of the man at the piano. Meanwhile, the phone continued to ring. Alex doubted that he could

5

have misdialed his own number. But there was nothing to do but hang up and try again.

When the ringing stopped on number four this time, Alex discovered how long he had been holding his breath. The carbon dioxide whooshed out of his lungs. He inhaled carcinogenic tobacco vapors, but he was grateful for the sound of his daughter's businesslike telephone voice.

"Checking out the midnight hour, kiddo?" he said. "Let me talk to Suzanne, okay?"

Maria didn't answer, nor was there a sound of her clunking down the phone. Alex could feel that she was standing, thinking, running her tongue between her upper gum and upper lip. "Suzanne left," Maria announced finally. Alex thought he heard an underlying quaver in counterpoint to the enforced calm. "She said not to answer the phone, but when it rang again I thought it might be you. She's really sorry, it was an emergency. I'm watching TV. It's okay."

"She left?" Surprise and perhaps alcohol made Alex stupidly repeat his daughter's words. "When?"

"Um, about ten. You didn't give any number where she could call."

"Yeah, but—okay, okay, listen, we'll be right home. In the meantime, don't answer the phone."

"Okay. I did hear noises upstairs, too, so I think somebody's home up there."

"Well, that's good. You can always call Anne or Frank in an emergency. Remember, their number is right on the list by phone, under LaFarge?"

"I know," Maria said impatiently. "Um, Alex?"

"Yeah, kiddo?"

"She said it was an emergency," Maria repeated, as if backtracking to get ready for a flying leap. The next sentence came out as a statement inflected like a question. Am I missing some grown-up code the inflection meant, or am I supposed to take this the way it sounds? "She said the emergency was that somebody was dead."

"Um, well, then I guess she really had to go. Listen, maybe, you know, it was like her grandmother or something. It was my fault not to leave a number. It's not *your* fault, anyway. Watch the rest of your show. We'll be right there."

* * *

6

Three nights before, Wednesday night, Alex and Maria had watched eight inches of light, dry, swirling flakes fall on rooftops, on small lawns, on sidewalks and streets. Every time it did this it was new. The flakes left room for an easy kind of joy and wonder as they floated in the glow of the streetlights. "Snow day tomorrow!" Maria had called with a nine-year-old's confident enthusiasm. In the morning she had hopped onto Alex's bed and flashed a quiet told-you-so look as the radio announcer plodded through his long, alphabetical list of school closings. It had been a day of late breakfast, shoveling out, sledding over at Fresh Pond. Alex had let his message machine handle the nervous customers. From long experience, his home number was unlisted. Let them wait; he knew that, deep down, automobile owners were happy to have somebody else car-sit for them on a day like this.

Then the snow had been followed by a half-day of sun and a cold snap. Now Alex cursed both climate and baby-sitter as he and Meredith crab-walked their way along sidewalks where slush had frozen into ice. A crab was what Alex felt like much of the Boston winter—an inefficient, prehistoric, stiff-jointed creature, knees and shoulders and elbows locked, picking its way awkwardly over the slippery ridges and troughs of bootprints fossilized by cold. When he felt his body working against itself like that, he would wonder why he hadn't stayed in California way back when. Especially these days, when his body needed to work for itself, not against. But tonight he thought mostly about getting through the four blocks to the car. He followed Meredith single file along the narrow paths. Once in the car, he repeated out loud the assurances he had been making to himself. "I know she's all right," he said. "I mean I just talked to her, and she sounded fine. But whatever happened, I don't see why Suzanne had to tell her something scary—that somebody died. It's bad enough to run out, I mean, she better have a good explanation for that. But to scare the kid on top of it..."

"It *might* have been a lie," Meredith said doubtfully. "It *is* the handiest excuse. American college students seem to have more deaths in the family than any other group I've met. Mine have lost seven relatives in a month. I've given up trying to guess which ones are true. If it *were* a lie, she might have been mostly conscious of its being untrue. She might have forgotten how real it would be to a child who wouldn't expect her to lie."

"Yeah. Maybe." That could be, Alex thought. He noted this surprising woman's surprising eye again. Meredith had some internal mechanism that spotted pretense as swiftly as ... as a carpenter's level, he had told her once, but he didn't bother with analyzing what he admired in Meredith right now. He was concerned that what she had said clicked with a thought he'd come to by quite a different route.

"It's not only that," he said slowly, trying to slow down his own intuition, to put it into words. "She said *dead*, not *dying*. You might be in a hurry if somebody was dying. You'd want to rush for a last word, or a last look at them breathing. There's not the same kind of hurry if they're dead. Your last chance is gone then —no more consciousness, no more breath."

Meredith brushed Alex's cheek with her hand. Her touch was light, as if she were fearful of intruding. Yet it didn't hesitate or flinch back. "That's perhaps when people are in the biggest hurry," she said. "When it's too late to do anything, that's often when they hurry the most." Alex grunted as he turned sharply but skillfully onto the icy ruts of the small North Cambridge street where he, and half of the time his daughter, lived.

2
OBITS AT LUNCH

In the morning, Sunday morning, they did make love. Alex closed his eyes toward the end, but he thought that Meredith kept hers open. He was glad that ohhh-Alex was part of what came out of her mouth as well as the just plain *ohs* and the *mmmmmMMMMM*. After breakfast, Meredith went home to her word processor, which Alex joked was how she paid her devotions now that she no longer went to church. Maria's friend Georgia came over to play. They played store, and then Georgia robbed the store, and Maria chased her shrieking through the apartment. "Stop, thief!" Maria cried.

Alex was surprised that this archaic phrase stayed in use among children generation after generation.

When that game wore out, he organized them to bake cookies. The baking kept them busy and it also warmed up the house. Meanwhile, he kept himself busy reading, doing laundry, and practicing the new positions he'd be showing Terry tomorrow. He also tried to call Suzanne Lutrello, seven times.

Always the same, no answer. When his own phone rang, he half expected the sitter to be calling him, anxious to apologize or explain. When somebody died, Alex thought, didn't the survivors keep themselves busy with concrete tasks like a phone call to clean up yesterday's social mess? After Georgia left, he went over again with Maria what Suzanne had said. He didn't mind letting her know he was worried. If Maria was worried also, he wanted her to talk. But Maria simply repeated what she'd told him the night before. She added only that she and Suzanne had gotten along well and talked earlier on about "lots of things."

"What kind of things?" Alex pressed, but Maria only said, "Lots of things. I don't know." Alex didn't see what difference it made because on the circumstances of the sitter's departure Maria was very clear: Suzanne had put her to bed but allowed her to stay up reading. Then she'd come into Maria's room and explained that it was an emergency, that somebody was dead, that she was sorry but she had to leave. "She said I was very grown-up, I shouldn't answer the door, and I could stay in bed or I could go in the living room and watch TV until you got home. When I got settled on the couch, she left."

Alex asked whether Suzanne might have meant dead in the sense of "If you don't do that, man, you're dead." Maria's eyes opened wider, as if this was a daring and attractive idea. But she answered, truthfully, "I didn't think about that." She added, "I didn't think it was the right thing for me to ask who died."

Suzanne lived in Dorchester, across the river and on the other side of downtown Boston. When Alex had called her home number last week to set things up for Saturday, she'd answered the phone herself. He didn't know—and neither did Meredith —whether she lived with parents, with roommates, with a boyfriend or girlfriend, or alone. She'd told Meredith that sitting in Cambridge would be okay, because she had friends nearby where she often stayed over. Maybe she was there now, but Alex didn't know where "there" was.

9

After dinner, Meredith came back. Whatever else happened, she spent every other Sunday night with Alex. That way, on the weekends when Alex had Maria, he could still leave the house in time to make Terry's Monday-morning class. At five minutes to seven he was crab-walking down a boot-stamped but unshoveled sidewalk, bitching to himself about the absentee owner of the long brick building where Terry's tai chi studio was.

It was an old industrial building, near the train tracks that separated North Cambridge from the rest of town. It was the kind of building in which they had once cut nuts and bolts from dies, or built radios out of vacuum tubes, or printed catechisms on ancient letterpress machines. Now the place housed a few cabinetmakers, odds and ends of artists, the one-room offices of tiny mail-order firms. The owner sat in Florida collecting the rents, and wouldn't give any thought to hiring a kid or a snow-blower service to clean up the walk. Any day he'd sell to a developer who would make the place over into condos or software firms.

Alex turned the knob on one of the double doors and found that it was unlocked. Terry was already here; Alex wouldn't have to stand around waiting in the cold. He was grateful the Sifu's powers had helped his tires to root themselves firmly and propel the old rusting Rabbit out of any rut. Alex knew the Rabbit well, because he bartered repairs for lessons. *Sifu* was Chinese for "teacher." SIFU TERRY NEWCOMBE was what it said, in copper-colored aluminum letters, on the studio door.

Inside, Alex joined three other students in their warmups, letting the stiffness in joints and muscles slip away. His morning tiredness began to evaporate like the steam that clanked in the pipes. He bent, straightened, arched, tried to remember to breathe. Each warmup posture stretched quadriceps and hamstrings and God knew what other inner components tightened by cold and age and improper use. Alex tried to smooth out the curve in his back, tried to relax the muscles that weren't being used. He tried to let the *chi* begin to flow.

The seven-fifteen train whistle sounded, joined by the higher-pitched clickety-clack as the wheels clattered over the track. Commuter train, bound downtown. Alex told himself to let the noise and the mental image go by as inexorably as the train. Don't shut it out, don't hold onto it either. Would Meredith remember to ask Maria to remember her homework, her extra sneakers for the classroom, her lunch? Would he be able to get that 144 with the frozen fuel pump started, so he could drive it into the shop? These minor worries drifted by as another train passed the other way. Terry said, "Okay, Alex, let's see Punch Under Elbow. Let's see it from, uh, from the Slanting Single Whip."

Alex smiled. He shuffled his long and angular body for one more loosening, then tried to square his hips, sink into his legs, and feel the connection between his feet and the floor. He watched himself in the full-length mirror—a black-bearded, curly-haired scarecrow, thin lips pulled back, eyes glittering, sharp nose parting the air before it. He assumed what he hoped was a presentable bow stance, feet spread, one forward of the other. Then, very slowly, he shifted his weight back onto the right foot, stepped forward with the left, extended his arms, stepped with the right, swiveled from the hips, and rotated one arm counterclockwise and the other clockwise as his hips swiveled back the other way.

Make yourself light, he told himself in Terry's voice. Spread your wings like a bird about to fly away. He tried to feel his arms and legs as porous, as collections of molecules moving insubstantially through a denser space. Through oil, through honey, through dry beach sand. He ended on his right foot, the left one emptied on the heel, the right hand punching under the left elbow. All movements ceasing together, motion becoming stillness before it would become motion again.

Alex smiled a second time. Punch Under Elbow had been impossible two weeks ago, but it wasn't now. He checked himself in the mirror, relaxed his stretched lips and hunched shoulders, and moved into the Repulse Monkey. That meant walking slowly backward along invisible tracks while fending off an attacker with smooth, alternating extensions of the arms. On each step his working knee trembled as it took all his body's weight. When he'd counted five steps he stopped, considering his bearded stork self in the mirror.

"Not bad," Terry said, laughing. Terry's dark brown face creased and his eyes stayed soft. "You're all up here in your arms, though. Let the energy sink into your belly, into your legs. Do it again, with me. Slower."

Alex did, and as he practiced the motions again and again he gradually forgot snow, ice, daughter, lunch, homework, girl-

11

friend, future plans, job. Other concerns came and went—the injured foot of Celtics forward Kevin McHale, the balance in his own checkbook, the war in El Salvador grinding on and on—and by the time he was doing his warm-down stretches, only two puzzles presented themselves to his conscious mind. One was how best to phrase the question he wanted to put to his doctor later today. The other was what he would do if Meredith returned from school without seeing or hearing from Suzanne. At the end of class, after silent standing meditation, everyone sat cross-legged in a circle where questions and comments were in order. Alex asked about the label of his latest accomplishment.

"Tell me something," Alex said. "We've warded off, and whipped, and spread our wings. We've embraced tiger, and according to the list you gave us, we're going to creep down like a snake and part a wild horse's mane. But Repulse Monkey is the first time we've walked backward, *away* from something."

Terry nodded. He was shorter than Alex but twice as wide, an Afro-American with a classic Chinese build. Everything about him seemed so solid. Maybe that was why Alex felt the need to probe, to tease.

"The only time?"

Terry nodded again.

"And yet a monkey is the smallest and least powerful animal we're dealing with. I mean, compared like to a tiger..."

Terry blinked his eyes. He always invited the students to ask questions, but he rarely answered them except with a question in return. Even when Alex had asked whether he might be related to Don Newcombe, who'd pitched for the Dodgers when Alex was a boy, that was what Terry had done. Alex's question had been only half a joke, because after all Newcombe wasn't all that common a name. It sounded British, especially with the Terrence. Maybe West Indian, Alex had thought. Anyway, Terry had countered with another question: "Do you want to bring your bat next time and see what my fast ball can do?" And that had led to a discussion of planting one foot, shifting weight, directing energy through the hips and ribs into the arm and hand, and other intricacies of the art of tai chi.

"Well, why?" Alex asked now, a little petulantly. "I mean, does a monkey have some especially dangerous significance in Chinese tradition?"

"I don't know," Terry said. "Does a monkey have some especially dangerous significance to you?"

"Well," Alex squirmed. It did, he realized, have one that related to his disease. That was why he didn't like the idea of retreat. "I mean, sort of like a monkey on your back?"

"If you say so," Terry replied.

After class, Alex had a habit of taking himself out for breakfast before going to work. When he'd moved into North Cambridge, there had been at least six breakfast joints scattered along the stretch of Massachusetts Avenue above Porter Square. Now they'd become an Indian restaurant, a Mexican one, a sushi bar, a fast-food franchise, and a video rental place. Still thinking about the monkey, Alex downed his eggs and toast at the one place left. He looked up and said, "Thanks, Mary," when the waitress refilled his cup and cleared away his plate. He was off nitrites (no bacon, no hot dogs) and food coloring (no M&Ms), but once his chemotherapy had ended, he had decided to let himself drink all the coffee he pleased. Mary, the waitress, was a cousin or aunt of his landlady, though he couldn't remember which. "Listen," he asked her, "do you know anybody named Lutrello that lives around here?"

"Lutrello? Not that I know about, dear. Manny Lucibello, he comes in once in a while. He brings in the baby, his granddaughter. He buys her a doughnut, she's a sweet kid. Lutrello, you said. No, doesn't mean anything to me. You could ask one of the other girls. Maybe they would know."

"That's okay," Alex said. Mary was probably sixty, though maybe not. With that pleasantly puffy Irish face, it was hard to tell. Meredith could pass for Irish sometimes, she said, because of the hair color and the eyes. Alex thought her hair was too dark a red and too limp for this purpose, and her face was distinctively oval, not round. Still, at the University of Massachusetts at Boston, the possibility that her accent was some kind of upscale Irish rather than British did get her past initial hostility at times.

Meredith's image stayed with Alex as he drove a crowded half-mile to his shop in Somerville, near Union Square. So did what she had said about the vanished baby-sitter, in her clipped, logical tone. "Probably Suzanne's afraid," Meredith had reasoned. "First she met Professor Phillips's boyfriend, and then she

13

let him down. She'll skip one class for real or pretended mourning, and then she'll come, sit way in the back, and be relieved when I ask her to stay and talk with me to clear things up. I'll suggest that she call you, and you can give her a proper bawling out."

You're Maria's parent, not Suzanne's, Alex had interpreted this to mean. Suzanne isn't your problem to worry about. Meredith was younger than Alex, only thirty-two in fact, but even she said she always had to remind herself that she was a teacher, not a mother, to these kids. Suzanne was a grown woman anyway, about twenty-three, hardly a kid.

It's getting tough when people in their twenties seem so young, Alex thought as he pulled his '75 Saab to the curb in front of the sign depicting a horned, Viking-esque half-man/half-animal on wheels. BLOND BEASTS, it proclaimed. NORTHERN EUROPEAN AUTOS REPAIRED. Inside, the digital display on the phone machine announced that there were five messages waiting. The first three and the last one turned out to be customers who hoped (vainly) that calling in during the weekend got them on some kind of preferential waiting list. The fourth message, though, was from Suzanne.

"Look, Mr. Glaub—um, Alex," her voice said. It was rendered thinner and higher-pitched by the poor electronics of the machine. "I lost your number, but this one was in the book. I'm sure your little girl's okay, isn't she? She's a smart little kid. I'm really sorry to let you down. The thing is, the only choices I had were bad. While I've got you, can you tell, uh, Ms. Phillips that I'm kind of tied up in a family problem so that's why I'm not gonna be in class Monday I don't think."

Alex rewound so he could listen to Suzanne Lutrello again. Then he reset the machine, changed into overalls, and was about to get to work on the Scirocco, already up on stands, that needed two new universals. But he remembered the Volvo 144 with the broken pump, parked along the narrow driveway, half in and half out of the snow. Its owner had brought it in just before quitting time, pushed down the street by a friend's Ford van. Alex threw on his coat and trudged through the snow to pour two cans of Drygas and a gallon of fuel into the tank. Couldn't hurt, might make it start. He'd a lot rather do the work inside than out. He left the Volvo to sit awhile and went back inside the shop.

The U-joint bolts were rusted and recalcitrant, as always. Alex, underneath, hoped the *chi*—the harmoniously flowing energy he'd freed up during Terry's class—wasn't being driven screaming from his back and shoulders by the rigors of reaching and twisting a pair of wrenches at this angle. Still, the process had a ritual about it that was comforting, that was like the Chinese discipline in a certain way. The bolts came off finally, and soon the new, well-machined joints were nestled safely in their spiders, ready to handle thirty thousand miles of torque and stop-and-go. Alex rolled his creeper out from under the Scirocco and went in the back to wash his hands. Then he called Meredith, who he thought would now be back in her office after Women Fiction Writers 1910–30. This was the class Suzanne would have missed.

"She sounded sort of scattered," Alex told Meredith after reporting what Suzanne had left on tape, "but not especially worried or scared. I won't hire her to baby-sit again, but I guess she's probably all right. It's funny, though. She said 'family problems,' not 'my grandmother died' or 'one of my family passed away.'"

"Well," Meredith said, "perhaps you'll figure that out, and if not, then she'll eventually explain it to me. Good luck this afternoon. I'll call you tonight, all right?"

After Alex hung up, he wriggled into his sweatshirt from Maria's school and covered it with an old parka from which the synthetic fiber was spilling. He trudged out into the cold to try to start the Volvo. The engine turned over but wouldn't fire. He got out, opened the hood, and reached inside. The fuel-pump bolts were a long reach from above, but happily they came out right away. Even with a new pump, though, the engine coughed and died twice before he could drive the car in. He connected a fully charged battery, started the engine once more, listened to its complaints with a stethoscope applied to various critical points. He called the owner at a downtown office to talk her into a tune-up on top of the new pump. Then, when the Volvo was done, he showered and changed back into the clothes in which he had started the day. Terry's class already seemed like a long time ago. This was his lunch break, but today he was using it for business of another sort. On his way out he bought a newspaper. There would be a wait at the blood lab, as always. Maybe the paper would reveal who in Suzanne Lutrello's family had picked Saturday night to die. Alex ate his tuna-salad sandwich on whole wheat as he drove.

At twelve o'clock, the Commonwealth Community Medical Plan was already a zoo. Alex's doctor, though nowhere to be seen, had left a lab slip at the desk. Alex sat in the waiting area under a poster advertising an exhibit of French Impressionists that had taken place in Amsterdam five years before. On his left, a large teenage boy in a leg cast was reading *Hollywood Husbands*. On his right, a small, elderly woman who looked perfectly healthy read a thick, oversize volume called the *Smithsonian Collection of American Comics*. All that his neighbors had in common was never looking at their watches and never looking up. He tried to emulate their example, to concentrate on the local news and obituary pages of the *Boston Globe*.

The news pages yielded five Saturday deaths, none unusual. On Route 128, the belt highway surrounding Boston, three persons were killed in a late-night crash involving two vehicles; blood alcohol tests revealed that one of the drivers had been drunk. In the suburb of Boxford a woman had been shot by her estranged husband; two hours later he had turned himself in to police. In New Hampshire, a Massachusetts woman had been the victim of an accidental vehicular homicide, hit by a car driven by a Massachusetts man; local police theorized that she had not been able to move quickly enough because she was crossing the road while wearing her cross-country skis. None of the victims, killers, or survivors lived in Dorchester; some had Italian names, but not like Lutrello.

The obituary stories featured a retired linotypist, two retired businessmen, a director of nursing, a high school teacher, and a graduate student. Again, none of them seemed to match up with Suzanne. On this page of the paper, the causes of death were not so clear—only short illness, long illness, in the hospital, or unexpectedly at home. Alex, however, allowed himself to speculate further.

Since his own diagnosis, Alex read obituaries neither more nor less than he used to, probably once every two weeks, usually as a form of procrastination when he didn't want to put the newspaper down. He did, though, now spend more time guessing at the concealed medical facts. Today he suspected the unlucky nursing director of a malignancy in breast or lung, and the graduate student of adult leukemia. He had never yet seen his own disease, a relatively slow overpopulation of malignant lymph cells, listed as a cause of death. He assumed, however, that a few of the long illnesses of relatively younger persons had been it.

Alex knew it might seem, well, unproductive, but he didn't consider this hobby of reading obituaries macabre. Like everything else in the newspapers, he thought, obituaries were a blend of entertainment and propaganda. To *learn* anything, you had to read between the lines. Besides, he was almost always generous in the way he imagined the subjects. For instance, he gave both the nursing director and the graduate student fulfilled lives, good medical treatment, a will to live, and a philosophical acceptance of their deaths before the end. Still, searching for a clue to Suzanne's family tragedy gave him an added purpose for his hobby today. He had just started to scan the fine-printed alphabetical death notices when his name was called. He skipped to the *L*'s, but they provided only a Larabee, a Lipkin, a Luciano, and a Lynch.

Carrying the paper with him, Alex chatted with the technician and gave up two test tubes of rich, dark-looking blood. The technician wore surgical gloves to protect herself against AIDS. Alex wanted to reassure her that his blood was not dangerous. The cells of his immune system multiplied too fast, but they were infected by no virus. As far as fighting off diseases was concerned, they did their job.

Once his blood was taken, he went upstairs to Medical Specialties, where he began again to work his way carefully through the death notices from the top: Abrahams, of Brookline, seventy-two, survived by her loving son and daughter, six grandchildren, two great grandchildren, flowers may be sent to...One of the *B*'s, Brady, had no children and was survived not only by loving parents and siblings but also by a beloved friend. Was that obit language, Alex wondered, for "gay"? He was midway through the alphabet when his name was called again. He folded the paper back to the front page but brought it with him to the examining room. He undressed, sat on the Naugahyde examining table looking at the headlines without reading them. He tried to make his breathing regular and slow. Finally his doctor's cheerful voice inquired, "Alex?" as she gave the door a proprietary, I-assume-I'm-not-intruding knock.

"Yeah," Alex said, and she swooped in to announce that he certainly looked fine, and how had he been? "Fine," Alex said, so Dr. Wagner smiled and said, "Now let's see what else there is to see." She asked him bright questions about the car-repair business while feeling carefully the flesh below his ears, in the front and back of his neck, in his armpits, belly, and groin. "Relax your jaw," she said once, and Alex tried to, though he felt that this kind of instruction was Terry's department, not hers. She turned away to wash her hands, giving him the sense she was taking time to memorize the shape of whatever she had just perceived. The whole thing was strangely unscientific—no numbers, no instruments, just a laying-on of hands.

"I don't feel a thing," she announced when she was ready. "Do you?"

"Well," Alex said. "Not really, but it's hard for me to tell." Now it was time to pop the question. "So—how soon would you be surprised if they came back?"

"Well, in cases of complete remission, which is what I would call yours . . . as you know, with your particular cell type, we don't think there are any complete remissions in the sense of cures . . . in what's called clinically complete remission, the literature says that tumors can recur as soon as one month later, or as late as three or four or even more years. Then they commonly respond well to treatment again."

"I understand that," said Alex. "But in my case—I mean, given, I don't know, age and history and response to drugs and all that—if they came back in another three months, say, would you be unhappily surprised?"

"I'd be un*happy*," she said. The smile slipped away, but there was no indecision, no considering, no wrinkling of the brow. "Your last course of treatment was, what, two months ago? It would put you on the less . . . fortunate end of the curve to have a recurrence that soon. It might indicate that we should consider a different kind of treatment. So let's hope they don't, all right?" The smile reappeared. "But surprised? I don't think I get paid to be surprised."

Alex wondered if the implication was that she did get paid to be unhappy—that the contact with failure was one justification for the exorbitant salaries that doctors received. He didn't think so. She was talking fast, making up her answer as she went along. Alex understood this. No matter how difficult the questions,

18

doctors, like mechanics, were always supposed to have answers on the tips of their tongues.

"Okay," he said. "Let's hope it doesn't. When do you want to see me again, two more months?"

"Yes. You can call on, let's see, Wednesday, to check your blood work. And call me, of course, if you notice anything wrong. How's your daughter?"

"Great."

"And . . . Meredith?"

Alex noticed the hesitation. It might mean that she'd had trouble coming up with Meredith's name. Or it might mean that she considered a two-month information gap quite a long one in an unmarried relationship. Meredith had insisted on meeting this Dr. Wagner, of course. By now, they had each been in Alex's life approximately the same amount of time.

"Twelve months and still counting," Alex said. "I'll tell them both you said hello."

"And . . . no more adventures?"

This was the problem, Alex thought, about being in a Medical Phase of one's life, such as he seemed forever destined to be. He liked his doctor fine, but it was a drag to have to tell her everything that might be remotely relevant to his condition—such as the emergency stitches he'd received to close a knife wound in a time that already seemed very far away.

"Not yet," he smiled. And added, holding onto the opaque smile, "So far, I don't have any planned."

Like a good patient, he went back to work. Aside from replaying the conversation about recurrence several times and studying it from several angles, he didn't think about much besides the job he had to do. Customers came by to pick up their cars. Just as the last one left, and he was punching himself out on the antique time clock he had rescued from a Vermont junk shop, the phone rang one last time. He listened to the recorder click on, listened to his distorted voice dully repeating that Blond Beasts had been reached and, without enthusiasm, advising that a message could be left. I wouldn't wait that out, he thought. But this caller did.

"Oh shit," she began. "Oh, fuck this machine. Are you there? This is Suzanne."

Alex was across the room in a leap. Obscurely, he felt he was confusing Meredith's student with his daughter—as if he needed for Suzanne to be all right in order to make her abandonment of

19

Maria okay, no harm done. Or was it the opposite, that he needed her to be in trouble? Anyway, he soared over a heap of parts to embrace the phone. "I'm here. This is Alex. Suzanne."

"Tell Ms. Phillips, please, that I'm kind of in trouble and I need her to help me out. I want her to meet me for a drink, up in Saugus where I am." Alex thought she was breathing fast, catching her breath. Now that she was talking to him, rather than railing at the machine, her speech had a rehearsed rather than extemporaneous sound. "Do you know the Typhoon, that restaurant, the Typhoon?"

"Yeah, the one—"

"Good, then tell her, ask her to meet me there, please, in an hour, or as close after that as she can."

"Okay, I'll—"

"Good. Thanks a lot. Good-bye."

3

SERGEANT TREVISONE'S CALL

The Typhoon Restaurant was housed in a huge imitation Polynesian temple along one of metropolitan Boston's finest strips of Americana, the old Route 1, heading northeast toward New Hampshire and Maine. Alex had not been inside the place in years, but he remembered the ambience as roomy, dark, and anonymous, and he remembered the long list of exotic cocktails available to drink. The *pièce de résistance*, the Typhoon Tahiti, mixed rum with three different French liqueurs. Like a storm aboard ship, Alex supposed, it would either knock you over or make you throw up.

The restaurant lay along the same stretch of Route 1, he explained to Meredith, as the steak house with the giant steer and saguaro cactus out front, and also the restaurant that was shaped like a ship. These big eateries were scattered among car stereo places and snowmobile dealers, bargain outlets and tuxedo renters, nightclubs and Italian restaurants moved out from the North End. Alex said that besides being concerned about Suzanne, he wanted to be along to show Meredith, a foreigner, these important sites. Meredith saw through this explanation, he was sure, but she didn't object. All she said was, "All right. But remember, Alex, I'm the one Suzanne requested to come."

So they had all three arrived at the Typhoon, a picturesque family group. Alex and Meredith and Maria would have dinner. Meredith would talk with Suzanne and find out what kind of trouble she was in. Now the waitress lit the candle, handed Alex three oversized menus, and asked whether he wanted anything from the bar. Alex declined. He drummed on the red tablecloth, his index fingers making soft, muffled thuds. He paid no attention to this drumming until he noticed what the rhythm was. The Beatles, "With a Little Help from My Friends." The song was twenty years old by now, though Alex believed he could remember clearly when it had been new.

Suzanne did not exactly qualify as one of Meredith's friends. She had taken one class from her during the summer, and then had dropped by Meredith's office in December, when Meredith had just returned from her half-semester's work in London. Suzanne had said that she wanted to know what Meredith would be teaching next. Then they'd talked a bit about Suzanne's plans. Suzanne had originally planned to be a nurse. If she could get a nursing B.S. under her belt, she'd thought, she would always be able to make a living. But she was considering switching to anthropology or psych. Why, Meredith had asked, intrigued. "You see a lot of the world if you're an anthropologist," Suzanne had answered. "Maybe the Amazon, the Andes, some little village in Tuscany. Or with psych, you see a lot about people if you work with their minds." And was she worried about getting a job? "Not if I don't have kids to support. I used to be in a rush to grow up. Now I'm in a rush to slow down."

A young woman with a handle on herself, Alex concluded. He tried to figure out why she had chosen this setting tonight. The restaurant was dark, simulating an outdoor Polynesian garden, illuminated by hanging electric lanterns and by spotlights that shone upward from behind large green leaves and through the waters of the goldfish pools. A lot went on here, Alex guessed. It was probably a place for putting out all sorts of

21

feelers, business or romantic or otherwise. While the Typhoon served predominantly the North Shore towns, it was definitely a highway stop, not a neighborhood place.

Meredith and Maria appeared from behind a tangle of leaves and vines. Meredith shook her head behind Maria's back. They had completed their tour, that meant, and Suzanne wasn't here yet. When the waitress came back, the three of them agreed on spareribs, fried rice, thousand-flavor chicken, and pineapple pork.

The food was, as Alex remembered, greasy and sweet. When it was gone, the adults took turns testing Maria on her spelling list. Then, by candlelight, Maria finished her homework, building the words into sentences in her book.

"Writing is different by candlelight," Meredith said. "The words hover, they're less exact. Somebody or other claims the way we react to printed words in electric light is completely different from the way people used to see handwriting by sunlight or lamps or candles. Though it seems to me more important that now so many more people can read."

Maria said, "It's hard to remember there was a time I couldn't read. That letters were just marks on paper, they didn't mean anything."

"You may never learn to do anything else that makes such a big difference," Meredith told her, winning a broad smile in return.

"I don't know," Alex said. "Wait till you learn how to drive a car." The inner voice wondering who would teach her, whether he, Alex, would be there to teach or watch, was soft and unobtrusive, almost whimsical tonight. In fact—Alex noticed, and congratualated himself—it wasn't all that different from the voice in which Meredith speculated about the effect of lamplight. Alex's self-compliment did not keep him from noticing the tall, graceful, broad-shouldered woman with her Afro cut in a punkish style, severely short on the sides. She passed their table slowly, stopped, and backed up. She regarded Meredith steadily with eyes that seemed a bit too determined, or a bit sinister, on her otherwise fresh and open face. "You're Professor Phillips," she said. There was no question in the tone.

"That's right," Meredith answered politely.

"Suzanne couldn't come herself. She says I should bring you to her." The accent was hard to place. Not New England, nor an accent of the ghetto or the South. A kind of absence of accent, like California. She kept her eyes on Meredith. They weren't slanted, exactly, but they were somehow angular, that was what it was. Maybe she was part Indian—something about her nose seemed Indian to Alex. Her skin was a deep but reddish brown. Her forehead glistened in the wavering light. From nervousness? Alex wondered. But she said calmly enough, "Do you mind if I sit down?"

Meredith slid over on the bench. "I recognize you, but I don't know your name."

"Natalie. You maybe saw me outside of class with Suzanne."

Maybe, Alex thought. Or in the hall, or the cafeteria, or anywhere else. An attractive black woman in a hairdo like that would stand out at UMass, though the last thing anyone, white or black, would do would be to admit it. Alex had one of his infrequent twinges of longing for New York, where, for all the tension, at least people were upfront about matters of race.

"These are Alex and Maria Glauberman," Meredith said.

"Hi." Natalie smiled, but tightly, not showily. Alex watched his daughter try to smile back. She was worried now that Suzanne had failed to appear. Maria didn't like it when a substitute teacher took over at school without explaining why the real teacher wasn't there. She liked to know what was wrong. So did Alex. He put the question both for Maria and for himself.

"Is Suzanne okay?" he asked. "She told Maria that somebody died. Like it was somebody in her family, or a friend."

"Sort of. Let her explain it, okay?"

"Uh-huh," Alex said. "Well, I guess we'll hear it from Meredith, then. I ought to be getting Maria home to bed." He studied the bill and put money on the table. They all walked out together through the parking lot, huge and bare, surrounded by the big snowbanks that multiple storms and plowings had made. The lot was lit as brightly as the restaurant was dark. A safe place, the lights advertised. No muggers, no auto theft. Alex felt like one of the toy figures in a modern Christmas diorama, all Styrofoam snow, midget plastic consumers, and die-cast model cars. Natalie led them to a battered brown Civic four or five years old. There was a City of Cambridge resident sticker on the rear window. Meredith kissed Maria goodnight. The Civic sped out of the lot and turned right, north, onto Route 1.

Alex took Maria's hand and led her to his own car. At the lot exit, he waited patiently for a break in the traffic and turned left, south toward home. The highway was no diorama, more like an old amusement park funhouse. Neon and fluorescent signs at the entrances to stores, motels, and nightspots loomed and disappeared. Most of the names were Italian, though the Irish and the Jews also had their place. This was commuterland, home of the building boom that had followed World War II. This was where the old immigrant groups went as they leapfrogged out of Boston. Suzanne might pick a rendezvous here because she had been nearby. Or she might pick a rendezvous because she had not. Meredith had thought Suzanne once mentioned growing up somewhere out here—Saugus, or maybe Lynn or Revere. She thought Suzanne's mother had commuted in to work at the Schraffts candy plant in Charlestown, no longer operating now.

"Strange stuff," he said to Maria. "Maybe Suzanne has to explain to Meredith that she's going to miss more classes or a paper or an exam."

"Or she has to stay at home with somebody," Maria said. "Somebody that can't go out, and she wants Meredith to give her some work to do there."

"That's true," Alex said, and though neither of these explanations was at all convincing, father and daughter had communicated that there were no worries or more adequate speculations that either one of them felt confident enough to discuss. Maria fell asleep on Route 128. Her own black curls, looser than Natalie's, in fact so much like Alex's, mashed against the door. Alex had always thought she had his ex-wife Laura's face with his hair around it, but now this seemed to be changing. Her face was getting thinner; not so cute, but shrewder. He liked seeing more of himself—partly from possessiveness, partly because it was intriguing to see some of his own expressions in female form. However, it was also disconcerting to watch her face change. The face would alter a lot before she learned how to drive, and so would the thinking that went on behind it. She'd be able to get herself stuck, entangled, in her thoughts. She would have those adolescent and becoming-a-woman times when, as Suzanne Lutrello put it, "all the choices I had were bad."

Home, he parked in front and carried Maria inside. She woke up enough to get into pajamas, then dropped right back to sleep. Alex tucked her in bed and returned to his living room to wait. He was jealous of Meredith, summoned so mysteriously.

24

She would face the task of winning Suzanne's trust, of delivering the wise guidance or decisive action that Suzanne seemed to hope Professor Phillips could provide. No adventures planned, he'd told his doc. That didn't mean none hoped for. He shook off these thoughts, began to stretch and then to move slowly, sinuously, through the tai chi form. He didn't push, just allowed his muscles to remember what Terry had told him in class that morning. He had nearly reached the end of what he knew, halfway through the Repulse Monkey, when his telephone rang. He broke off and picked it up. A brusque, official voice asked, "Alex Glauberman there?"

"Yeah. You've got him." Much to his surprise, he thought he recognized the voice. It belonged to the time his doctor had referred to, a strange, eventful time in September, in the midst of chemotherapy, when he had brushed close to other people's deaths, violent ones, and had had dealings with this man. A rush of smells and sensations washed over Alex—nausea and excitement, acrid smoke, sweetness, sex, fear, and determination. But all the cues and all the associated memories floated amid a haze, a chemical haze that made what had gone on only partly real life, and partly a kind of parentheses. He told himself a lot of male, brusque, Boston-accented voices sounded the same.

"Sergeant Trevisone," the man contradicted him.

Efficient Sergeant Trevisone, who must have pulled Alex's unlisted number out of some closed-case file. He was a small, lean, suspicious, intelligent man—a homicide detective, Cambridge police. Alex swallowed.

"What—is something wrong?"

"Your girlfriend. You'll need to come get her."

"Come get her?" Harm to Meredith was not something he'd imagined.

"She's okay. She just hasn't got a car, is all. She arrived at the scene of a homicide. We had to bring everybody down here."

A homicide. Alex heard again the voice that had called his shop for help.

"Was it . . . Suzanne Lutrello?" he asked.

"Suzanne Lutrello," Trevisone repeated. "You knew her?"

"She baby-sat for my daughter," Alex answered. She was only twenty-two or twenty-three, he wanted to add. That's much too young to be dead. The previous time he'd dealt with this detective, the victim had been a much more proper age; that is, he'd been older than Alex by quite a few years. Suzanne's death was too sudden, and Alex had spoken with her only hours before. But sudden was what homicide generally meant. Slowly Alex realized something else, which was that Trevisone did not need to call him up to tell him Meredith needed a ride. Surely Meredith had a dime. Trevisone was bothered that Alex Glauberman had popped up again. Trevisone wanted to talk to him face to face. "If you want to see me tonight," Alex said, "I'll need to bring my daughter along."

"Somebody'll take care of her," Trevisone replied.

Somebody didn't take *enough* care of Suzanne, Alex wanted to say. He didn't relish explaining any of this to Maria as they drove across town to the police station. Cambridge, a city of about one hundred thousand, maintained only one. The station house was located discreetly in Central Square, out of sight of the universities that dominated Kendall and Harvard squares on either side. How was he supposed to explain this death to Maria, to put it in context, to take the menace out? *Meredith went to see Suzanne and when she got there Suzanne was kaput.* He shrugged angrily. Maria knew about murder. It was there every night on the cop shows, on the TV news, the broadcaster hawking his wares like a carnival barker in an excited, pretend-shock voice. Somehow Maria would sort it out, would put it in her perspective. How would it stack up anyway, to a nine-year-old, against the question of whether or not she'd go to the police station in pajamas? She'd said absolutely no to that.

He didn't explain anything yet. First he wanted to find out the story himself. Dressed, Maria sat silently with the policewoman behind the desk. Alex turned and followed Sergeant Trevisone through the doors. Trevisone's office had not changed: same insurance-agency calendar, same steel desk, same battered, padded-seat, straight-backed chairs. Meredith was waiting in one of these, her own back straight but eyes tired and shoulders slumped. Alex walked toward her, but her eyes lifted and shoulders straightened to say hands off. He didn't know whether that meant *I'm handling this my own way* or whether it meant *Don't show off any ownership of me.* He stopped short and sat down in the empty chair.

"When Suzanne arrived to take care of your daughter," Trevisone said abruptly, "how did she seem?"

"I don't know. Kind of distant and vacant—the way most baby-sitters seem. Do you have kids?"

"They're grown up." The detective let Alex know that he didn't appreciate the attempt to turn the tables. He added, "And we weren't in the hired-sitter class." Then he relented, waved away the implied criticism, and pointed as if at something in the near distance. "My sister's kid we used, up the block. Go on."

"I mean, she listened to me talk about bedtimes and stuff, but she wasn't really there. Baby-sitters have heard all this shit a hundred times, and they know it's really up to them and the kid. I thought she was taking in Meredith's scene, that I was Meredith's boyfriend, and figuring what kind of kid Maria was."

"Ms. Phillips says you didn't leave a number where you could be reached, and Suzanne didn't ask. Why didn't she? Could she have been distracted by something, afraid, worried, maybe?"

"Maybe. But usually they leave all those moves up to the parent. If the parent doesn't offer, they might not ask."

Trevisone did not seem interested in Alex's baby-sitter generalizations. It's because you've never been a single parent, Alex thought. The detective stroked the ends of what Alex had once thought of as a Billy Martin mustache. It was a Billy Martin *mouth*, really, he decided this time. There was something about the lines radiating out from the mouth, and the set of the jaw. Trevisone was skilled and crafty and probably not the type to pick fistfights either in bars or in the line of duty, but he was still a Billy Martin rather than, say, a Sparky Anderson type. His tenacity was not just a craftsman's, but was powered by some untold anger or hurt.

"Forget the baby-sitter angle," he said. "Just tell me, as a person, a girl, a woman—how did she strike you?"

"I really didn't know her. I'd recognize her again, but that's about it. She was about—shorter than Meredith, taller than Maria—about maybe five feet two. Seemed like a lot of people her age. Black hair, teased into kind of a mane, you know, kind of loose sweater, I think, tight jeans, cowboy boots. Alert, with it, like I said. Not to what I was saying, but to what was going on, the situation..."

"Attractive?" Trevisone asked. "If you'll answer a question like that in front of your girl—woman-friend."

The phrasing was meant to provoke someone, Alex or Meredith, but Alex chose to let it go by and Meredith, he saw, was directing her attention not to Trevisone but to him, knitting her brows in teacherly disapproval as if he'd made some mistake, leaped to some incorrect conclusion that she was waiting for him to see. Whatever it was, Alex let it go, too. He realized he'd been trying to fix Suzanne Lutrello's image for the past two days: an interesting face, dark eyes, penciled eyebrows but no lipstick, a narrow mouth, a straight nose, not turned up— altogether a face that was alive but also haughty in a certain Italian way. She moved with confidence, he remembered that; her breasts had swelled the loose sweater and her hips had been wide without being fat. He remembered all of this, and he wanted to give Trevisone a truthful answer if only because painting an accurate picture of Suzanne was all he could do for her now that she was dead.

"Listen, can you tell me what happened to her?" Alex asked.

"Could you please answer the questions first?"

Yes, Alex thought, I know, you're asking the questions here. He hesitated in part because the detective was a short man himself, maybe five-six or five-seven, and Alex didn't want to give any needless offense. It was just that, from Alex's height, women of Suzanne's shape and size often looked as if they suffered from too much gravity—as if they'd be quite beautiful if only they could be stretched back out.

"Yeah, she was attractive, I guess," Alex said at last. "I'm more turned on by taller women, if you really want to know." Trevisone let his eyes roam across the room to Meredith and back. If he wanted to think the comment had been flattery, that was up to him. Probably he didn't give a shit what kind of bodies Alex preferred. Probably all he wanted to know was whether Alex was holding something back. "What are you after, Sergeant?" Alex asked then. He said it in a deferential, assistant-investigator way, yet implying their previous cooperation gave him the right to ask.

"Standard question. I'm just eliminating something, if you really want to know. You ought to hear the stories baby-sitters come in with about the guys who hire them. Anytime you've got a father and baby-sitter in a violent case, any good cop's ears will perk up." He looked at Meredith again. "So," he went on to Alex, "you agree with Ms. Phillips that it was completely unexpected, her running out on your daughter like that?"

"It was completely unexpected to me."

"And she was just there to baby-sit your daughter. No other connection between the two of you?" Trevisone let that question hang in the air for Alex to interpret any way he wanted. Alex didn't risk a glance at Meredith now. Presumably she had told Trevisone about the restaurant, but if not, Alex wasn't going to volunteer the information. So he took the question as referring to his and Suzanne's relationship as of Saturday night.

"That's right," he answered. Trevisone sighed and turned to look at the big round clock on the wall.

"Okay, that'll do for now anyway," he said, extending his hand for Alex and then Meredith to shake. "Thank you. Both of you can go on home."

"Thank you," Meredith said. "As Suzanne's teacher and somebody she trusts, is there any chance I could be kept informed about your investigation?"

"No," Trevisone said. "But feel free to call if you have any new information to add."

"Yes," she agreed. Alex thought it was unlike her, failing to face up to a situation, continuing to talk about poor Suzanne Lutrello in the present tense. In the dingy hallway she looked back. Trevisone had stayed in his office and shut the door.

"It wasn't Suzanne," Meredith said.

4

SCAT

Alex came out of the small hallway that separated the living room from Maria's room in the back. He found Meredith stretched out on his couch, an old blue plush one, threadbare but still comfortable. She had propped her bare feet on one padded arm of the couch. She was apparently studying her toes as she sipped from a glass of the Scotch, Glenfyddich, that she had carried back from London as a gift for Alex in November.

It was a prosaic gift, bought at the last minute in the duty-free shop, and Alex had suspected this was her way of saying she wasn't sure yet whom she was coming back to. But then, Alex almost always found presents to be disappointments. What lurked inside the wrappings never lived up to the surrounding secrecy. He lifted her feet so he could sit, then let them back down, her legs on his lap. He traced patterns on one knee of her woolen slacks. He rubbed the toes of one bare foot with his other hand, waiting.

"Asleep?" Meredith asked.

"Yup. That was true? What you told us about Suzanne?"

"Of course."

"She's not dead?"

"Not dead, but apparently missing."

Alex nodded. Meredith offered the glass, so he drank. "I'm glad," he said. "But Trevisone is a homicide cop. Somebody has to be dead."

Meredith took back the glass and drained it, not lifting her head. She stared someplace behind and above Alex, toward the oil paintings on the wall, though he knew that she couldn't be seeing them at this angle. She pursed her lips, as if preparing a lecture. Alex would have leaned to kiss them, except that he was more interested in seeing them form words. Was that what a year did? he wondered. Just the facts, ma'am. He understood, also, that it might not be distaste that kept her from explaining. It might be the fact that telling him, now, was giving him a present that could meet his expectations.

In part, investigating a murder—or anything else that people tried to hide the truth of—was like fixing an engine. You took the mechanism apart until you could see each piece and how they all fit together, until you found the piece that did not work the way it should. But that was not the really compelling thing, and Alex knew it. The compelling thing was to try to understand the circumstances that led to untimely deaths. Call it a hobby; call it a way of answering questions for which doctors had no answers. Whatever it was, Alex knew it was a magnet for him now. Meredith knew that too. Once she began, she told the story clearly and without gaps.

"Natalie took an exit right off," she began, "and turned back onto the highway going the other way, toward town. She drove us to Cedar Street, not four blocks from here. As soon as she turned the corner, we both saw a police car out in front. She sort of gasped and then smothered that, and then she parked at the beginning of the block. She said, 'You better wait till I find out what this is about.'

"I waited in the car fifteen minutes, but Natalie didn't come back. So then I went where she had gone, to the house with the cop car in front. It was a regular two-family house. The postbox for the upstairs flat said 'Mr. and Mrs. John Reilly' and below that, on the same card, 'Natalie Cooper.' When I rang, someone buzzed me in. At the top of the stairs there was a policeman, whom I told I was looking for Natalie. He led me to the kitchen. They had put a sort of plastic shower-curtain affair over the parlor doorway. Natalie was in the kitchen. I said, 'Suzanne?' My voice had a crack in it, I suppose. The policeman looked at me sharply. Natalie shook her head, you know, as a sort of warning. 'What's in the parlor?' I asked. The policeman looked at Natalie, like, 'It's your house, miss.' 'Scat Johnston,' Natalie said. 'A guy I knew. He's stabbed. Somebody cut him. Officer, this is my professor Ms. Phillips. I called her earlier, to tell her I was worried about Suzanne disappearing. Ms. Phillips, I'm sorry I got you here at this time. It was really nice of you to come.'

"'Yes,' I said. I turned to the policeman. 'A man has been stabbed?'

"'Dead,' he said. He took out his notebook and asked for my whole name and address. He said Sergeant Trevisone was on his way and would probably want to bring us all down to the station. Trevisone took Natalie's story first. Before she went off she thanked me again for coming. She said, 'I'll talk to you later.' When my turn came I told Trevisone all about Saturday night. But I didn't want to contradict Natalie, not yet, so I told him nothing about tonight except to parrot what Natalie said in the kitchen. I'm expecting that we'll see Natalie here soon."

Alex didn't ask any more questions. Suzanne was not dead, not tonight, but somebody was. A guy Natalie Cooper knew, stabbed where Suzanne Lutrello was supposed to be. That was the observable trouble, like, "Yesterday it made a funny noise whenever I slowed down, and today it just won't start." All else was guesswork, so far. "A guy" was an unknown, an abstraction, a piece of a puzzle. He was already beyond feeling, beyond pain, before Alex became aware he'd ever lived or breathed. That was what Trevisone's job must be like, day in and day out. But Alex also felt Suzanne's fear. He wanted to know why she was missing, how much trouble she was in. The doorbell sounded, as if on cue. It rang again, and Meredith swiveled her legs off the arm of the couch and off Alex's lap.

He listened to the front door open and close, to Natalie's voice protesting that she couldn't track ice into the house. When she and Meredith came into sight, Natalie was trying to say something else, but she kept breaking into silent tears.

Alex stood, awkwardly, as Natalie's fingers rubbed past her eyes again and again, as if the tears could be erased. Meredith put an arm around the younger woman's waist and then sat her in the armchair opposite the couch. Natalie was trying to keep her mouth in a straight line. She seemed to have put on fresh lipstick, a brighter color against the brown that was like rich soil or like some expensive, deeply colored wood. She was wearing black corduroys and a bright yellow turtleneck. Alex couldn't remember, but he thought she'd had on something more subdued before.

"Natalie," Meredith said, "would you like some tea, or a drink?"

Natalie kept wiping until she succeeded in drying her eyes. She looked at Alex. She asked, "Is it possible that you might have a J?"

"A jay?" Alex said, and then understood. It had been a while since he'd heard the term. He came back from his bedroom soon with the marijuana, lit, and a seashell that passed for an ashtray. Natalie took three measured puffs and handed the joint back to Alex. Alex inhaled deeply, enjoying the taste. He'd been more or less on the wagon, himself, since chemotherapy. He'd smoked a lot of weed during the chemo, using it as a medication, or rather as a counter to the other medications that left him raw in body and mind. Since then, he'd been giving his lungs a break. Now he breathed out, slowly, and sighed sort of the way Trevisone had done.

"Thanks," Natalie said. "Professor Phillips, thank you, too."

"Meredith," Meredith said.

Alex said, "Alex," for symmetry if nothing else.

Meredith added, "Nothing is going to stay secret for long." She stopped, waited, and then said, "Alex has run into that sergeant before. Alex knows how to keep a secret while it lasts. He also has some experience in things like this."

"Experience? He's not a cop, I hope?"

"No. He's a car mechanic. An honest one, by the way."

"Most mechanics are honest, I think," Natalie said. "I mean, as honest as lawyers or legislators or newspaper reporters. It's just that educated people feel uptight around people who understand things they don't." Alex wasn't sure this was entirely true, but he knew that he'd happily lie for Natalie from now on. "My stepfather used to be a mechanic," she added. "He got less honest when he got into sales. That's how I got to be buddies with Suzanne. On account of our stepfathers."

Alex said, "They work together, selling cars?"

"No, they don't know each other at all." For the first time, Natalie laughed. It was an infectious laugh, but an unusual one. It was an old woman's laugh.

"A little white girl from the suburbs and me, what we had in common was stepfathers nobody would expect. It came out in papers we had to write about our view of marriage, in class. Her mother married a black man. My mother married a white. She came up to me after. She said, 'I forget your name, but you and me have got to talk.'"

Meredith perked up. It was as if she had let go of something, tossed it out to sea to let it drift where it would, and then a wave had washed it back to her. "Sarah Greenwood's class," she said. Natalie nodded. "She told me about the day that happened. It surprised her no end. I never knew it was Suzanne."

"You'll find out there was a lot you didn't know about Suzanne."

"Where *were* your parents?" Alex asked. He added carefully, "They weren't home when this guy's body was found?"

"They're in Barbados. That's where my mother is from. Scat, this guy, was kind of staying there for a few days."

West Indian, Alex thought. So Indian was close in a way. Of course, there had been Indians in the Indies, Columbus had named both out of the same mistake. And why was he drifting like this, thinking about Columbus? Oh, it was the dope. Alex tried to focus in on the name Natalie had let drop.

Scat. Alex thought of scat singers, though he'd been under the impression that scatting was a female form. He wasn't sure now who was in trouble, Natalie or Suzanne. He pictured a corpse that looked like that piano player, a trim black man with a thin mustache and rimless glasses, his formal white shirt slashed open and stained. "On Saturday night," he said, "Suzanne left here suddenly. She told my daughter somebody was dead. I thought she might have meant somebody *ought* to be dead. This guy you knew, is that who she meant?"

Natalie picked up the joint, looked at it, put it down. She asked, "Did you tell the police about that comment?"

Alex and Meredith both nodded. "Yes," Meredith admitted. "But about tonight I said what you said, that you called me because Suzanne still hadn't turned up."

"Oh shit," was all Natalie replied, and then she reached for the joint again herself. Was she trying to relax, Alex wondered, or did the drug help her think? Probably she was thinking hard. Alex knew he would be doing that, in her situation. The problem was that he didn't know what her situation was, or what she needed to be thinking about. "Well, the cat's loose, for better or worse." She looked at Alex. "What I mean is, she meant what she said. But *they'll* think she meant what you said. Because Scat was her boyfriend. I mean, he was past tense even before tonight. She still saw him, though. Off and on."

"Do you mean between other guys?"

This time Natalie mimed smoking the joint. She also mimed sniffing something up her nose.

"She still saw him," Alex interpreted. "But only when she needed to buy."

"Yeah, that's it. Coke mostly. Sometimes pills. She was off the needle stuff for good, no thanks to him."

"And . . . he was kind of staying with you now. Were you involved with him after Suzanne, is that what you mean?"

Natalie laughed the same laugh. "Who gets laid the most?" she asked. "Football players, acrobats, or mathematicians?"

"Acrobats?"

"No. Mathematicians. Three points."

"I don't get the joke," Alex said.

"Three points. To a football player that's a field goal. To an acrobat it's when you stand on your hands and your head. To a mathematician it's a triangle. The more you make everything into a triangle, the more you get laid. It's a stupid joke, told by a math major, of course. But I think of it whenever somebody sees a triangle that's not there. I was taking care of Scat to keep him *away* from Suzanne. I don't hold with violence, but I won't pretend to be real sorry he's dead."

"If I *were* a cop," Alex said, "I'd be suspicious when some-body answered a question with a joke. You described Scat to Meredith as a guy you knew, not one that Suzanne knew. Was he an old friend, or an old boyfriend that maybe you introduced to Suzanne?"

Natalie smiled this time, but didn't laugh or explain what was funny. "I think you've got the wrong idea about Scat," she said finally. "But yeah, there is something in what you just said. Because I let him stay at my place this time, he got the wrong idea about me. It was the dope, I think. He didn't usually do shit very often himself, but Saturday night he was fried, I don't know what on. When I told him he had the wrong idea, he threatened me with a knife. The knife he got killed with, I think. Now I hope you won't run and tell *that* to the cops."

"What happened?" Alex asked.

"Oh, not much. Scat was a jerk a lot of the time, but no real rapist, I don't think. I just locked myself in the bedroom and told him good night." She looked at Meredith as if Meredith ought to believe her, even if Alex didn't. "I didn't see him between then and the time you and me got there tonight."

"Well," Meredith said. "Why did Suzanne leave Maria so suddenly that night? And what did she want me to help her with today? And where is she now?"

"I'm sorry. I really would like to tell you that, but that's Su-zanne's affair, not mine. I can tell you that she didn't kill Scat. Shit. She'd have killed him years ago if murder was in her mind. She ran away because she knew they'd blame her, or because she's running from whoever did."

Right, Alex thought. Exactly. But... "Who do you mean when you keep saying 'they'? Do you mean just Trevisone, the cops, or do you mean somebody else?"

The laugh came once more, but this time Natalie stifled it. She wasn't an old woman, and didn't have the knack yet of laughing at danger. "You think Scat Johnston is some no-account representative of the minority colored underclass, am I right? No. We are talkin' about Lowell Johnston, a no-account represen-tative of the minority Brahmin aristoclass. When I got home, the cops already knew who they had there, stuck with more holes than the junkies that were his customers, bled to death all over my folks' rug. They had somebody that they were supposed to act like he as a fine young man, somebody that had folks who are like rich, WASP, Brattle Street types. And the Johnstons always blamed 'that mixed-up little Italian girl' for their boy going bad."

"My friend Trevisone," Alex said, "might not take that mixed-up Italian bullshit too much to heart."

"Now that Scat's dead," Natalie answered, "the Johnstons are going to want blood for blood, and the blood they want ain't gonna be blue. Your friend Trevisone may know the score, but you know he can't make the rules. So listen. I'm not asking you to take my word for anything. Just—if she gets back in touch, give her a chance to explain before you decide who you ought to be telling what."

When Natalie left, Meredith said she needed a hot bath before anything else. Alex sat at his kitchen counter for a while, doodling question marks and likenesses of Suzanne Lutrello on a pad of phone-message paper. Then he dropped these in a drawer of the small desk he'd built when he redid the room. The apartment had two bedrooms, neither very large, a living room, and this showpiece kitchen Alex had crafted. It was a good size for two people, not so good maybe for three. He slid the drawer shut and followed Meredith to find out what she was thinking now. Her eyes were closed, her head buried in the spray from the hand-held nozzle as she washed the police station smells out of her hair. Alex watched the water run down her back.

Meredith finished rinsing, then turned to face him as she twisted the water out of her hair. Her skin was flushed from the hot bath, and her nipples were redder still. Alex felt thankfulness and desire, felt that a year was surely not too long, that two or even three years were not going to make him blasé about her after all. "We could have a tub big enough for both of us," he said. "Instead of the piano and pool table, maybe." He started to undress so that he could find room for the two of them even in this one. He suspected, though, that this had been a wrong thing to say. He didn't know yet that nothing would have been right.

"Don't leap to conclusions," she said. He was surprised at the sadness in her voice. He stood, unsure, more of a stork than ever, with one leg raised halfway out of his jeans.

"About us, you mean?"

"No, I don't mean about us. Earlier this evening you leaped to the conclusion that Suzanne was dead. Or you let Trevisone point you there." Meredith reached toward a towel hanging on the wall. Alex handed it to her and watched her wrap herself away. He put his foot back through the leg of his pants and back onto the floor. "Take another look at your newspaper," Meredith said, sharp now, not vulnerable or sad. "The one you left in the wastebin over there."

Alex looked at the wastebasket, white plastic, just now sweating bubbles of condensed steam. Her accent annoyed him. The way she said *nyewspaper* instead of *noospaper*, the way she said "bin" instead of "basket"—there was something unconsciously superior about it. He saw the morning paper, the one he'd studied while waiting for his doctor's appointment, folded to one of the news pages and resting on top of the trash. Wet streaks darkened the newsprint like tracks, like stains. He understood that Meredith had been reading this page while she soaked in the tub, solving some puzzle that had so far eluded him.

"You found something I missed?"

"Not missed. I found something that didn't mean anything then but will now. That skier in New Hampshire who was hit while crossing the road. The driver of the vehicle was Lowell Johnston, twenty-five. Suzanne was telling Maria the truth, though she really meant more like 'somebody killed,' transitive verb, than 'somebody died,' intransitive. Scat Johnston can't have been staying at Natalie's on Saturday night and have run down a skier in New Hampshire at the same time. Natalie has got us both lying to Trevisone, and in the meantime she's been lying to us, too."

Alex picked up the paper and read the short item over again. Then he turned to the obituary page and located the death notice. So. "Caroline Davis, 19, died suddenly" was an automobile fatality. And tomorrow's list would include "Lowell Johnston, 25, died suddenly," and he had been stabbed. The steamy room felt like a greenhouse—warm but too close, hard to breathe, full simultaneously of life and rot. Alex wanted to be out in the open, to be doing instead of talking. He did not want to see Suzanne Lutrello's name added to the list.

"So what do you think?" he asked Meredith. "Maybe you ought to get dressed and we ought to go right over and confront her with this."

"Not me," Meredith said. "I am getting dressed, and drying my hair and then going home, where I've got my own work to do. I have nineteen other students in that class. Of course I'm available if Suzanne herself asks for my help again. But otherwise neither she nor her personal life is my job." She wrapped her head in a second towel, brown, and rubbed vigorously at her hair. When she looked out, her face was framed by the towel as by a hood. The pose gave her a wise-woman, sorceress sort of look. "In my own way," she added, "I do understand why you think it is yours."

5

TWILIGHT AND DEW

Every other Tuesday morning Alex walked Maria to the schoolbus stop. Tuesday was her swing day, the day she moved back to the home of whichever parent hadn't had her the weekend before. Laura would pick her up at the end of school today. Maria was not very communicative on Tuesday mornings, as a rule. Noisy, yes. Communicative, no.

Over breakfast, today, she chattered about the police station as Alex toasted her frozen chicken nuggets and sealed them in a thermos container that would leave them lukewarm at lunchtime. Still good enough, apparently, that one chicken nugget could bring half a bag of potato chips in return. "It was different," she said, with a dark fist propped under her soft chin, "than when we got taken there in second grade. That time it was like getting taken to a play."

"A play?" Alex asked. "You mean like a police play, mystery play?"

"No, they sat us down in seats and talked like somebody on a stage."

"In the lobby?" Alex remembered only a controversy that had raged beforehand, when the school had sent home a notice for parents to sign, consenting to have their children fingerprinted. The cops and the teacher had thought it would be fun. Some parents thought it would put their children down in FBI files for life. Alex had doubted this, but as a matter of education he had sided with the "anti" faction nonetheless. He thought the procedure taught children to be too trusting of police. In the end, the solution had been pluralistic: those with signed permission had gotten fingerprinted, and those without it had not. Alex had worried that he'd been a killjoy in Maria's eyes. If she'd afterward described what else happened in the visit, he apparently hadn't listened.

"No, in some kind of room where the police had classes."

"Did they talk about how crime didn't pay?"

"I don't know. They talked about strangers and stuff."

Then Alex remembered. A leaflet of do's and don'ts with strangers had come home afterward. "So how was it different last night?"

"Realer, even though nothing happened. The guns didn't look real, but they wore them. The policewoman told jokes she might not only tell to kids. They brought in a woman that was swearing and waving her arms, and Officer Crowley, the policewoman, told me she was drunk. I knew she was drunk, or just really mad. I told the policewoman you helped to solve a murder once. Will you call me if you find out anything more about where Suzanne is?"

Alex packed the thermos container, a brownie, and a few carrots into Maria's backpack. He thought that Maria seemed to accept the explanation Meredith had given on the ride home last night: that Suzanne was okay but hiding from something; that both her friend Natalie and the police were trying to find out why. He waited for more, but Maria dropped the topic of police and talked about the trip she and Laura and Laura's husband and baby were taking the next weekend. Alex realized he was going to have to call Laura and explain something about the missing sitter and the police. He could come up with an explanation, but what was the truth? Was Suzanne hiding out, or was it worse?

On the way to the bus, Maria asked Alex whether he would have a new tai chi posture to show her next week. Until they were within sight of her stop, she consented to nestle her gloved hand in his as they walked. They watched their feet, avoiding both the icy patches and the shit left by the local dogs.

"No," he told her, "I think the next thing I do is repeat some old ones."

"What's the use of that?" Maria wanted to know.

39

"I'm not really sure. Most of the motions seem to get repeated a lot. That's true in real life, isn't it? Take chewing. We repeat that a lot, though we do some new things in between."

"Well," Maria said, "let me chew on that till I see you again." She let go of his hand and ran to join the clump of children waiting for the bus.

The only other parent was a Haitian mother, to whom Alex smiled and from whom he got a nod but no smile in return. He spoke no Creole, so as usual he left it at this. If the news from his country had been like the news from hers, Alex didn't think he would smile either—especially on a cold morning in this icy place.

The bus arrived, nearly on time, and Maria and others piled in. Alex watched her sit down and pull off her hat, which he hoped she would not lose. He waved as the bus drove away. What would she be like, what would her worries be, when she reached the age at which Caroline Davis had died? What, in fact, had Caroline Davis's worries been? Alex chose the second question over the first. He nodded at the Haitian mother again, and as they went their separate ways he practiced walking the way he'd been learning in Terry's class.

Weight low, back straight, pelvis tucked; let the heel touch first, roll onto the toe, empty the other leg before you step. It was easier on the smooth studio floor. Allow yourself to be right here, right now, he told himself. He tried that, long enough to get home, but then while he warmed up the car he reread yesterday's obituary notice for the woman, or girl, whom Scat Johnston had run over:

DAVIS—IN JERICHO, NEW HAMPSHIRE, CAROLINE, AT 19 YEARS. BELOVED GRANDDAUGHTER OF ROSEMARIE (STURGEON) DAVIS OF BOSTON. DEAR DAUGHTER OF JAMES AND SYLVIA (MCCANN) DAVIS OF SAN FRANCISCO. CHERISHED SISTER OF FRANKLIN DAVIS OF BILLINGS, MONTANA, AND HELENA (DAVIS) ENGEL OF HONOLULU. A SERVICE IN HONOR OF HER LIFE WILL BE HELD AT THE MEMORIAL CHURCH, HARVARD COLLEGE, ON TUESDAY AT 3:00 P.M. CONTRIBUTIONS IN HER MEMORY MAY BE MADE TO THE INSTITUTE FOR CONTEMPORARY ART.

Then, in today's paper, he found Scat's as expected. There was only the notice however; apparently the family had been able to keep the murder out of the news, at least for a day.

JOHNSTON—OF CAMBRIDGE AND JERICHO, NEW HAMPSHIRE, SUDDENLY, LOWELL TOWNSEND. DEAR SON OF GRAHAM AND BARBARA (PEPPERELL) JOHNSTON OF CAMBRIDGE. BROTHER OF GARDNER JOHNSTON OF NAHANT AND MRS. ELLEN SIMMONS OF PARIS, FRANCE. A FUNERAL SERVICE WILL BE HELD THURSDAY AT 2:00 P.M. IN THE GOODE-KEATING FUNERAL HOME, BELMONT, TO BE FOLLOWED BY INTERMENT IN THE MT. AUBURN CEMETERY. PLEASE OMIT FLOWERS. EXPRESSIONS OF SYMPATHY MAY BE MADE IN HIS MEMORY TO THE GREATER BOSTON UNITED WAY.

Belmont and Mount Auburn, Alex thought. That fit. He wondered where Caroline Davis would be interred. San Francisco, he supposed. But he remembered that, aside from the old one in the Mission Dolores, graveyards were not permitted within the municipal boundary. Where then? Daly City? He let the car keep warming while he went inside to pack a change of clothes. He drove to his shop, where the first customer brought him a Saab that needed a valve job. He pulled the cylinder head, covered it with a plastic garbage bag, and lugged it out to his own car.

Later he pulled the rear hubs of a Triumph and covered and carried them out as well. At two-thirty he was ready, showered, and dressed in a pair of new gray walking shoes, creased brown wool-blend slacks, and a blue oxford shirt. He dropped the parts of Saab and Triumph at the machine shop he patronized, to get the valves and disks ground. By five past three he was parking in a "Harvard University STICKERS ONLY" lot; he told Divine Providence that he was going to church and would appreciate not being towed. His sport jacket across his arm, he sprinted along a neatly plowed asphalt path that led through an ivyed brick arch and past nineteenth-century red brick dorms. He turned left in front of an older building, built to last out of large, hand-quarried stones. He ran past two Japanese visitors posing for VCR pictures under the statue of John Harvard. Did they know the man cast in bronze, on his granite pedestal, had merely been a minor Colonial preacher who happened to bequeath a fledgling seminary some books?

The church came into view around the corner—a newer building, a low, sprawling mix of brick and wood whose lines looked almost suburban. The architecture spoke more of secular, ecumenical Protestantism than the training of the stern Puritan theocracy. Its broad steps had been shoveled clean of snow. These were the same steps from which, in the warm days of June, passports to wealth and power were annually issued. In the church vestibule, Alex shed his winter coat and caught his breath while tying a solid, square-cut tie. Then he slipped into the sport jacket and studied the traces of automobile grime on his hands.

It wasn't as if Alex Glauberman never crossed the physical barriers that separated his part of the city from the university. He ventured occasionally into the college lecture halls, sometimes for a movie, sometimes for a speech. The social barriers were porous, too, in their way; the woman in his life before Meredith had been a medical technician, but the one before her had been a graduate student here. He'd never had a reason to step into the church, however, and he couldn't help feeling that this was a place where they might look at your hands to make sure they were clean and your blood—he remembered Natalie's comment—was blue.

For Alex this feeling was heightened because, though he did not practice the religion he'd been only lackadaisically taught, still he felt there was something tainted about setting foot inside such an unequivocally *goyische* place. This made him all the more conscious of a particular fact: Lowell Townsend Johnston of the Brattle Street Johnstons had committed vehicular homicide against someone whose grandmother would and could call a memorial service here in the Harvard College church. It seemed that the dead and the agent of death were required to come from the appropriate circle. Alex rubbed his hands unconsciously and took a seat in the rearmost pew.

A gawky young minister and a white-haired woman in a powder-blue suit stood at parallel lecterns. They took turns reading from selected works. Alex studied the woman and did not at first focus on the words. It must be unusual, he thought, to wear that color to a memorial service, even one "in honor of the deceased's life." Aside from this choice of dress, her looks reminded him of his landlady's aunt or cousin Mary, who had served him breakfast yesterday morning after tai chi. Only her looks, however—not the discipline of her voice, the careful crafting of what she said and how she said it. Alex realized that the minister and grandmother were reading something—a poem—in series, each taking a stanza at a time. The minister read with slow emphasis on each word, not a very good way to read, Alex thought, but rather as if the poem were in a foreign language and if he didn't pronounce the words carefully, the audience might not know the meaning of what were actually very ordinary words:

> Come, heart, where hill is heaped upon hill:
> For there the mystical brotherhood
> Of sun and moon and hollow and wood
> And river and stream work out their will.

The verse described the place where Caroline Davis, whoever she had been, had died. In the White Mountains, where hill was heaped upon hill, when it was blanketed in white snow and she had made the mistake of disdaining to take off her skis when her communion with the snow was interrupted by a road. Now the grandmother, more eloquently, read the stanza that came next:

> And God stands winding His lonely horn,
> And time and the world are ever in flight;
> And love is less kind than the grey twilight,
> And hope is less dear than the dew of the morn.

The kind grey twilight and the dear morning dew. Meredith would be able to identify the poem, but he hadn't invited Meredith, and if he invited her she probably wouldn't have come. Alex was ambivalent about this—both glad to be on his own and also a bit confused by her attitude. Tonight they could talk it out, maybe. He didn't need to worry about it now.

Instead he absorbed the grandmother's words, loved the words though he couldn't say quite what they meant, and his heart went out to the woman who read them. He felt she was revealing something about herself, her own old age, and also about what makes people, even much younger people, leave the city to go live where the brotherhood of nonhuman forces work

43

out their will. And this thought took Alex from the north bank of the Charles River to the north bank of the Platte, near Grand Island, Nebraska. There hill was not heaped upon hill, in fact the prairie had barely even begun to roll. But the river flowed shallow and fast, spending the force it had picked up in a thousand streams of the Rockies far out of sight to the west. The thought took him to all the twilights and dewy mornings he'd spent there, during those two years when he'd apprenticed to his trade and paused in his rushing from coast to coast.

At the same time, Alex tried to get the chronology straight. He tried to lay the events in a line like a series of bolts and washers and nuts. If you lay them in line right away, Hans Heidenfelter of Grand Island Motors had taught him, you could put them back together in the right order; you needed no manual, no puzzling it out, no muss no fuss.

Caroline Davis's grey twilight had been Saturday, some hours before Suzanne Lutrello had announced to Maria that she had to leave because someone had died. In that twilight, Lowell "Scat" Johnston had run into her. In the dew of the next morn, Alex had tried to locate Suzanne but failed. Then there had been another dusk and another dawn, and Scat Johnston had been cut up in less pastoral surroundings with a knife.

Those were the only facts that Alex knew for sure. He studied the mourners; there were only fifteen, scattered in small groups or single, as if they did not know each other. They ran the gamut of generations. He tried to place them in order, to remember who was with whom. After the literary passages, Rosemarie Davis gave a brief account of her granddaughter's life, as if she were bringing this disparate crowd up to date. Caroline Davis grew up in San Francisco, she traveled and wrote poems and had her first love affairs and began to figure out who she was. She came east to college, decided that was not who she was, and moved to New Hampshire to wait tables for a while and spend as much time as she could outdoors.

When her grandmother finished, Alex did not join the receiving line but dashed back the way he had come. His car had not been towed, and he got to the machine shop in time to pick up the hubs of the Triumph. The Triumph's disks were once again smooth and shiny, the way they would have been anyway if the owner had brought the car in for new pads on time. Putting the wheels back together, Alex thought about time and the world

44

being ever in flight. Suzanne Lutrello was in flight. The question was whether all these things fit together or not.

Once the Triumph was done and returned to its owner, Alex was through for the day. The Saab had to wait until its valves were ground, probably tomorrow morning. Judging by the direction of bequests to the ICA, either Rosemarie Davis or Caroline Davis was or had been a patroness of the arts. Alex punched out, washed up, and called the only artist he knew.

6

ROSEMARIE

The only artist was also his oldest friend—the only friend, in fact, who dated back to before he'd come east from Nebraska with Laura and settled in Boston. Her name was Kim, and she was the one who had painted the Viking car that advertised his shop, as well the abstract oils in shades of gray and blue that hung above his living room couch. He called her up and asked whether the name Davis meant anything in the art world. Kim reminded him that the art world was big and snooty, that she still classified mainly as an interloper, and that if he was flattering her there must be a reason why.

"Reason coming," Alex said. "But what about it? Caroline Davis, or Rosemarie. That's Rosemarie (Sturgeon) Davis, by the way, parentheses courtesy of the *Globe*."

"No," Kim said. "Rose-mah*rie*, not *Rose*-mary. Rosemarie Sturgeon was once well known, oh, in the thirties, I guess. She's mostly forgotten now, how did you hear of her? Anyway she's something of a legend in my circles. She's the oldest known dyke painter in town."

"She's the grandmother of Caroline Davis," Alex said.

"Even lesbians can be grandmothers. Most of them probably got to be, in her day. Now, reason for asking, please."

"Her granddaughter was hit by a car in New Hampshire. Killed. The guy who ran into her was the ex-boyfriend of a student of Meredith's. Then he got killed, murdered, in the apartment of that student's friend. The friend says she's afraid the student will be suspected. There's a lot of fear and lies flying around. I'd like to talk to Rosemarie, but I can't call her up and say, 'You don't know me but I think this is too much coincidence.' I don't have any good reason for thinking it, either."

"A damsel in distress," Kim said. "Not a bad reason. Not a good one, though. I met Rosemarie once. If you do have information, I think she would want to know. One condition."

"Okay," Alex said.

"Don't be a middleman. Bring the source of your information too."

Alex would have preferred to learn what he could from Rosemarie Davis and then tackle Natalie again. However, one of the bases of his and Kim's twenty-year friendship was that each knew better than to argue with the other when the other had made up his or her mind. So he agreed, then called Natalie Cooper, but got no answer. He went home to an empty apartment and called her again. He found her suspicious but willing; if Alex told her when and where this meeting was going to take place, she would come on her own. He said nine o'clock at Petros's coffee shop in Central Square.

Petros's was a small, unpretentious place featuring nice china, Greek or American coffee, and Greek desserts or spinach-cheese pie. Alex liked it much better here, where old men chatted over papers from Athens, than in Harvard Square's French and Italian cafés, where doctoral candidates sat studying every word of papers from Manhattan instead. The last time he'd set up a meeting here, it had been late summer and hot. He'd carried a sick feeling in his stomach and the air conditioner had wheezed above the door. Now a few customers turned to stare at Alex as he let in a piercing arctic draft from outside. Rosemarie and Kim were seated drinking coffee at the farthest table, with their backs to the wall. A Day-Glo image of the Parthenon shone above their heads. Alex felt a small twinge of embarrassment—was he making something of nothing?—and a strong tug of expectation.

Rosemarie Sturgeon Davis was no longer in her powder-blue suit. She was wearing loose blue jeans and a sweatshirt. When she stood, Alex could see that the sweatshirt displayed a woman with a paintbrush. Its legend said, FRIDA KAHLO, LA PINTORA MAS PIN-

TOR. Alex knew hardly any Spanish and did not recognize the name. He did see that Rosemarie Davis's hands were stiff, almost contorted, and he wondered whether she was still able to paint. He shook her right hand gently and said, "I'm pleased to meet you, Ms. Davis, please sit down."

Rosemarie said, "This afternoon, I wondered who you were. I thought of mentioning you to the detective, but I decided I'd better not."

Alex felt the wind on his back and turned to see Natalie Cooper coming in the door right on time. He signaled, and when she got there he made introductions: "Natalie. Ms. Davis. Kim." He added, "Natalie, thanks for coming. Can I get you anything?" When he came back from the counter with two more coffees, he thought the three women were waiting for him to start the show. But before he could, Natalie laughed the wise laugh of the old lady. She pointed an index finger across the table. "Rosemarie Sturgeon. That was really your maiden name? Your father was named after a fish?" Alex sat down next to Natalie and tried to figure her out. She would be a woman accustomed to getting a lot of mileage out of her presence and her looks. She liked taking control. It helped that she had such a ready tongue.

"You won't believe this," Rosemarie Davis said, "but it's a case not of named *after* but of named *himself*." She said this gravely, not lightly, as if to disbelieve her was a serious step, not to be taken without thought. "The name was Sullivan when he was born. He made the change after he made enough money to forget he was Irish. Not that he would have admitted to such a charge, of course. The lines that made you sit up at the service today, Mr. Glauberman, those were from Yeats. They were about Ireland, really, not just any hills and dews. But that's what it's all about, isn't it? There's nothing truly new anymore. The challenge is to take something old and make it somehow your own."

"You saw me sit up?"

"Oh yes, seeing is still my strong point. My eyesight hasn't suffered in the general deterioration, not yet. Besides, there weren't many people there. Friends of mine and of my children. None of Caroline's, so far as I know. Except, I thought perhaps, the two lone men, one of whom was you."

"I'm afraid not me," Alex said. "Then, the younger people..."

"Groupies is not a kind word," Rosemarie said. "So I will not use it. But devotees would be too kind, and I'm not sure what fits in between."

"Fans," Natalie said. "There's nothing to be ashamed of about having fans."

To Alex's disappointment, Rosemarie Sturgeon Davis did not pick this offer up. "I'm afraid that comes from 'fanatics,'" she said. She paused, waited, and then said, "There was that one other man, younger and more substantial than you, who didn't introduce himself either. Well, later this afternoon I was visited by a detective from the Cambridge police, who did. Detective Sergeant Trevisone told me that the person who plowed over Caroline was murdered last night. He said he was visiting not so much as a part of his investigation, but as a courtesy. Yet my sense was that he wanted to know whether someone might have been exacting revenge. I told him that as far as I knew Caroline had no connections in Boston except for me. And she visited me as much out of duty as anything else." She let unasked questions hang in the air: Who was Natalie, and what had she come to say?

"I didn't know your granddaughter," Natalie said. "I'm sorry she got hit, I don't know what else to say." She followed this with a rush of words directed to the older woman across the table but apparently intended also to answer the questions Alex hadn't yet had a chance to ask. Alex was conscious of her persuasiveness, her sincerity and warmth. At the same time he wondered whether everything she said was always so full of gaps and shadows.

"I didn't know *her*," Natalie repeated. "But I knew *him*. He was a, you know, a fuckup. But Suzanne, my friend Suzanne had hooks in him and vice versa. Suzanne was taking care of Alex's kid that night, the same day your granddaughter got hit. She claimed she saw it on the news, but I think he called her up and she didn't want me to know. She wanted to make it seem like it was all on her initiative. Anyway she went right up there, to New Hampshire, and the first I knew was when the two of them showed at my house Sunday with a story about how Scat had killed somebody in an accident and was all broken up about it and needed to get out. I didn't know how to take that, but I told him to stay at my house a couple days. The last thing I wanted was for him to move in on Suzanne. Monday, Suzanne told me the trouble was more serious than that. She didn't say more serious how. She said he wanted help."

"Meredith's help?" Alex asked. He looked at Kim, who nodded, meaning she had already explained to Caroline's grandmother who Meredith was.

"Yeah." Natalie nodded eagerly—maybe too eagerly, Alex thought. "Uh-huh. So I went to collect Professor Phillips, at the restaurant. Alex knows this, he was there. When I got back, the cops were at my house, Scat was dead, and Suzanne was gone. Listen. In this company, I'll be upfront. If Suzanne killed him, he must have deserved it. If she didn't—and that's what I think—then somebody set things up to make it look like she did. Either way, she's got good reason to run and hide."

"What about that story you told me," Alex said, "about how Scat made advances and threatened you Saturday night?" He thought "made advances" made him sound like Trevisone. Well, better than "made sexual advances," which would sound like a copywriter for the news. *Came on to you? Put moves on you?* He wanted Natalie to trust him. He wanted her to trust him with the truth.

"I didn't want to get into all this yet, okay? So I admit, I told you the first thing that came into my head."

"You made up a story that would make me sympathetic to you, and give Suzanne a reason for doing him in that I might approve of."

Natalie lifted her chin, and her face lost its softness while her eyes seemed to become sharp-edged jewels of ice.

Kim said, "Okay, you two, cut it out."

"Why do you think," Rosemarie interjected, "that she wanted to consult with this Professor Phillips, the sweetheart of Mr. Glauberman here?"

"I think," Natalie said, and she put her elbows on the table, leaning across, "that she talked Scat into confessing." Her head was almost touching the grandmother's, the black curls on top of one reaching like Velcro for the white curls on top of the other. "But she wasn't sure she was doing the right thing. She wanted some kind of authority figure to back her up."

"Confessing?"

Natalie looked down and twisted a silver bracelet on her left wrist. She did not move any closer, did not try to take Rosemarie Sturgeon Davis's hand. "Confessing that your Caroline's death wasn't an accident."

Rosemarie's face lost none of its composure. It only looked a

49

bit more tired in the creases between her pink cheeks and pale eyes. She sat back, and thought, and didn't say anything right away. She didn't seem the type to leap to conclusions, nor would she want to have to abandon one, once it was reached.

"If I were confessing to that detective," she said, "I'd want a lawyer, not a professor of Literature and Women's Studies."

"If you were Scat. I'm talking about Suzanne Lutrello. Suzanne wanted Professor Phillips, somebody she could talk it over with, somebody that might be able to tell her how to go."

"Uh-huh," Alex said. Maybe, he thought. But all this seemed beside the point. When Rosemarie didn't fill the silence, Alex did. "Natalie, did you ever hear of Caroline before this? Was she somebody that Scat or Suzanne knew?"

Natalie shook her head, twisting the bracelet some more but not speaking. Alex turned to Rosemarie. "So that's it, that's what I wanted you to know. Maybe I just want to make your granddaughter's accidental death make sense. Maybe Kim's right, I'm just trying to help out Suzanne, a damsel in distress." He waited for her to contradict him, to present the connection that would make everything fit.

"I hardly knew her," Rosemarie said. "She was my granddaughter, and so she turned to me when she arrived in the East. She registered for college, as she'd been sent to do, and after the first week of classes she dropped out. I think she'd planned to do that all along. I supported her in this decision. I lent her money to get started on her own."

Alex saw the creases threaten to collapse into valleys. He dropped his eyes and saw the taut fingers gripping each other on the table. This time Natalie covered them with her hand. Alex felt like the bull in the china shop, or maybe just like a man among women where he didn't quite belong. Kim said, "Whatever happened could have happened in the city, outside a dorm or a lecture hall. You know, Alex and I left college together. It may have put our futures at risk, but not our lives."

"Yes, but with my help she was able to get to this particular place, a particular road. She might have been somewhere equally dangerous instead, but she would not have ended up precisely there."

"Did she stay in touch with you?" Alex asked. To himself he sounded cop-like, Trevisone-like, again. "Did she talk about anybody in her life up there? A boyfriend, a girlfriend, somebody who'd want to exact revenge?"

"She visited me a few times, but only once did we really talk. She didn't tell me about her personal life, romance. She wanted to talk about some women she knew who were whores."

All three younger people stared. "She had friends that were hookers?" Natalie asked at last. She was trying to put a less harsh, more fashionable sound to what this bereaved grandmother had said.

"Yes. Whores, I think, was once a perfectly simple Anglo-Saxon word for the line of work. Do you remember the scandal about the female students at Brown who were 'recruited as prostitutes,' as the papers say? I think this was something similar, college women who serviced visitors to the ski resort, you see. The town is called Jericho, but there is a large, self-contained resort, Pepperell Woods. There are so many potential customers —vacationers and conventioners and skiers, single men and married men away from their wives."

"Why did she want to talk to you about this?"

"It was a moral problem, I think, that troubled her. She couldn't make up her own mind whether prostitution was just a job, or not. In her gut she found it degrading, but her friends apparently told her it was no worse than serving food all day. I think she was severely tempted ... to see for herself what it was like. She seemed to think that I had done something similar, and so she wanted to know what I thought."

"That *you* had?" Natalie asked. "Had somebody been spilling family secrets about you?"

"No. Or yes. I mean that I am a lesbian, unambiguously, and have been all my life. Yet I married, and lived as a married woman. That was what she wanted to know about, what that was like."

Natalie showed nothing, but she was apparently at a loss for words this time. She removed her hand from Rosemarie Davis's at last. "Well," Kim said, "your marriage accounted for her existence, after all."

"Yes. In those days, if we wanted children, or grandchildren, we had no other way. She wanted to know if that was what my marriage had been about, or whether it had been a means of survival in comfort, a career, a job. It was a very personal conver-

51

sation. As you can imagine, it's not something many people would ask." Rosemarie withdrew her hands from the table to her lap, indicating that this topic was, for now, closed.

"Well," said Alex, "do you know how she resolved this moral problem for herself?"

"No. After that, she was almost as reserved as before. But I do know *that* she resolved it. She stopped by to see me last week, for just a few minutes. She had driven down, she said, just for part of the day. She said the question was settled for her, but as yet she couldn't explain how or why."

"And these friends . . . you don't know any of their names?"

"Unfortunately, no. She didn't tell me very much about them, or even whether her friendship was with a group or really with one woman in particular. It was the problem in her own head she wanted to settle. I felt, actually, that the friendship may have been one-sided—that she was not as important to these women as they were to her."

Rosemarie had been making eye contact with each of her listeners as she talked, even in her private grief knowing how to behave before an audience. Now she let her eyes rest on Alex, and for the first time she seemed to have found something to smile at.

"It would be very simple for you to locate these women, you know—even without knowing their names. My husband, who traveled in the coffee business, once told me that in Brazilian hotels the custom was to ask the desk clerk for a blanket to warm you during the night. He said you requested a blanket, and you specified the race by the color: white, black, brown. Do you ski, Alex?"

"Yes."

"Yes," Rosemarie Sturgeon Davis repeated. "And how much are you paid for your time?"

"*My* time?" Alex had been imagining explaining himself, before a wood fire in a New Hampshire resort, to the ladies of the night whose time this grandmother had just been encouraging him to buy. The white woman was like Meredith, as he imagined her when she'd been twenty. The same as now, but less practiced, just trying herself out. The mulatto woman was like Natalie, tall and brash, though lighter-skinned, and in demeanor she was alternately hot and cold. The blacker woman was like certain

52

statues of African goddesses that he had seen. It took him a while to understand what Rosemarie was now offering to do.

"I've spoken to the police in New Hampshire," the dead girl's grandmother explained. "They believe it was an accident, without negligence on the driver's part. Even if I could now convince them it may have been something else, they would say that the driver is dead, so there's nothing more to do. But I would like to have the full story, because that was a sweet and honest girl who did not deserve to die."

"Why do you think," Alex asked slowly, "that I could get that story for you?"

"Perhaps you couldn't. However, I can see that we both distrust coincidence. After the police sergeant visited me today, I opened the Yellow Pages to detective agencies. The agencies trumpeted their skill at catching thieving cashiers, skipped debtors, runaway children, and nonmonogamous husbands and wives. I closed the directory and wondered where I might find someone more appropriate. Kim tells me you've done something of this sort."

"When I fix cars," Alex answered her earlier question, "I charge twenty-five an hour plus parts and machine-shop fees."

Rosemarie Sturgeon Davis took out her checkbook and a sheet of stationery, cream-colored with a thin violet border. "At two hundred a day plus expenses," she said, "I can afford to allow you to neglect your repair shop for a week. I'm writing you a letter of introduction, to whom it may concern." She wrote, and then she looked up at Alex to be sure. Her chin was the weak link in her face. Probably it hadn't always been, probably these muscles had merely succumbed first to the passage of time. In any case, her chin quivered now. She got it under control by speaking the question out loud: "Will you do this for me?"

Alex nodded, and then three things happened at once. He folded the letter and the thousand-dollar check and put them in his pocket. Natalie Cooper this time took both of Rosemarie Sturgeon Davis's hands. And Rosemarie finally lost her self-control and cried.

Home, Alex found the unaccustomed, eerie emptiness that always surprised him every other Tuesday night. He did not need to look in on Maria, to insist it was time to turn off the light or the radio, to try to discover what was on her mind or to watch her unconscious recharging of the batteries as she lay there, breathing quietly, oblivious and asleep. He pictured her in her other bedroom, next door to the sister she had in the other half of her life. It was late; she would be asleep there, too, the same person, dreaming the same dreams. He called Meredith and told her what had happened today, the service and the meeting for coffee and the letter and the check. The thousand dollars made this his job in a new way. Now I'm not just doing this on a whim, this fact let him say to Meredith.

"I think I should spend tomorrow looking into things around here, talking to the families," he went on, "trying to pin Natalie down some more if I can. I'm going to make reservations for Pepperell Woods for the weekend, starting Thursday." He waited for help but got none. "Do you want to come?"

"Maybe," Meredith said. "After my Friday class. Include me in your reservations, please. Keep me posted, and I will let you know right away if I hear anything from Suzanne."

"That's it?"

"No. I want to remind you to call about your bloods tomorrow."

"Oh, right," Alex said, surprised that he had, in fact, forgotten. The bureaucracy at the Commonwealth Community Medical Plan was not so good. If anything was wrong with his blood, the information would get to his doctor, and to him—eventually. The *eventually* was why the doc always asked him to grease the wheels by calling in first. "I will." He waited for an explanation of the cold correctness of her tone. "What's wrong?" he asked at last. The answer he got sounded like one that Meredith had rehearsed.

"Last time you did this, Alex, you were sick. I tried to watch over you as much as you would let me, which was not very much. Now you're supposed to be well—as you put it, as well as you're ever going to get. So, when you choose to go on investigating murders . . . well, dammit, I don't have to like it, that's all."

"I chose, yeah, but Rosemarie needed somebody to do it. You wanted me to send her back to the Yellow Pages?"

"I never said you invented the job. Neither do sailors or fishermen invent theirs. That's what it makes me, though, isn't it? One of those women waiting for men who've gone to sea. There's not much to do but stroll around the widow's walk and cast either fearful or hopeful glances out over the waves."

"Oh fuck," Alex exploded. "You're not talking about 'investigating murders,' quote unquote. I invited you to come up to New Hampshire and help me find out what Rosemarie wants to know, didn't I? You're talking about waiting for tumors to show their ugly faces again."

"Don't tell me what I'm talking about," Meredith shot back. "If I don't carry a rifle, I can't criticize the waging of war?"

Alex imagined the fury with which her fingers would be gripping the phone. He still thought he was right, but he knew that now he'd really pissed her off. Step Back to Repulse Monkey, he said to himself—or, better, Rollback, or White Swan, or any of the many postures whose purpose is to help the tai chi practitioner redirect an antagonist's energy without stepping back. So that a blow is deflected, goes somewhere else, so that it does not land. Rightly or wrongly, Alex rooted himself in the idea that her anger was primarily at his cancer, not his actions. He slid away from the anger, yet he remained aware that his block was itself an admission that she had a point.

Being a "recovering cancer patient," in Alex's view, was a difficult game because it was a game you had to play in the dark. Put another way, it was like playing a team sport, say basketball, against an opposing team whose strengths and weaknesses were completely concealed. Maybe the opponent had exhausted both his starting five and his bench—maybe those haywire, abnormally multiplying cells were all gone, done in by chemical warfare and the body's natural defenses, dead. Or maybe not—maybe the opponent had acquired new life in the form of an unheralded rookie, a late-round draft choice who soon would break out onto the floor and suddenly would dominate the league.

There was no way of knowing; the issue was to keep from being paralyzed by waiting, paralyzed by fear. One of the ways to avoid paralysis, Alex felt, was to take risks. To show he was not afraid to play aggressive ball. Even as he dredged up this analogy, however, he knew it would not be convincing to Meredith. Should one take up skydiving, she would parry, just to vanquish one's fear of an airplane crash? So he just said good night, and so did Meredith, and then each of them hung up a telephone and left the other one alone.

That was that, then. Alex turned in the silent apartment and dropped on the couch where she had told him about what happened after she left the restaurant that night. Okay, he concluded, she was being pigheaded. She wasn't going to help him enjoy this, help him take pride in unearthing guilty parties for Rosemarie Davis, or in piercing Natalie Cooper's web of words and helping her save Suzanne Lutrello from whatever threatened, arrest or frame-up or worse. Meredith would not be sucked into this. She was going to remain the parson's level-headed daughter with the unerring eye.

Women, Alex said to himself. Enough women for the night. His eyes focused on a windowsill that held an ashtray, and in the ashtray half of the joint that he had rolled for Natalie. He wanted to get smashed and go out and shoot pool, the way he used to do in Nebraska, many, many nights with Hans. Hans, the factory-trained VW mechanic who'd left Germany for a change of culture and a way out of the *Bundeswehr* draft—and gone straight to the heartland of America, where the great-grandchildren of German immigrants could be found. And then he'd been charmed and intrigued when a Semitic, black-bearded Glauberman had come along. Well, that was all far in the past now, and anyway, even if Hans Heidenfelter miraculously pounded on his door, Alex didn't know any pool halls without cigarette smoke, and breathing other people's tobacco was not an acceptable form of thumbing his nose at the odds.

So he dialed his friend Bernie, who would give him a hard time like Meredith, but once he did it he wouldn't stay mad. Besides, Bernie was a downtown lawyer and a keen observer of doings among Boston's upper class. Bernie would know some things about Graham Johnston and Barbara (Pepperell) Johnston and maybe Lowell Townsend Johnston or Rosemarie (Sturgeon) Davis as well. He and Bernie would go to an upscale bar with a no-smoking lounge where they would drink imported beer and see what loose ends might turn up to be unraveled. But he got only Bernie's answering machine, which he took to mean that Bernie and his wife Phyllis had gone to bed. So he smoked the rest of the joint and thought about the fact that Hans was married too—or had been, the last Alex had heard.

Because in truth, that business about Alex and Hans and the

pool hall hadn't lasted all that long. Soon enough it had been Alex and Ilene Paciorek, and Hans tagging along. And then after a while it hadn't been that, but Hans and Ilene, two real Nebraskans, who soon enough, in a mix of recklessness and tradition, drove off one night and came back a week later, married. And they had all gotten along, but from then on Alex knew he was leaving. He'd waited for an excuse, and the excuse had been Laura, passing through and needing her car fixed en route to Boston.

Well, life. Tonight there was no more to do about old family dramas or new ones either. In the morning he would start with the Johnstons. For now he spread his feet, hip-width apart, and tried to feel a connection between the earth and the soles of his feet. It was a relief to give both his mind and his body to the tai chi form, to surrender to its infinitely detailed pattern, its sequence, to strive without striving, to search for stillness in motion and for motion in stillness. It was a hell of a lot more wholesome than speaking in coded whispers to ski resort employees, searching for the college-educated hookers that Caroline Davis had known.

7

TESTING, ONE AND TWO

Wednesday morning, Alex again brought extra clothes to work. He felt enough loyalty to business and craft to finish up the valve job on the Saab that was sitting in his shop. But he told the customers with reservations for today that he was sorry, they'd have to come back in a week. He told them he had to get his boiler fixed. The cold snap had broken, the sun was out, and the weather forecast called for a high of thirty-nine. Still, he knew none of the customers would themselves work in a building without heat. They threw him sour but vanquished looks and left. Alex found a number in the phone book and called the Graham Johnston home.

"My name is Alex Glauberman. I don't like to intrude, but I'd like to arrange to speak to Mr. or Mrs. Johnston when I can. I'm afraid it's about their son's death."

"You're from the police, you mean?"

"No. No, I'm not. I'm a friend of a friend of Scat's. To whom am I speaking, please?"

"This is Gardner Johnston."

"Yes," Alex said. "Scat's brother." He riffled through a clip-board full of repair orders. It helped him act the part of some-body whose call should command respect. "It has to do with some things that happened in New Hampshire. I've been re-tained to look into those."

"You're an attorney?"

"Yes," Alex said. That would have to be the meaning of these oversized sheets of paper in his hands. He had a friend who was an attorney, anyway. Which was the capital of New Hampshire, Manchester or Concord? The second one, that's where you drove past the gold dome. "In Concord. I know this is a bad time. But I'm down here seeing to some property closings today..."

"Just a moment," Gardner Johnston's expressionless voice said. A moment went by—three minutes, actually, by Alex's watch. No one spoke to him, but the line did not go dead. There were probably laws against impersonating an officer of the court. Bernie would know. Trevisone would know, too. For now, Alex just tried to figure out what to say next.

"Well, Mr. . . . . Glauberman, he'll see you today then. He'll be at home here, at half past twelve."

"Thank you," Alex said. Apparently it was assumed that his property closings could be shifted to accommodate the schedule of a wealthy and mourning man. That was not surprising. What was surprising was that the senior Johnston would agree to a meeting without more explanation. Alex scribbled the house number on the topmost repair order. This reminded him he was supposed to call in for a lab report. He gave his name to the assistant, who told him he would be put on hold. On hold they played a kind of Muzak that was heavy on violins and guitars. The assistant came back. She said, "Alex, Dr. Wagner wants you to come down and get another test."

Immediately, Alex heard his breath go shallow. He felt some

58

live creature in his belly fill with air and float up into his face. Step back, he told himself. Roll back. Turn aside.

"Alex?" the clinical assistant said.

"Sorry?"

"Dr. Wagner would like you to come in for another test."

"Yeah," Alex answered. "I heard you. Did she say what was wrong?"

"No, but I have your slip. It's the blood counts and the LDH. Those are the ones she wants you to have."

"I had those Monday. Do you mean there was a problem with the results?"

"I really don't know. She's with a patient. She said to tell you these tests were to be repeated."

"*All* of them? Because they were all bad, or because she thinks there might have been an error?"

"Would you like to speak to her? I'll have to put you back on hold."

Alex looked at his watch. The doctor hadn't called him. Therefore—giving her the benefit of the doubt—it was not an emergency. Whatever had bothered her, she had decided not to do anything about it until she saw the result of another test. "No. If I get in there right away, can she order the new test Stat and get the result this afternoon?"

"I think so. If you can get in here before twelve."

"I'll have to," Alex said, and hung up. He needed a shower before he could see Graham Johnston. He gave himself five minutes. Five minutes to wash off the grease, and the same five minutes to think. He stood under the warm water, closed his eyes and let it soak his skin, soak his hair and his beard. With his eyes shut he could see the pink lab slip waiting for him, the little check marks indicating which parts or functions were being checked. Like a vacuum test, compression check, rpms or cranking volts or dwell. Only it was living things being measured: blood counts and LDH.

Blood counts were straightforward, he understood them well enough: white cells, red cells, and platelets. He'd gotten used to having his counts checked twice a week during chemo, because the medications had the side effect of killing off these vital cells. But now they were checked just every other month. Routine, he had been assured—in case of bone marrow involvement, which would not show up to the educated touch or on the ghostly black-and-white X-ray film. "Involvement" was the medical term for a small malignant mass. Such a mass might be reflected in lowered counts of blood components that the bone marrow produced. It was better not to get involved. And something else, too, some more remote possibility. Something about autoimmune reactions, which might prompt the body to devour its own cells.

LDH was the other bimonthly test. Lacto-something, Alex couldn't remember the name. A liver enzyme, the doc had said. Jaundice, hepatitis, what did impaired liver function look like? Yellow piss? Yellow for liver trouble, red for kidney. But no, that wasn't the point of the test. "A secondary measure of tumor growth." Those were the words she had said. How did that work, and why?

Alex shut off the shower and reached for a towel, feeling suddenly cold, wintry cold. He began to get ready for what would happen if the second test also made the doc unhappy—unhappy, but not surprised. Ultrasound, CAT scan, bone marrow biopsy, it would be. That needle in the hip, right through the bone, jabbing into the marrow like electric shock, inside the bone, just for an instant, where the anesthetic couldn't touch. And then what? Back to the medications? Back to that sense of his body not being there for him, running on only half of its cylinders, suddenly surging and then as suddenly missing, choking off? Back to that long, slow, perpetual lousy feeling in his gut?

Along this stretch of Brattle Street the sidewalk was well shoveled, from curb to the edges of the lawns where the noontime sun melted enough ice to show mud and tufts of soggy grass. Alex wondered whether the city fathers provided mini-plows for the old boulevard of the old rich. Or perhaps the lawn-care firms did this as a sideline in winter. He parked his car, tied his tie, and pulled the bandage off the inside of his elbow.

The needle hole had clotted nicely—no problem with his platelets as far as he could see. He'd gotten in and out of the lab quickly and efficiently, just as the needle had gotten in and out of his arm. Usually he liked watching the test tube fill up with the rich, dark blood. Usually it was comforting to see the life-sustaining fluid, and it was comforting also to be able to face it without flinching or faintness; it would be wimpy in the extreme to be afraid of the sight of one's own blood. But he'd given himself dispensation. Today it was okay if he didn't want to watch. He'd been tempted to hang around and try to talk to the doc. However, that dispensation he had not given. He had work to do. The appointment with Graham Johnston would not wait. There was something ghoulish about coming here to the bereaved father. Facing his own death, even remotely, made that feel a bit more all right.

Alex checked his appearance in the rearview mirror. These were the same clothes he had worn to Caroline Davis's memorial. They weren't what lawyers wore, but one of Alex's last claims to bohemianism was that he didn't own a suit. Brown slacks and a preppy tweed jacket, bought used; these would have to do.

The Johnston house was set sideways to Brattle Street, and well back. It was an old house, wood clapboard painted a light purple with a bluish tint. Probably it had originally been white, and had fronted on a farm or a large meadow. But for a long time the farm or meadow had been house lots and side streets. The Johnston property was separated from these lots by a solid cedar fence. As Alex followed the concrete walk, an invisible dog kept up an angry, monotonous barking from the other side.

The door was answered by a servant, a housekeeper—a young woman with wide Indian features, Salvadoran or Guatemalan, Alex thought. He said who he was, expecting to be shown into some wood-paneled study, but she pointed into the kitchen, which lay in the back of the house at the end of a short hall. The kitchen had been redone sometime, the renovation understated. The walls were still painted wainscot panels halfway up and painted plaster above—no Sheetrock, no polyurethaned new blond wood. The old fireplace held an antique Franklin stove. What had once been a pantry held a large electric range surrounded by work surfaces and hanging pots. Alex liked this kitchen. In fact, he was jealous. This one was still itself, not rigged together as he'd done his own, out of odds and ends of modern, functional designs. On the other hand, this one had been, even from the beginning, a cookhouse of the well-to-do.

The housekeeper pointed Alex to a chair whose rungs he'd bet had been turned on a hand lathe when electricity was used for telegraph messages and not much else. The tabletop was old walnut or oak, darkened with age and scarred with use. There would be a dining room somewhere, probably through the closed side door. Had this table been the place where the wife or the cook served breakfast to the kids? The housekeeper poured Alex coffee and set before him a tray of cold fish. In halting English she told him to wait, that Mr. Johnston would come soon. Alex wondered whether the cold fish was some kind of metaphor. He discovered it was seviche, and delicious, tender but retaining its texture, cilantro and garlic peeking through the taste of lemon. He decided it had been prepared along with other easy-to-serve dishes for the condolence callers who would be dropping in.

Graham Johnston's house put Alex in mind of a Puritan sea captain or farmer, grizzled, big-boned, austere. Johnston, who came in through the dining room door, was much closer to Tweedledum or Tweedledee. A round head with cherubic expression rested on a roly-poly body in a rumpled black suit. The only thing that destroyed the image of an overgrown boy was the heavy shadow on the cheeks and chin. Either he had not shaved, or some rugged ancestor's genes had given him a naturally heavy beard. He was not at all shifty-eyed, yet Alex felt a shiftiness nonetheless.

"Seviche," the cherubic man explained, shutting the door behind him. "Fresh fish cured in lemon. I'm expecting my wife back from Europe this evening, in time for the funeral. But Josefina is an excellent cook." He served himself some of the fish as he talked, and then he stopped talking to refuel. He shoveled the food in, but not absently. He enjoyed it. His tongue searched for any morsels that remained on his plump pink lips. "I understand you wanted to see me concerning Scatty," he said then. He blinked. "Concerning my son."

That answered one question Alex had not known how he was going to ask. The nickname was a childhood leftover, not part of the newer, shadier identity that Lowell Johnston had carved out.

"Yes," Alex said. "It does concern Scat. Frankly, it concerns the circumstances surrounding his death."

"I see." More fish disappeared. "My older son said you represented yourself as an attorney. Am I being sued, or do you have some sort of . . . proposition to make?"

"Proposition. I am . . . a friend of a friend of your son's. I wonder if you'd mind telling me about his nickname, by the way."

"Not at all." Not at all. Alex had a flash of the kind of jolly creature one should beware of in fairy tales—the friendly elf who feeds you a delicious meal, which you find out too late is a potion that turns you forever into a fish. Caroline Davis's grandfather had allegedly renamed himself after the sturgeon, the caviar fish. "Lowell was the youngest," the father said, "and so he was nicknamed by the older children. As an infant he would double over in laughter when they chased the cat. When he began to have words, he would try that one out whenever the creature appeared. 'Scat,' he'd cry at the top of his lungs. 'Scat.'"

The father seemed genuinely pleased to share the recollection. He stopped eating and smiled inwardly, lowering his innocent blue eyes. Because he was remembering a happy time? Or because he envied the boy's ability to scream that way, at the top of his lungs? It didn't seem that Graham Johnston would ever do that kind of thing. "We should have stopped calling him that, I suppose," he went on. "That's what he did from this house, as soon as he got that motorcycle at sixteen. He went. Scat. Gone." He blinked again. "I really didn't know my son very well. But he was my son. I gather that to you he was, or is, only a means to some other end. So now let's talk business. As you can imagine, this is a busy and difficult time."

What business? Alex wanted to know. Something to do with New Hampshire. All he could think of was that Graham Johnston knew or suspected his son had been in some deep shit. So now he was expecting to be approached by—whom? Lawyers? Why? Business? What? Could you sue a father for damages inflicted by his late son? Was it wealth he was protecting, a trust fund, against a claim upon Scat Johnston's estate? Or was he expecting to be hit up for money right now, hush money—as if the family name, the son's reputation, was all that remained of the son's life to be saved?

"As you know," Alex said, "your son was involved in a fatal accident in New Hampshire shortly before he died." He said this slowly, a man revealing his purpose bit by bit as the civilities and delicacies were put away and the men moved on to claret, business, and cigars. But in fact he could playact all he wanted; he had nothing more to say except the truth. "I'm trying to find out about that, and whether it could have any connection to what happened to him next."

"If you are a private investigator, I'm not interested. I'm content to leave things in the hands of the police."

"I'm not a licensed investigator, but I'm looking into this for Mrs. Davis, whose granddaughter was the skier in the accident." Alex laid Rosemarie's letter of introduction on the old, scarred wood. "You're welcome to call Mrs. Davis if you have any doubts about me. She thinks the deaths may be connected. I'd like to ask you some questions on her behalf."

Graham Johnston did not pick the letter off the table, but he read it carefully nonetheless. When he looked up, his face had lost its glow, and the shadow had become more pronounced. He rang a small Colonial-style bell, which he picked off the window-sill. Josefina appeared swiftly, and silently she cleared the two plates and what was left of the seviche away. "I see," Johnston said for the second time. There was no anger visible or audible in what he went on to say—only resignation, a sad fat boy's resignation at being the way he was, and the world being the way it was, too.

"I have nothing to tell you," he said to Alex. "Unless I find some reason to be dissatisfied with the police, I prefer, as I said, to leave it to them. They say that so far the trail leads right to that girl Suzanne. The two of them rode up to that other girl's apartment on that damn motorbike, his new one, though the temperature was twenty degrees. At the time they say Scatty would have died, she ran out the door, mounted *his* bike, and roared off. I don't think anything that happened anywhere else has any bearing on the case."

"I see," Alex said. "And suppose, as I look into this, I come up with any information about your son's life that I think you would want to know. Should I route this information through the police?"

"None of it can hurt him anymore," Graham Johnston replied.

"Well," Alex said. "Thank you for your time, and please pardon my intrusion."

"Yes." Scat's father stood and turned toward the dining room door. Over his shoulder he dismissed his visitor. "Josefina will show you out."

Josefina did, and Alex got no chance to see who or what else was in the house. He retraced his steps down the path and then turned right on Brattle, taking himself for a walk instead of getting in his car. Graham Johnston had agreed to see him on the expectation there was some kind of proposition, some buying or selling to be done. He had been nervous, blinking and shoveling in the food, yet he had also been circling, sizing up, preparing for a fight. Then, when Alex had laid his cards on the table, Graham Johnson had grown calm. He had overestimated Alex's hand, or mistaken him for someone else. When Alex turned out to be Rosemarie Davis's emissary, blundering in the dark, that had been the end of that.

Alex walked till he came to an open green. It was a green in summer, of course. Now it was a big open *white*. It lay between the Mormon church and the Quaker one. It would be a good place to stand in the sun.

The old Puritan-descended churches—Congregational and Unitarian—were close in to Harvard Square. The heretical faiths had somehow ended up out here, on either side of a large elliptical drive, and had maintained the space in the middle as an empty buffer between them. Alex crunched his boots into the softening snow and turned so the sun could hit his face. There were four more hours until he could call for his test results, just before five o'clock. He closed his eyes in the sunlight, tucked his pelvis, bent his knees, extended one hand in front of him palm out, and formed the other into a relaxed fist resting at the ready on his hip.

Just stand, he told himself, stand solid and breathe. Now imagine each breath entering through the hands and the feet and the toes. Let the four streams of healing breath travel inward through the marrow of your bones. Where the streams met, he imagined them rising through his spine and circulating also in the marrow of his skull. Then he breathed out, sealing off the marrow behind the escaping breath. The energy, now under a sort of pressure, was expelled through his open hand toward whoever or whatever might be in front of it.

Cleansing the marrow, this technique was prosaically called. Like all exercises related to the internal schools of Chinese boxing, it drew no distinct line between relaxation and power, or between medicine and martial arts. This technique helped the practitioner to become rooted and to develop power. It was also a meditation, a healing practice. Alex liked to cleanse his marrow at least once a week. He enjoyed it, and after all it could do no harm. It was as prudent as changing the oil every two thousand miles. Today it was more than prudent. Alex wondered whether Taoism, from which tai chi was derived, included a concept of prayer. Soon he was ready to walk back to his car. He would call Bernie again and convince him that he could spare half an hour. Then he would park near the subway and meet Bernie downtown.

The sun stayed out, its glow nice on the white lawns. Some of the tree branches had been sheathed in ice, which now dripped and glistened in the faraway heat. All that marred the effect were the gray, gritty snowbanks heaped by the plows at the edge of the street—dirty, jagged ramparts now turning to slush. Alex was thinking about springtime when he noticed the glistening pattern on the windshield of his car.

It was a beautiful pattern, an intricate spiderweb gleaming like strings of icy pearls in the winter light. At first he thought it was just a trick of that light, a shining effect of the melting frost. Then he realized that there shouldn't be any frost, or droplets, or any kind of lines. Because the window, when he left the car, had been dry. He felt that trapped thing again, that creature trying to fight its way out of his gut. He broke into a run. What he found was what he'd deduced would be there.

The windshield had been smashed—not just smashed, but worked over carefully, probably with a hammer. There was a gaping, jagged hole in the middle, and everywhere else spread a network of shatter lines. The same thing had been done to the back window, only the vandal had put two big holes there. Someone had stood here and methodically done this to the glass. Someone who wasn't afraid to do so in public on this peaceful but well-watched Brahmin street.

Robbery was not the motive. Number one, the side windows, offering easier access to the door locks, were untouched. Number two, the car was more than ten years old, and almost any other on the street would have been more enticing to steal or to rifle. Number three, no effort had been made to break loose enough shards to get inside. And number four, Alex saw, was that wrapped tightly around the passenger-side windshield wiper, like a bandage holding together a wounded arm, was a white piece of paper, a note. He unwound it and found that it was typewritten in all caps. It was almost a poem. At least it had a title, the way a poem would. It was almost incoherent, too. Yet it was sharply focused; an offer of a trade, a deal, backed up by a threat.

ICE CREAM SUNDAE(Y)

SHE IS NOTHING, DESSERT, VANILLA CREAM PIE.
DO YOU KNOW WHAT IT IS TO LOSE A SON?
DO YOU HAVE SOMETHING (SOMEONE) PRECIOUS
    YOU ARE AFRAID TO LOSE?
I GIVE THE ORDERS.
SERVE UP THE DESSERT
BY SUNDAY!
SERVE IT UP,
THE PRETTY POISON,
THE SCUM.
NO MORE TROUBLE NOW.
SUZANNE BY SUNDAY.
OR ELSE!!

Alex rerolled the note, taking care not to disturb the front side of
the paper. He found his keys, unlocked the door, put the note in
the glove compartment, and locked that. He unlocked the trunk
and then started the engine so it could warm up. From the trunk he
took one of the bricks he kept for blocking the wheels when
changing a tire. He hefted the brick, got a running start down the
concrete path, swiveled from his hips, and directed as much of his
anger as he could into the snap of elbow, forearm, and wrist.

The brick crashed cleanly through a picture window. The
picture window was to the right of the door, probably the living
room. Two voices, Alex thought, screamed as he ran back to his
car.

Accelerating away from the curb, heart pounding, Alex was
no longer surprised at what he had found, nor was he surprised at
what he had done. He understood that fury had a way of erupting.
You could be controlled and as methodical as all hell about it, but
still you couldn't control what you were about to do. That could be
true of himself, heaving a brick. It could be true of a Tweedledum
going bang-bang-bang with a hammer after hastily typing a note. It
could be true of a driver who rammed two tons of steel into a
nineteen-year-old skier as she tried awkwardly to slide or quick-
step across pavement. And it could be true of somebody who drove
a knife, again and again, into a well-born man who dealt heroin, a
man named after the act of scaring a cat.

If Alex wasn't careful, the message on his wiper blade proclaimed, that kind of fury could be unleashed on his daughter too. He drove home. He steered with one hand as he punched out the hole in the windshield with the other gloved fist. The glass came off like sections of jigsaw puzzle, the pieces still clinging together as you take the puzzle apart.

8

EMERGENCY ROOM

The house where Alex lived was a two-and-a-half decker, built close to the street. It had no yard, unlike the Johnstons' house, but it did have generous front porches on the first and second floors, each enclosed by a half-wall.

Alex lived in the first-floor apartment. The owners, Frank and Anne LaFarge, lived on the second and third floors. Anne liked Alex. Her youngest child had just gone away to college, the first to do so, at UMass's bigger campus in Amherst. The older children were married and working, with homes of their own. Anne had recently hinted that she'd like to sell the house to Alex if she could talk Frank into moving to a newer and smaller place the way she'd like. She mentioned that Alex and Meredith, together, might make enough to get a mortgage, even with rates and prices the way they were. Two-family homes weren't under rent control; either apartment could bring in a pretty high rent. If they couldn't come up with a down payment, maybe they knew some other "young people," as Anne said, to make the place into condos, one unit per couple.

Today Alex and Anne arrived home at the same moment. Alex wasn't quite sure why he'd come home, since he recalled that he had a spare set of windows in his shop. These came off a Saab 99 EMS like his from a customer who had skidded hard into a telephone pole the first bad freeze of the winter. It didn't take much, in the insurance company's view, to total a car that old. Thanks to the shoulder belts, both the customer's head and the windshield had survived.

Alex supposed he was coming home because of the screwy threatening note and the careful way his car had been mauled. He wanted to know that his apartment was safe and undisturbed, that nothing had been done to Maria's pictures and posters, her toys, her old stuffed horse, her desk with pens and pencils stacked neatly to be ready when she returned. This would allow him to feel the threat had been vacant, a blind flailing-out, not really aimed at Maria at all. However, when he saw Anne staring at his windshield, he wished he'd gone to the shop instead. He began to make up something about vandalism and insurance estimates as they each got out their keys to the separate entrance doors, side by side on the front porch. He didn't look around the porch. Anne, with pride and responsibilities of ownership, did.

"That girl..." she said, her glove coming to her mouth.

What girl? he started to say, what local scandal was this? Then Alex caught the real shock in Anne LaFarge's voice. Suzanne Lutrello lay huddled on her side in the far corner of the porch, hidden from the street, hidden as well from the sun. Her legs were drawn up in a fetal position. Her arms, instead of being curled around her knees, stretched straight, unnaturally straight, behind her back. Her head rolled forward, the left temple pressed against the floorboards. Her eyes were shut, and she looked as if she had been there a long time. She wasn't wearing a coat, only a black sweater. Anne went toward her, but Alex hurried past. His first guess was that Maria was no longer in danger —that Suzanne, the vanilla ice cream, was not just cold but dead. He could see that her hands, bare beyond the sleeves of her sweater, were blue. Her wrists were tied together with what looked like the cord from a venetian blind.

As he got to her, Suzanne opened her eyes and then let them shut. That made twice now that Alex had given her up for dead when she was not. He felt guilty, vowed to make it up to her, as he tried to sit her up. She gasped and then groaned. Alex fished for his pocketknife to free her hands. Meanwhile, Anne LaFarge crouched down and laid the younger woman's head in her lap. She began massaging Suzanne's face. Alex cut through the cord and tried to restore circulation in the wrists and hands. Suzanne gasped again and now she tried to move, so Anne and Alex both helped. Suzanne grabbed awkwardly for her left shoulder with her right hand. She missed. Alex felt her shoulder, to see what was wrong. She screamed a soft, whimpering scream.

"Hurts," she said. "Wicked bad." She closed her eyes and sagged against her rescuers' support.

"Hold her up," Anne said. "Don't move her. I'll call the ambulance." Alex remembered that Anne had mentioned being trained as a nurse. You didn't have to go to college for it in those days, she'd said. It had been in one of the conversations where she'd expressed the hope that Alex would someday find a way to finish school. She didn't work now, but Alex took comfort from the fact that she ought to know what to do.

"No ambulance," Suzanne pleaded suddenly. "You take me. No ambulance. No cops."

Anne LaFarge only threw her a practiced, motherly, disapproving look. She shifted the weight of Suzanne's body to Alex and hurried inside to phone. Alex held Suzanne up while trying to let the injured shoulder alone.

"Are you bleeding?" he asked. What he meant was, had somebody stabbed her, shot her, was there any other injury he couldn't see?

Suzanne forced a smile. "No," she said. "Fell on it. Maybe broken. But that's all. I can walk, if you help me." Her eyelids drooped again, but she forced them open. "We got to go. Alex. Now. Help me up. No cops, please."

She put her good arm around his shoulders, and he wrapped both of his arms around her waist. He raised her up, slowly, until he felt her legs begin to take some of the weight.

"You got a car?" she said. She gasped again, but didn't groan or cry. Maybe it's not broken, Alex thought. Maybe it's only bruised.

"Most of one. Can you walk?"

"Walk," she said.

Bent over, step by step, Alex helped her across the porch and down the steps. He heard a storm door open and slam behind them.

"I said don't move her," Anne's voice commanded.

Alex put Suzanne in the passenger seat, threw his landlady a puzzled and helpless look, and drove off. He felt like a thief stealing a baby from a hospital ward. He thought the police would feel that way about him too. He stopped and tucked his coat over her like a bib, and turned the heater on full blast. Still, the wind was going to pour in through the hole he'd widened in the windshield. Now it looked as if a basketball had gone through the glass.

"A hospital," he said. "You need to get that looked at. If the circulation got cut off, you could have frostbite too."

"No cops," she repeated. Alex thought of the note resting in the glove compartment. He had a lot of questions to ask her. In the end, if he couldn't talk her into turning herself in, he might have to do it himself. The first thing, though, was her arm.

"Okay," he promised. "Just doctors." Up till that moment he had forgotten he had to call a doctor of his own. What was wrong with him was invisible, if indeed there was anything wrong. But suppose he had to check in for a biopsy tomorrow, and subject himself to "more aggressive forms of treatment" after that? How was he going to take care of a daughter and a fugitive from justice then? He banged out more of the broken glass.

"Not here," Suzanne said. "Someplace farther out."

Not too far, Alex thought. He compromised. "Middlesex Memorial is supposed to be okay."

Suzanne nodded in a resigned way. Alex did the best he could on the twists and turns of the Alewife Brook Parkway, but he could tell she was bracing herself against the pain, trying not to show it. She didn't ask about the window, or explain anything, and this was not the time to press her to talk. Alex followed the parkway, which followed the Alewife Brook to its confluence with the Mystic River and then downstream.

WHAT FISH HAS A MILLION SQUARE FEET? the promotional billboard near Alex's house riddled the commuter traffic on the parkway. ALEWIFE CENTER, LEASING NOW, it answered itself. An alewife was a small fish, and it gave its name to the waterway and now the subway terminus and a mammoth four-story garage. Beyond the station were new office parks, and soon these would be joined by twice as many offices, a hotel, and a mall. A connection that had been vague suddenly became clearer. Scat's mother, somebody Pepperell Johnston. The ski resort, Pepperell Woods. Development, land, property—was that somehow what these deaths would turn out to be about?

Past Medford Square, Alex turned onto Interstate 93 heading north—toward New Hampshire, where the explanation of

71

one death, maybe two, ought to be. But he left the highway after a mile, where it bisected the rocky hills known as the Middlesex Fells. This land was a public reservation, immune to development for the moment at least. He slowed down on the winding park road. A couple carrying cross-country skis emerged from the woods. The skiers' dog leaped onto the road. Alex braked sharply and Suzanne said, "Oww. Jesus."

"Almost there," he said. "Listen, Suzanne. Did you know the woman Scat hit?" Seeing the skiers, he couldn't help but ask. "Caroline Davis. Did you know anything about her?"

"Uh-uh. Except it wasn't an accident. I know that. That's why somebody wanted Scat dead. I just haven't got any proof."

Back to square one, Alex thought. Okay, the first thing was Suzanne's arm. The hospital emerged around a bend, pleasant, surrounded by the woods. The emergency room wasn't busy, surprisingly, and they took Suzanne as soon as her paper work was done. She swore she'd pay Alex back, but she didn't want to use her real name, and anyway she insisted she didn't have her ID. She said she was Sharon Smith, and Alex vouched for her, signing on enough dotted lines to satisfy the intake clerk that the hospital could always come after him. Just stepping into the ER and seeing an M.D., the fee schedule said, would cost a hundred fifty bucks. Alex hoped that qualified as "expenses" on Rosemarie Sturgeon Davis's account. A man in a white coat gently lifted Suzanne's arm by the bicep and turned it this way and that. He asked her to scream as loud as she wanted to when it hurt the most. She groaned but didn't scream. The intern, or whoever he was, told Alex it was *probably* a dislocated shoulder. He looked at Suzanne's hands and face. Had she been outside, skiing or something? he asked.

Suzanne said, "Something," and the man in white frowned and took her away through swinging doors. Alex looked around for a pay phone. There were two, mounted on the wall, not in booths, at the angle of two rows of plastic chairs. A sign hanging from the ceiling said WAITING AREA. Both phones were in use, so Alex stood and waited. That was what a waiting area was for.

"...ten stitches," he tuned in to the man in front of him saying. "And he'll be in a cast three months. He'll need to lie in the backseat to get home." He tried to tune in on the woman at the other phone. "...false labor..." he made out. But the woman obviously wasn't pregnant. She was stuffed into a tight ski-slope-style windbreaker, high heels, tight jeans. Either she was talking about some other kind of labor, or she was talking about somebody else. Then the man who was talking about the cast hung up. Alex moved in on the phone, picked up the receiver to claim it, but didn't drop his dime in yet.

"...with her luck, she'll have the kid in the car on the way home. What? I don't know. I'll put her to bed and hope the contractions are gone by tomorrow so she can go to school." It dawned on Alex that this was the grandmother-to-be, that here was the national problem of Teenage Pregnancy right before his eyes.

The woman on the phone turned and stared at him. Her face was lined but tight, her lips twisted just a little, her arched eyebrows seeming to ask him something. Her jacket said *freestyle* in silver script over each breast. She puffed rapidly on a cigarette, not inhaling. Then she said, "Yeah, I hope so," and hung up, still staring at Alex as if he'd been following her, or blaming her, or checking her out in a way that demanded some response. He said, "Good luck. I have a daughter, too." The woman didn't answer, but she smiled and shrugged as she went past. Alex took three deep breaths and dropped in a dime and dialed. A recorded message told him it would cost thirty more cents to reach that number from here. Alex followed orders. The clinical assistant said, "Oncology. Can you hold please," and gave him over to the Muzak without waiting for an answer. Alex said yes anyway. The grandmother-to-be sat down.

"Yes, please, who were you waiting for?" said the voice on the phone.

"This is Alex Glauberman," Alex said. "I'm calling for a test result. Is Dr. Wagner still in?"

"Dr. Wagner is with a patient. Would you like to hold?"

"That depends. Can you see if you have the result, or if she left a message for me?"

"Hold on, please, I'll check." He was delivered over to the pacifying string orchestra again. The tune was "Do You Know the Way to San Jose," though all the life and meaning were drained out. Alex looked around at the people waiting for good or bad news. If it was good, they'd forget being here, forget the details. If it was bad, they might remember everyone, everything. What would he remember? Dionne Warwick? That musical lament about a future that never came?

"Alex." His doc sounded chipper, maybe a bit breathless though. Shit, Alex thought, I don't want to take any more motherfucking drugs. But he gave himself credit for that thought. It was honest. It was to the point. It was not *Don't tell me I'm going to die.* "Your second tests were all fine," she said. He could hear her catching her breath. So she had been worried, and she'd hurried to the phone from somewhere, to reassure him herself. "It was just the leukocyte level that concerned me. It was on the very low end of normal the first time around. But not the second. So. I think we can assume it was all a false alarm. The lab is under a lot of pressure, mistakes happen, we'll assume that's what this was. But why don't you come in after one month instead of two, just to be sure?"

"Okay," Alex said. He didn't see the point of calling something a normal range if the low end raised so many suspicions, but now was no time to care about that.

"I'm sorry if you got fearful," she said. "But a stitch in time saves nine. So. Relieved?"

"Yes," Alex said. "Thanks. Yes, relieved."

"Okay. 'Bye, then."

"Okay. 'Bye."

Alex hung up the phone. He was more than relieved, he was ready to jump in the air and kick his feet. Yet he was also a little bit let down. It was that feeling of gearing up for something you turn out not to have to face. Not right then, anyway. It was the same feeling he'd attributed to Graham Johnston that morning. Had the letdown somehow contributed to his later fury—set off, perhaps, by seeing Alex's car still insolently waiting outside his house? Or, Alex thought for the first time, had it maybe not been Graham Johnston at all? It had to be someone who'd been there in the Johnston house, unless someone else had been following him, waiting for a chance. He called Bernie's office and kept demanding attention until Bernie's very brusque voice sounded in his ear.

"What, Alex? I'm up to my ass. What?"

"You got my message last night?"

"Yeah. I know some stuff. Architect, development, real estate. Lawyer, artist. I'll call you tonight, okay?"

"Graham Johnston's son Lowell was murdered Monday night. A suspect fled and is being looked for. I've got the suspect

74

with me. Now we're both being looked for, probably. We both need a lawyer. And Maria's been threatened, indirectly at least. So I need to see you, the suspect and I need to see you, as soon as we can."

"Alex—oh fuck it, never mind. I'll try to be out of here in half an hour. Where?"

"I'll call back and leave a message. Thanks Bernie."

"You shouldn't be getting mixed up in this," Bernie said, but Alex heard grudging admiration through the advice. Maybe because of it, Bernie hung up without saying good-bye. Alex smiled as he sat down in an orange plastic chair. Two phone calls, and things were looking much better. He wanted to share his relief with Meredith, but that was hard because he hadn't had a chance to share his problem. The *freestyle* woman moved to sit next to him. "So what happened to your daughter's arm?" she said.

"What?"

"I saw you bring her in. I saw the way she was holding her arm."

"Oh God," Alex said. "Do I really look old enough to be her father?".

"Sorry to tell you so," the woman said, then winked. "She's sure as hell too young to be your wife."

"I'm divorced," Alex said. "But you're right. My girlfriend is ten years older than her. What about you?" He had already looked for a ring on her finger, so he knew it wasn't there.

"Yeah. Divorced. Maybe it's simpler today. They don't bother to get married."

"What's going to happen about the baby?"

"Bring it up together, I guess. Hope that our two heads make a better mother than one." She jerked her chin in the direction of the swinging doors. Alex turned to see Suzanne walking out, looking about warily. The right sleeve of her sweater dangled empty, limp. "So just tell me. Who's that—if she's not your daughter, not your girlfriend, and not your wife?"

Alex looked back and forth between the *freestyle* woman and the one with her arm in a sling. He could imagine going off with the woman next to him, disappearing for an hour or a day, comparing their lives. He wouldn't be responsible for her, nor she for him. He was, all of a sudden, responsible for Suzanne.

"Are those the only choices?" he asked.

The woman winked again. "They used to be," she said. "Maybe not now. You tell me."

9

VIOLENT FEMMES

Suzanne waved jauntily with her good arm, but gave the woman next to Alex a stony and suspicious look. Alex walked over to Suzanne, slowly, asking himself whom he saw. A lively woman, in her early twenties, in cowboy boots with wooden heels, bleached jeans below a long sweater, black, down over her hips. Maria had once told him these jeans were called acid-washed, to distinguish them from stone-washed, which had a more lived-in, less fashionable look. The word seemed to mean like *sulfuric* or *nitric* again, apparently; acid meaning *lysergic* was gone.

Suzanne's hair was styled for exuberance, but her face was what he'd said to Trevisone: alert. She looked as though she liked fun but not nonsense. There was no giggle and no pout in her rather delicate lips, no freckles and no dimples in her round cheeks. Just a natural face, no longer very innocent or very young. She was short, as he'd remembered, and solid, but not at all fat. The jeans were tight around nice calves and thighs. Her hidden arm made a funny bulge above her waist.

"Feel better?" Alex asked.

"Believe it. It just hurt like hell when they popped it back in. It's in a sling now, under here. I got to rest it, that's all, so it won't pop out again. They say I'm stuck in the sling for a couple months. I guess you want me to explain some things."

"That's right. But I called a lawyer, a good friend. I want you to tell it to him while you're telling it to me. If either of us gets busted, I want him to already know what's going on."

"What about Professor Phillips?"

"No. Though I am going to call her, after. We need to pick a place to meet the lawyer. I've got a spare windshield in my shop. Before we run into any rain or snow, I'd like to put it in. My shop has got no windows, itself, by the way. Nobody would know anybody was there."

"Uh-uh. They might search it. That lady—she would have called the cops, right?"

"Anne. She owns the house. She might not. But she wouldn't cover for me if they came to her."

"So they know I'm with you. Can you get your lawyer to meet us at the Burlington Mall?"

"I guess. Why there?"

Suzanne laughed. "It's close to Billerica." Pronounced *Bill-ricka*, like a street in a new housing development named after the builder's children, the next town from Burlington was actually the site of the Middlesex County jail. "No, seriously, my brother Tommy works in the record store there. I want him with us too."

"What about my windshield?"

Suzanne pointed through the glass double doors. She said, "It'll be dark in ten minutes. Right now it's not snowing or raining. And no cops'll be able to see it, so they won't pull you over." Right, Alex thought. The shortest days of winter were gone, but it still got dark before five. He also thought she had everything figured out too well.

"What if I hadn't come home when I did? What if Anne had found you, without me?"

"Yeah," Suzanne said. "There was a record they used to play for us, in music-appreciation class in junior high. *Peter and the Wolf*, you know the one I mean? The grandfather comes on in the end, in this deep, deep voice. He says, 'What if Peter had not caught the wolf? What then?' Look. Suppose the cops are calling hospitals, asking if anybody like me has been brought in by anybody like you. Call your lawyer friend. Tell him the Town Meeting in the mall, he should look for us at one of the tables on the side."

On the highway, things were crowding up. The cracked glass glowed red from the taillights of the traffic, homeward bound. Alex squinted into the wind, bitter now, that tore at his eyes and whistled in his hair. Too late, he remembered he had a pair of safety glasses in his toolbox in the trunk. Suzanne, for all the tough talk, huddled by the passenger door, withdrawn into herself, covering her face with her free hand. Alex was glad he had a beard to do that. He turned on the radio and got National Public Radio news. He pushed the next button, which gave him the late-afternoon reggae music show instead. He preferred both the music's politics and its sound. So did Suzanne, apparently. She began to bob her head, a little bit, in time.

At Route 128, Alex turned west. The wind wasn't so bad there, because in rush hour the traffic always crawled. The road was three or four decades old and could no longer handle the flow of cars. Back in the suburbs, Alex thought. Back in the building boom.

The *old* boom, he corrected himself. Today's boom was in the city, as the middle-class migration imploded and industry, in the form of high-tech and services, followed. It was a cycle. It was happening everywhere. He noticed it all the time in the watershed of the Mystic that he was now leaving behind. A river valley —no bridges, no pavement, no highway, no brick—a fertile river valley was what the first settlers would have seen. Alex knew— because Meredith had learned it from Puritan chronicles—that a female Indian chief known to the English as the Squaw Sachem had once reigned along the Mystic. Her people's land had become settlers' farms, then shipyards and docks, then factories, and each year now more and more of the factories were gone. The Schraffts plant where Suzanne's mother had worked was all condos now. The Ford plant that had once assembled Edsels was a shopping mall. So was the drive-in movie near where Alex had turned from Alewife Brook Parkway onto I-93. The old jobs had disappeared, but somebody made a lot of money turning the old into the new.

City and suburb, Alex thought. City and suburb and mountain resort. Real-estate development, Bernie had said. Alex's father had been a construction craftsman, plaster and carpentry, before prefabrication had pushed him out and political connections had found him a place as a shop teacher instead. Big money, he would say. You got big money killing big money. You got to expect that somewhere there's money involved in that.

Alex reached the end of the thought, and now he was impatient with the jam-up, frustrated by the lilting, syncopated music from an island and a culture far away. He wanted to keep moving forward, taking this New England thing apart. He didn't want to have to sit still and worry. He didn't want to worry about Suzanne, and he didn't want to worry about himself. Wondering loomed large in his nature, but worrying did not. Over the past year he'd worked hard to keep it that way.

At just before six on a nondescript weekday night, the Burlington Mall was not the hyped-up place it had been when Alex had rushed through it before Christmas as part of the stampede of last-minute shoppers. Santa was gone, and barely a child was to be seen. The Muzak had reverted to old show tunes in place of Better Not Pout and Ba-Rum-Pa-Bum-Dum. Alex supposed this was the emptiest hour, the time everybody was home making or serving or eating the family meal.

"I don't want to go into Tommy's store," Suzanne said. "I don't want anybody to be able to prove he saw me. He's cute. He's got black hair, a mustache, he's younger than me, he'll be shooting the shit with some girls, and if the music is good he'll be boogying. He gets an hour off at six. Bring him down here, where we can sit and talk and not worry anybody'll listen to what we say."

Down here, where Suzanne had led him, was the species of place that seemed *de rigeur* for every enclosed shopping center from coast to coast. It was an open area full of small tables, surrounded by a ring of fast-food counters representing a dozen different national cuisines. A faint, unpleasant smell hung in the air, disinfectant, as if the brown brick floor had been mopped recently, perhaps when the late-afternoon crowd thinned out. Now the place was only about one-quarter full. Nonetheless, Suzanne was correct about the sound: the acoustics were awful. Piped music and footsteps and voice babble rebounded off hard surfaces to make a loud, perfect background din. Despite the localized name, Town Meeting was supposed to approximate an open-air plaza in a climate where people habitually sat and dined and conversed outdoors. In this plaza, everyone was well dressed, looked as if he or she had a nice home to go to, and under the fluorescent lighting showed off skin that was, conventionally speaking, white.

As Alex and Suzanne stood by the edge, a security guard under an old-fashioned Smokey the Bear hat ambled by. He had a policeman's swaggering gait, the one that came with the knowledge you wore a uniform, a badge, and something on your hip. On his was a walkie-talkie. Alex stayed put until the guard passed. He thought that, in sending him off to find Tommy, Suzanne was stating that she had already trusted him plenty, so now he was going to

79

have to trust her. He told her Bernie would be a studious-looking Jewish guy in heavy black-framed glasses and a three-piece suit.

When Alex had called Bernie the night before, it had been for both companionship and information. He knew Bernie loved and studied the intricacies of Boston Brahmin society the way only somebody who came from outside it could. It was like British Egyptologists, or Americans who went gaga over Indian peyote rites. Only in reverse. But now he needed Bernie in his official capacity as well, because Bernie specialized in criminal cases within the downtown firm where he worked. He said his clients might tell bald-faced lies to stay out of jail, but they were still less hypocritical than the types he'd get in commercial law.

Bernie and Alex had met soon after Bernie first passed the bar. He'd gotten Alex off when Alex was nabbed by a federal park ranger for smoking hash on the beach; later he'd also handled Alex's side of a relatively amicable, we've-come-to-the-end-of-the-road divorce. In fact, Bernie had held two-year-old Maria while Alex went up to speak his lines before the judge. Maria's shit had leaked through the Pamper and overalls onto Bernie's three-piece suit. He'd hung on, but he'd factored the cleaning costs into his bill. Bernie's daughter Elizabeth was the same age as Maria, and now the girls were friends. Alex kept an eye out for Bernie as he retraced his steps back to the main promenade of the mall.

It was quiet here, with few shoppers and the muted show tunes whose melodies Alex knew, though not the names. The trees, growing out of wide wooden boxes, were the same as the ones in the make-believe plaza. They had spindly branches and light-colored bark. They reminded Alex of miniature eucalyptus with sadly stubby leaves. Looking up, he realized they grew under skylights, dark now, the only admission of an outside world that could be cold, or lightless, or cruel. He also saw exposed steel beams and sheets of plywood, alike painted in muted blue and gray. He realized that a second level was about to be added to the mall. Soon he reached a doorway from which hard-driving guitar and drums poured out. Just inside the store, Tommy Lutrello lounged behind one of the two cash registers, exactly as described. He rolled his shoulders to the beat and talked over it with two blond teenage girls. He wore a white shirt with his name on a red pin bearing the music store's logo, and no tie. His dark hair was brushed upward in a way that reminded

80

Alex of Paul Anka from one decade and John Travolta from another.

Tommy stood about half a foot taller than Suzanne, and looked more distracted. His face was harsher and more closed in, with a slightly pocked effect. He wasn't a bruiser type, far from it, but Alex got more of a whiff of submerged violence from him than from his big sister. Maybe that was just a stereotype, though. Alex guessed that Tommy might be nineteen. He asked for some help and drew Tommy down an aisle of compact discs away from the pair of teenagers. "Can you figure out the price on this?" he asked vaguely, and then added, "I'm with Suzanne. She wants to see you on your break, over at the fast food."

"Suzy?" He looked at his watch, a watch with hands, mounted on a wide pigskin strap. "I'll be there," he said. "Who're you?"

"Alex. I'm a car mechanic and sometimes I look into things for people. I know that sounds like a line, but it's a short version of the truth." Alex asked himself why he was showing off. "I was hired to look into that auto accident Scat Johnston was in. Your sister thinks her situation will get better if I find out."

"Uh-huh," Tommy said. He reached down into a rack of compact discs, pulled one out, and handed it to Alex. "Well, that's the price that's on there," he added loudly, and went back behind his register to pick up the conversation he had left. Alex looked at the CD, which was titled *The Blind Leading the Naked*, performed by a group called Violent Femmes. He looked at Tommy again. Tommy could just as easily have picked Velvet Underground or Volkswagen Tyres, the groups filed on either side. There might have been a message in the album Tommy chose, and there might not. On impulse, Alex turned to the rack of tapes across the aisle and picked out the same album on cassette. He paid the other cashier, with plastic, and left. Tommy caught up with him halfway back down the main drag of the mall. Tommy said, "Over here, you mean?" and led the way.

10

GOOD WITNESS

The black-uniformed security guard sat in a white imitation wrought-iron chair in one corner of the Town Meeting. Suzanne and Bernie sat in identical chairs at a wood-and-Formica table in the corner opposite. Suzanne was working on soup and a sandwich. Bernie was drinking coffee and looking at his watch.

The place was about as crowded, or empty, as before. Half the diners seemed to be finishing business left over from work. The men had their jackets off and their pale yellow, blue, or pink sleeves rolled up. The women kept their jackets on, but gesticulated energetically with cigarettes or pens. They would all have gotten off work in the sprawling low-rise complexes that seemed to pop up like mushrooms along the highways hereabouts. Besides the dressed-for-success set, other pairs of diners sat and chatted or munched, relaxing after a day behind cash register or counter or keyboard or wheel. A few noisy clumps of teenagers flirted and showed off. Aside from having one arm under her sweater, Suzanne did not stand out here. Bernie, however, was the only customer in a downtown three-piece suit.

"That's our lawyer," Alex told Tommy. "Suzanne dislocated her shoulder, or somebody did it to her. So far she hasn't told me who or why. I took her to the hospital. I've stuck with her and stayed away from the police."

"Thanks, man," Tommy answered. If Alex was playing hotshot hero, Tommy was playing big brother, not little one. "Do you want a taco or a hot dog or anything?"

Alex restrained himself from saying, *No nitrites.* He also restrained himself from asking, "Where were you Monday night when your sister's no-good rich ex-boyfriend got killed?" He said. "Taco would be nice."

* * *

"Okay," Alex prompted. Suzanne had gotten some food inside her and introductions were done. "I want you to start about three years back, or whenever it was, when Scat was dealing you scag."

"Scag?" Suzanne looked puzzled. She knitted her black brows as she licked the residues of soup from her Styrofoam bowl.

"Outmoded term, I guess. Natalie said he was supplying you with heroin. Whatever you call it nowadays."

Suzanne put the bowl down and licked her teeth. "Nowadays," she said without smiling, "I call it shit. In those days, I called Scat and what came with him a way out. My father—our father—died, okay? And our mom remarried, too soon for our taste." She looked at Tommy, to see whether he had anything to add.

"Too dark for our taste, too."

"Dark," Alex said, feigning ignorance. "You mean he was shady, something like that?"

Tommy looked at Alex. He gave the impression that what he saw was somebody not quite in the real world. "She married a nigger, that's what I mean. I wouldn't call him that now. But who I was then, who Suzy was then, that's what we felt, okay?"

"Tell me about him."

"His name is Harold Simms," Suzanne answered. "She brought him home from work one day and introduced him as Flash. He doesn't look anything like a Flash. He's got heavy glasses, like Bernie there. He's got kind of a fat, baby face with a beard hiding the bottom half. He smokes a pipe. He looks like a Harold. But to her, when she brings him home, it's easy to see he's Flash for real."

"For reasons you couldn't understand at the time?"

"He was, I thought, younger than her. I didn't trust that. He worked with her, he was an assistant manager where she worked, taking orders over the phone. She said it was one of those things where he'd always had a crush but she hadn't been available before. She said, you know, she knew that deep down there'd always been some action between them."

"She said that," Tommy broke in, "but we thought it was all a crock of shit. We thought, 'What does this dude see in her except Dad's insurance policy and a piece of easy white ass when he doesn't feel like running around?'"

83

Bernie had been taking notes on a yellow legal pad. Now he stopped and ran his finger around the inside of his collar, though he didn't loosen either collar or tie. Alex bet himself he knew what Bernie was thinking. Tommy would not make a good impression on a jury, calling his mother a piece of easy white ass.

"So this is ancient history, okay," Suzanne picked up. "But you wanted to know, Alex, what I was looking for a way out from. Mom and Flash, that was one thing. Mom and Tommy, that was another."

Alex nodded. "And your way out was Scat?"

"I was in school, part time, at Salem State. I quit. I went up to New Hampshire. I worked in a restaurant where a girlfriend of mine used to work summers. Tommy stayed at home, but it was pretty much open warfare, so I brought him up with me as much as I could. Until I met Scat. Then Tommy didn't want much to do with me, either."

Alex turned to him. "Because you saw what she was doing as rejecting your father, too?"

"Scat was a rich kid who had strange ideas about how he got his kicks," Tommy said, more confidently this time. He had the same nose, straight and proud, as Suzanne. Alex wondered whether this was what was meant by a Roman nose. Tommy's nostrils flared over the precisely cut mustache. "One day this kid shows up at our house on a big Harley, black jacket, all that shit. He says, 'How do you do, I'm your sister's new old man. She sent me to get you for a party.' Then he drives up to where she is, Pepperell Woods, on that thing, me hanging on behind. It's a bitch of a night, sleeting and shit. The party turns out to be a lot of his friends mixing coke and liquor, and some of them going off to the john to shoot up. I didn't like my sister in that crowd, and I didn't like her getting laid by him."

Alex could see that—could even imagine, if he had a sister, feeling the same thing. But there was still something wrong with little brother as the arbiter of who all the grown-up womenfolk chose to sleep with. Alex didn't think Tommy Lutrello was as much of a redneck as he was making out. Maybe all this tough talk was not a giveaway but a ploy to divert suspicion away from his sister, to him instead.

"All right," he said, and then stopped. The blond, ready-for-Ivy-League cashier from the soup-and-salad counter had sat down at the next table with her dinner. Now the security guard, who had used up his quota of sitting time, detoured in a slow and consciously casual way to talk to her. But Alex couldn't make out what either of them said, so he assumed the reverse was also true. And Suzanne's picture hadn't been in the paper or anything. "You're up there, and you're hanging with his crowd," he prompted. "Tell me about them."

Suzanne slid her eyes toward the guard without turning her head. If she'd been spotted somehow, Alex thought, it was too late to run. Apparently she decided the same, because she shrugged and went on. The shrug brought a grimace, though.

"They were mostly pretty rich, plus some locals and some ski bums who were more like me. For a while they seemed kind of cool. They had been places, done stuff, and none of them even *knew* anybody black. Also, they didn't care if I didn't care about my future. So it all took me away from what went on at home. So I'll skip the grisly details, okay? Sca—my boyfriend didn't do so many drugs himself, but he kept everybody else supplied. I got hooked, and pretty soon that was all I did. After almost a year of it, I was down to eighty-five pounds. I looked like a scarecrow, and that's how I felt, too. My boyfriend would take me places, park me like I was the car and he had the key. He'd even bring me home, you know, to visit my family. Like they had tossed me out and he had picked me up, and now he owned me and he was going to rub their noses in that."

Alex noted the word *owned*, and noted she hadn't said how she paid for the dope. All along he'd been looking for a connection to the fact that Caroline Davis knew some prostitutes who worked Pepperell Woods. He wondered whether maybe he had found it. He remembered, guiltily, thinking that Suzanne would be more attractive stretched out taller. He didn't think starved down thinner would be the same. But he believed emaciation did turn some men on. It made the woman more of a china doll, something that it was up to them whether to take care of or break. He knew better than even to hint about any of this in front of Tommy Lutrello.

"How did that mess end?" he asked instead.

"I ran away. I mean *ran*. One night in the spring, mud season, I packed sneakers and a change of underwear and a couple of pictures and things that meant something to me. I stood on the road with my thumb out, at sunrise, shivering from cold and fear and my heart pounding. Time I hit Boston, I felt ready to pass out. I asked the last driver to put me in a phone booth so I could call a hotline. I got lucky. I got into a treatment program, an alternative treatment program. It was in Dorchester, but no-body—not anybody—knew where I was."

"That was luck," Alex said. "And guts."

"All I wanted was to crawl in a hole and never come out. Somebody happened to match me up with the right program, and they happened to have room. I was allowed to give out a post-office box, but no other address. The idea was to get away from all that kind of pressures—family, love interests, every-body—until we could set about liking ourself again. I was there for six months. I applied back to college, UMass this time, and I started while I still lived there, in the program. When I got out on my own, and I had this new identity, this new me, I started little by little making bridges to who I used to know. To my mom, to Tommy, to my older brothers, to my stepdad. By now I had a different idea about black and white. My counselor, well, you know her, Alex. She was my age, we had a lot in common, and she was black."

"Natalie, you mean." Alex had been engrossed in Suzanne's telling, hadn't noticed that both the cashier and the security man had gone. He looked around, bewildered. Bernie pointed at the cashier behind her counter and the guard strolling back toward the main drag of the mall. "And Scat?" he asked. "You got back in touch with him?"

"Sooner or later I had to face up to it, to him. I wouldn't ever trust myself if I couldn't."

That made sense to Alex. Yet it also sounded like catechism, like a maxim learned in the drug program. From Natalie? One thing was sure: Suzanne's story meant she had known Natalie before they ever wrote papers about their stepfathers in sociol-ogy class. Or Natalie's story meant Suzanne's story wasn't true.

"Did you buy drugs from him anymore?" Alex asked. "Not needle drugs. I mean, you must have still bought an occasional ounce of grass—"

"Why 'must'?" Tommy demanded. "Because you do, you mean? You think somebody has to be weird if they say no to drugs?"

Not really, Alex thought. Though frankly I get confused about any issue when Nancy Reagan and Jesse Jackson say the same thing. He didn't want to be drawn into this argument, but he did want Tommy to feel taken seriously. Kid brothers tended to have a problem about that.

"In my generation," he said, "doing certain drugs was a way to confront reality—to believe we and it didn't have to be the way we and it were. In your generation, doing drugs may be a way to blend in or space out. Like watching TV, I don't know. If it was up to me, I'd repeal the prohibition and ban handguns and unemployment instead. But I asked the question because Natalie implied Suzanne still bought from Scat."

Suzanne stuck out her chin and reached her free hand to fluff up her hair. Alex imagined the arm in the sling had to be getting stiff or hot or something, there inside the sweater. She had to be dying to soak in a bath or just lie down and conk out. It was no time to be sympathetic, though, not yet. "Well," she said, "truth is I buy from him for Natalie once in a while. She likes to keep her hand in that stuff. As long as anybody's not an addict, I don't care what they smoke or snort or guzzle at the bar. I've been an addict. I know that's in me, that tendency. So I stay away from narcotics, and alcohol, too."

Bernie was still taking notes, without comment, but for the first time Alex saw him smile. He thought Suzanne would be a good witness. He might or might not think she was telling the truth.

"I saw Scat sometimes," she went on. "He wasn't in such good shape, but he seemed to think he was into big things, big plans. I don't know if he cared about me anymore, really. He was jealous of Natalie, like she'd stolen me from him, and he—well, the thing is, I hadn't seen him in maybe six months until Saturday night. When I was sitting for Maria. I liked Maria, Alex. She's a smart little kid. We got to talking. She . . . told me about how you used to have cancer, by the way."

Alex felt his eyes pop open, and felt them turn to Bernie in surprise, for support. He watched Bernie smile again. "That's good," Bernie said. "Alex always thinks she's afraid to talk about that."

"Used to?" Alex repeated. "Were those really the words she used?"

"Used to." Suzanne nodded. She started to lean forward and reach out for Alex, in a sisterly way. She thought better of it, and stopped. Her fingers walked in place on the table. For her, Alex thought, that asterisk had been there next to his name the whole time. What did it mean about her decision to trust him with this mess? He didn't want to owe her anything. But he did want to know what she'd learned about the things that went on inside Maria's head.

"She said you took 'medications,'" Suzanne added. "She sounded like a little doctor, 'medications.' She said it was hard, you worked hard, and you were as healthy as the next person now. Is that true?"

Alex shrugged. "Sort of. What did they tell you about your shoulder?"

"The more I wear the sling, the better it will probably heal. After a few months I don't have to go easy on it or anything. But because it once popped out, it'll never be quite as good as new."

"That's what I thought. Well, it's sort of like that for me. Worse, probably. But sort of like that. I don't have to go around acting like I'm sick. I shouldn't expect never to be sick again. If you care about Maria, there's something I have to show you. In a minute. But tell me what happened Saturday night, why you left."

Suzanne closed her eyes, took some slow, deep breaths. She seemed to be waiting for something, maybe counting to ten, maybe what Terry would call opening her channels for the circulation of the chi. Alex studied the smudged lines of eyebrow pencil, the streaked eye shadow, the chapped and burned look of her cheeks and lips. Suzanne Lutrello, a success story. Bruised, maybe knocked off track, but definitely not giving in. He looked at Tommy, to see what Tommy thought about her, but Tommy was watching him. Caught, the brother dropped his eyes hurriedly. Alex wondered how the asterisk changed Tommy's view. Had Alex Glauberman, scraggly sixties dinosaur, metamorphosed into Alex Glauberman, battler against the Big C?

"I was feeling pretty good," Suzanne said in a sudden rush, "about how you licked your illness, and how you and Professor —you and Meredith seemed nice together. I had licked my addiction, I was thinking maybe I'd find somebody nice, like you, for myself soon. Maybe I'd have a cute, smart kid like Maria someday, after I finished school, made some money, was ready. I put Maria to bed and turned on the TV. I wasn't really paying attention, half paying attention, and they had this little story on the news about this girl, this woman, getting hit by the car. They said, you know, something like, 'A tragic incident in New Hampshire claimed the life of a nineteen-year-old skier.' They said she 'blundered over a snowdrift' and flopped onto the road. They said the driver, 'Cambridge resident Lowell Johnston,' was treated for shock, questioned by police, and released without charges. And I don't know where it came from, but I had this impulse, you know, to take care of him. I should have stood up to it, but I thought, he's surrounded by people who don't give a shit, and here he's gone and done something really tragic that for once isn't his fault. I called and asked if he wanted me to come up. I had to catch the last bus, that was why I left so fast. You were going to be home real soon anyway. But it wasn't the right thing to do, for Maria. It wasn't the right thing to do for me."

Alex took from his inside coat pocket the message that had been rolled around his wiper blade. He spread it in front of Suzanne. He said, "Whoever busted my windows left this." Tommy and Bernie edged their chairs closer to Suzanne so that they could read it too. Tommy started to say something, but Suzanne shut him up with a look. Alex had a speech ready, but Suzanne made that unnecessary.

"Okay," she said. Her eyes were wide, and the bones seemed to be trying to press their way through the scraped skin of her cheeks. "It's Wednesday. I know I can't run forever. I promise, I swear that on Sunday you can turn me in. I don't know if I've got the strength to tell the whole story now. But I know from Natalie that you were hired to find out whether it was an accident. I know it wasn't an accident. And I think that's how come Scat got killed."

"I want to hear about it," Alex said. "Whenever you're ready. This note may be bullshit, is probably bullshit, but I'm taking it at face value. As far as I'm concerned, I don't have any choice. Bernie is going to get a message to Trevisone and another to Graham Johnston that Suzanne will turn herself in by Sunday at the latest. I hope by then we can hand Trevisone some evidence that convinces him there's more to this than the Johnstons want him to think. But if you disappear on me, Suzanne, I'll go to Trevisone right away and do anything I can to help him catch you."

He turned to Tommy. He needed to give Tommy something to do. "There's a bunch of motels out there, across the street. I want you to take Suzanne over there before your break from work ends. She should register under some other name—not the one from the hospital—and pay cash. If you haven't got cash, we'll get some from a machine. Suzanne, you stay in the room, don't leave, and get some sleep. Tommy, you go back to work. I'll stop by and get the key."

"Where are you going?"

"Bernie and I need to talk. Then I'm going to fix my window. Then I'll come back to Suzanne."

"Okay," Tommy said. "C'mon, Suzy. Let's go."

11

OLD MONEY

For a long minute Bernie just leafed through his notes, saying nothing. Then he took off his thick glasses and wiped them on his solid navy blue tie. After he was satisfied, he rested the glasses back on his nose. He put both elbows on the table and rested his forehead on the heels of his hands. He drummed very slowly with his fingers, a kind of slow massage of his scalp to get his thoughts in motion.

Bernie was deliberate where Alex was headstrong. His hair, which Alex saw was thinning faster than ever, was cut and styled, where Alex's grew thick and wild. Yet he could also be headstrong, in his own way, in places and times where Alex would be deliberate. When they skied together, Alex cared about finesse and technique as well as speed. Bernie went all out. He almost always reached the base of the mountain first.

Bernie sat up straight, drained the coffee cup, and said, "I've got a wife and two children waiting. What's all this about fixing your car?"

"I'm driving it to New Hampshire, but not with shattered glass. Also, I want to see whether Suzanne will run."

"Because without her you won't be in this so deep?"

"Maybe. In the meantime, let's go buy a coat at Jordan Marsh. If she keeps to the deal, I have to take her with me, and I

90

don't want her to freeze. You can tell me what you know about the principals while we shop. I don't guess you can get out here again in the morning..."

"No. We'll buy a tape recorder along with the coat. You can send me the tape by courier. All I can say now is she's a good, sympathetic witness, if we end up trying to get it down from murder to a lesser charge. Everything else depends on the facts about Johnston's death, which you'll notice we still know none of."

Alex stood up, and Bernie did too, and they walked slowly out of the fast-food arena and back toward the main corridor. It was a little busier now. Alex supposed that the evening shopping time had begun. He said, "Graham Johnston told me the police told him she was seen on Scat's motorcycle, leaving the apartment where he was killed around the time of death."

"Well, find out how much her movements can be pinpointed. And get her to be exact as possible about what exactly she did and saw."

"And my own legal situation, assuming she does turn herself in, and I helped talk her into it?"

"Depends on how much your sergeant ends up thinking it screwed up his investigation not to have her right now," Bernie said. He was talking fast, as the doctor had, as Alex did when his customers asked him how bad the damage was before he knew what was wrong. "You're going to be aiding interstate flight, it looks like. I can't encourage you to do that, but I don't think you'll end up spending more than maybe a night or two in jail, if Trevisone gets spiteful. I guess Tommy has the cash for the motel, by the way. Who's paying for this jacket, and the cars you're not fixing while your whereabouts are unknown?"

"Rosemarie Davis," Alex reported. "She hired me to look into her granddaughter's death. I can still do that, regardless of what Suzanne's story is. Let's start your information on the principals with Rosemarie."

"I can tell you more about the Johnstons, really. But if you want ancient history, then Rosemarie's father, Paddy Sullivan, does happen to figure in the annals of the Boston Bar."

Alex and Bernie turned the corner, heading toward the big department store that anchored the mall's south end. Alex felt that he didn't need Bernie showing off right now. Besides, he bet

Rosemarie's father wasn't really called Paddy, certainly not to his face. He said, "Patrick?"

"Yeah. Michael Patrick on his birth certificate, but Paddy to his friends and enemies alike. He studied the law at Trinity College in Dublin, and they say he played some part in the patriot game. They say he had to go west, after the Easter Rebellion, to stay out of a British jail. He became Boston's leading Irish lawyer when there weren't so many Irish lawyers to lead."

"Uh-huh," Alex said. "If he was a patriot, why did he change his name?"

"The legend goes that it was the price for losing a bet: if I don't bed a certain young lady by Friday, I'll rename myself after a fish." Bernie sniffed. He couldn't resist the story, Alex saw, but he couldn't accept it either. "Anyway he did good and he did well, too, and they even let him teach at Harvard toward the end."

"So," Alex said. They drifted into Jordan's without having to slow down to open a door or take off a coat. His thoughts were half on extracting useful facts from Bernie's recitation, half on how expensive a coat he was going to buy. It was a present from Rosemarie Davis to the woman the police said killed the man who killed her granddaughter. He said, "Goosedown. If she runs, Maria will grow into it someday. What about Rosemarie? Does she figure in the annals too?"

"Not much. But she was a rebel, too, of course. She painted a mural somewhere, a memorial to Sacco and Vanzetti, that depicted Governor Fuller and Judge Thayer as Puritan clergy, hanging witches. With huge erections, I'm told. But she married George Davis, a coffee importer who didn't know Dali from doily, and didn't care."

"It was a marriage of convenience," Alex said. Department stores always disoriented him—too perfect, too clean, too hard to breathe. He finally spotted a sign for Women's Outerwear and pointed the way he wanted to go. "She wanted cover, and also children, I think."

"Aha. Do you want to know about her money? She would have inherited some real estate from Paddy and stocks from George, though it might all be sold by now. The Johnston money is bigger and more interesting. It's old, old. Shipping, I think—probably slaving, sugar, lumber, rum. The Pepperells, that's the mother, are as old as the Johnstons, but they didn't used to be as rich. Lowell Townsend Johnston. A name made up of three last names will get you into any club in town."

"Uh-huh," Alex said. He had found a coat that would do, a navy blue parka, inconspicuous, on sale for only a hundred and seventy bucks. "Pepperell as in Pepperell Woods? How do the Johnstons and Pepperells turn money into more money now?"

"Graham Johnston is an architect. I don't remember the firm's name, but they work with Sloan, Garrity—that's one of the hottest developers, not big yet, but hot. They specialize in research parks and conversions; take an old rubber plant and turn it into gene-splicing and software shops."

Alex heard "rubber plant" and thought of the decor at the Typhoon. He tried to imagine how you dissected a tropical tree down to its genes and put them together with something else. "Oh, like Firestone, I see what you mean."

"Yeah, good, Alex. That's a pretty fancy coat; I hope it buys you some solid facts from her in return. All these old factories, built to last, only the buildings outlasted what went on inside. Maybe that happens every couple centuries in Europe, in China. It's never happened here before."

Alex folded the coat over his arm and stepped around a mannequin that was too perfect, like the rest of the store. Her skin was too smooth, her lips parted just slightly, not scared or laughing or happy or sad. He hoped Suzanne didn't run away. He liked how real she was. Since he didn't interrupt, Bernie rambled on.

"We represent a guy who calls his outfit New Habitats. Know what he does? He tears down old rooming houses and three-deckers in the old town centers. He guts what's left of the old affordable housing stock and puts up health clubs and little motels..."

"Okay, so Graham's an architect." Alex moved into line at a cashier's station, behind a woman with straight blond hair piled high on her head. She laid a credit card and a pile of children's hats and mittens on the counter. "And an investor?" he asked.

"Sure. That way he keeps himself assured of work. Take Pepperell Woods. The Pepperells had farmland in New Hampshire. Graham Johnston put his in-laws in touch with some Boston money and the ski place was born. Graham and wife made a mint off selling the land, they got to be partners in the resort corporation, and Graham's firm got a healthy cut of the design work. What I'd like to know is why Lowell Townsend Johnston had to sell narcotics. He had no need to do anything but sit on his ass and cash checks."

The blond woman, her purchases bagged, shot them both a quick, interested glance as she went by. She had a high forehead and a turned-up nose. She might own a condo in the Woods, or she might have been interested in the word *narcotics*. Alex paid for the coat with plastic. He said, "Maybe he was bored. I would be. I have a hunch that his rackets, whatever they were, might have been costing the family as much as they were bringing in. Graham seemed to think I was there to discuss business at first— like people had made a business before of keeping quiet about his son."

12

REAGAN/BUSH

Alex knew he'd been right about fixing the window when a fine drizzle began. A drizzle like this, early on a winter night, meant worse was to come. The wipers scraped on the jagged glass, producing an ugly sound that might be made by claws. Then they stuck. There was no point in burning out the wiper motor, so Alex pulled to the side of the highway and banged away still more of the shattered window. He remembered to get his safety glasses out of the trunk. When he edged back onto the road, the rain picked up. It sprayed through the hole, drenching his face and beard as he drove. Maria would spray him like this, in the summertime, but then it was just a quick dash until he could wrest away the garden hose. Both of them would end up screaming, part in fun and part in anger, and soaking wet all through. Driving into the cold rain was not fun. Alex slowed down.

He fiddled with the radio till he got a weather report: rain in the city, possibly turning to snow. Snow in outlying areas, heaviest to the north and west. In his pocket was the room key he'd gotten from Tommy. Days Inn, room 314. Tommy had reddened, handing it over, as if he were handing his sister over to a stranger—which, as far as he was concerned, was the case. Spend the night there, Alex thought, and get the rest of the story. If it made sense, bring her along to New Hampshire tomorrow. Behind him, a semi driver blinked brights angrily and then pulled beside and ahead, throwing another gallon of spray through the hole.

What should have been a half hour's drive at this time of night took Alex twice that long. At last he turned into the driveway leading to his shop. His teeth were clenched; his lips made a sputtering noise like an engine getting under way. He got out, unlocked the garage door, and blew out a long sigh as he drove in. Then he pulled down the big steel door behind him, walked back out through the pedestrian entrance, and padlocked it.

This was not a special precaution, just something he always did when working nights. He didn't want anybody cruising for likely B&Es to note that here was a garage sometimes left unlocked. But tonight it felt especially spooky being here alone. Inside again, he quickly hit the lights and the forced-air heat.

The sound of the blower was comforting. It promised warmth and drowned out the rapping of the icy rain on steel. Alex walked to the back, past a jumble of engine blocks and heads, spare wheels, and other large and rusty parts. He splashed his face with a sinkful of warm water. Then he waded through the old parts to his stash of miscellaneous auto glass.

He found, as remembered, both a rear windshield and a front one. He lugged them out and began removing the screws that held the fittings in place. For the moment he decided to ignore the sound of someone or something banging on the garage door. That happened often enough when he was working late. Probably a drunk, or kids liking to make noise. The window job was a painstaking one, because if the gaskets were not positioned just right, the windows would leak. Alex did not like rushing it, constitutionally, but this time he used extra silicone sealer to make up for his haste. He had wanted to test Suzanne's confidence in him, but he didn't want to strain it for too long. He did not want to commit himself and then find her gone. He tightened the last screw, cut the lights, and stepped cautiously outside.

The driveway looked fine—wet and cold, but empty. There were no cars awaiting repair in the driveway, for a change. A faint light filtered in from the street, and another from the barred storeroom window of Freddy's Liquors. At a bit after nine, Freddy still had almost two hours to closing. On the street, Alex could see two cars with lights on and wipers going. They would be in a line waiting at the red light; sure enough, they growled off, revealing only the lighted window of the used-furniture place across the street. Alex undid the padlock and backed his car out. He was bending down to snap the lock closed when he heard the screech of wet rubber and the loud racing engine bearing down.

He wasn't quick enough to slide the door up, or even to stop the motion of snapping the lock. But in the next instant, all in one move, he turned and jumped onto the hood of his car. Brakes squealed. The incoming car bumped against the Saab and banged its front bumper into the garage where his legs had been. Alex perched on the hood, pelted by the icy rain, head down behind the new glass. He felt the Saab's body shudder on its springs as the pressure was relaxed. The other car had backed away.

In the murk and the headlights' glare he couldn't make out much. It was a big American car whose vertical hood ornament made him feel he was in the sight of somebody's rifle. Then the lights went out, both front doors opened, and from each door stepped a figure in a bulky coat, each wearing a mask.

That was his first thought: each wearing a mask; and then, as they stood there without moving or speaking, details began to seep in. The car was dark, maybe black or dark green. It was a full-sized car, not new, with traditional lines. No light hit the grille or the ornament, but the upright, rectangular shape of the symbol suggested a Ford, a Granada perhaps.

The figures in the bulky coats kept behind the doors, hands down, visible only from the waist up. They wore identical dark hats with brims all around, the kind the army-surplus stores sold for use in sun or rain, with dark handkerchiefs or bandannas hanging down around their ears and the backs of their heads. They might be dressed up to play desert commandos except for their winter coats and their Halloween face masks. It finally dawned on Alex that the faces were supposed to be Ronald Reagan and George Bush.

He wanted to laugh, but the situation was both too dangerous and too surreal. The one in the Reagan mask raised his or her hand, and in the hand was a revolver, silvery and suddenly wet. It glistened in the weak electric light, a poor version of the way shattered glass had glistened in the sun. The figure was of medium height, medium height for a man anyway. The hand that held the revolver was gloved. As the gun came closer, Alex slid more to the center of the Saab's hood. The hood was getting slick, too slick for his toes and knees. The gun pointed over the edge of his open driver's-side door. Its owner twisted away to look all around the inside of the car. He or she seemed to study the new down parka as if somebody could just now have been wearing it, somebody who had softly and suddenly melted away.

The Reagan mask emerged from the car and turned toward Alex, seeming to study him in the same way. The gun hand wagged at him, the barrel like an admonishing finger, but without a word. His own words came back to him, legalize drugs and ban handguns instead. Then, suddenly and without a word, both Reagan and Bush retreated into their car, backed out quickly onto the street, and sped away. Alex could now see that the car was green. He'd been able to make out the emblem on the rectangular ornament—a sleek jet plane pointed toward the sky— which, for reasons he'd never understood, meant Oldsmobile. Probably an Olds Cutlass, not a Ford after all, but your basic General Motors family car. Not much of an identification, he thought, as he considered the idea of reporting this. Look, Sergeant, he could say, see this telltale dent in my garage door? And I know the make of the car. Shit. They assembled them out in Framingham, off and on, when the plant wasn't shut down anyway. There had to be five Cutlasses, of various years, parked every night on Alex's block alone.

But there was one thing more—one thing he thought but couldn't be sure of. The driver, the one with the Reagan mask, had bent his or her head to check out Alex's backseat and the floor between the seats. At that moment the bandanna had ridden up enough to show just a bit of neck. Though the dim light made it hard to tell, Alex thought the skin of the neck had been brown.

Natalie, he thought. Or maybe Harold "Flash" Simms. But that made no sense, and then he thought, Who the fuck knows? In a land of equal opportunity, that might have been anybody's colored chauffeur or hired hand. It might have been any well-heeled Caucasian, just back from a month in Puerto Vallarta or

Honolulu, too. His legs trembled as he eased them to the pavement. His garage door *was* dented, but not seriously. The Saab's bumper, not like some, had held its own. He sank into the bucket seat, started the engine, and backed out into the street. When the light turned green, he drove slowly past the muffler place, the Dunkin Donuts, the radiator shops and weather-beaten apartments, checking his rearview mirror and the parked cars. Plenty of full-sized American cars, some of them Oldses, some of them dark green. Near the on-ramp of the Monsignor McGrath Highway sat another of these long dark cars, headlights on and motor running.

A traffic light halted him just before that car. Alex stopped dutifully, shifted into first, held down the clutch, and waited for a small break in the traffic. When he got one, he let up on the clutch and roared through the red light. He ran the next red, too, then swerved in front of a truck laboring at the beginning of the grade that led up the ramp. With the truck's horn blaring and its bulk filling all his mirrors, Alex couldn't tell whether the suspicious car had followed or not. He spun sharp right, skidding but regaining control, and took the side street that led away from the ramp at ninety degrees.

Now nobody was in his mirror as he sped past three-decker apartments and corner stores, past the old trade school and the machine shop where he had taken the hubs and valves to be ground. He saw a car three blocks back, but caught a green light at Broadway and soon was climbing the hill and then winding down past the housing projects and the Accurate Speedometer shop, toward the Mystic River once again. Once he hit the Interstate, he gunned the engine and enjoyed the efficient response and the fact that he could now hit sixty without a gale in his face. Whoever had been behind the masks, they had apparently come looking for him in hopes of finding Suzanne. Now he had lost them and—assuming Tommy had kept his mouth shut—there was no other way anybody could locate her. He drove north at a steady sixty through the rain. He bit open the plastic surrounding the tape Tommy had sold him, and slipped the cassette into the player. Judging by the cover, Violent Femmes was a trio of young men. The first song on the album, called "Old Mother Reagan," did not compliment the former President.

Alex grinned, happy with the sentiment of the song. He

98

tried to decide just what it meant that someone would choose to masquerade as Reagan and his successor while pursuing Suzanne Lutrello with a gun. Probably those were just the first dime-store masks that came to hand. Politics could be a deadly business, as far as military murder or economic strangulation were concerned. But killings, individual killings, were much more purposeful and stemmed from different sorts of dark, undersidish things—things like family secrets and family vengeance, business deals and corners cut, women as merchandise, the money in white powder you sped over on skis, the money in white powder you shot into your arm or sniffed up your nose.

Violent Femmes and violent thoughts kept Alex company till he parked his car outside the motel just off the Middlesex Turnpike exit from Route 128. Out here the precipitation had turned to big splats that left a white film on the plowed motel lot. Alex backed into a space in the double row of cars in the middle. He saw a generic temporary living space, a three-story rectangular block with three rows of twenty-five identical picture windows separated by identical strips of brick. Though some rooms were lit up and some were not, none of the picture windows was in use; all the curtains were closed. It was a good place to hide, an unmarked plain brown wrapper of a building.

The builder had tacked a single-story entrance lobby onto one end of the big block. The only exterior door besides that was a glass one in the middle of the first floor. Alex grabbed the new coat, which contained in one pocket the tape recorder he and Bernie had also bought. He hurried through the sloppy weather toward the isolated glass door. He found it locked, an emergency exit, leading from a crossways hallway that had an identical exit door on the back side of the building as well. He jogged around to the lobby, his boots punching their shape into the half-inch of new snowy slush. Caution made him wait a moment in the lobby, leafing through a tray of tourist information. He thumbed a tabloid circular full of coupons, ads, and entertainment listings. He had no interest in any of this, but he was glad he had waited when he saw a long dark green car, not new, circle the lot and come to a stop in front of his Saab. It was the Cutlass, and once again it had boxed him in. He got on the house phone and called room 314.

Suzanne's hello was tentative, opaque. She might have been

peeking out her curtain, but Alex didn't take the time to guess what she had or hadn't seen. A plan came to him and he gave orders, that was all.

"It's Alex," he barked, "but somebody followed me. I'm in the lobby. There's a fire exit on the middle of the first floor. There's a door to the lot and a door out the back. Get out the back way as soon as you can. If I'm not there when you are, see if you can find someplace to hide on the embankment below the highway. Got it? They're carrying guns. Go."

Suzanne's voice showed no terror, only decision. All she said was, "Got it. I'm gone." He heard her hang up. He watched, but no one got out of the car. He waited a minute more, crossed the entrance lobby, and then sprinted down the long, empty corridor past faceless doors and walls. At the crossway he turned right, ducked, and frog-walked to the emergency door, counting on keeping low and on the backlighting to make him invisible to anyone keeping an eye out from the lot. The green car hadn't moved. The passenger window was down. He thought, but couldn't be sure, that the face looking out was masked.

He heard a door slam and turned to see a preteen girl staring at him with an open mouth. He had a flash of Maria, getting off the school bus in front of the drugstore on Huron Avenue, two blocks from Laura's house. As she ran her tongue between her upper teeth and lips, trying to decide whether to stop in for a candy bar or a comic, this same long green car coasted to a stop. He forced the picture down and then swallowed it, a bitter fear to digest. He told himself right now he had to do one thing at a time. He ignored the girl behind him; she probably knew better, anyway, than to talk to strange men. He checked the window and then waddled back.

Suzanne came running, panting, a one-armed marathoner in the middle of a race that never seemed to end. Alex put his shoulder into the red-painted lever on the rear door, the one that said EMERGENCY USE ONLY, ALARM WILL RING. The alarm did, piercingly. The girl covered her ears and ran the other way. Suzanne and Alex were out the door and across the grounds before lights began going on in half of the darkened rooms.

The embankment was steep, but the old snow was still soft from the sun that had temporarily warmed it this afternoon. Alex kicked steps in it like a mountain climber. Suzanne gripped his wrist and used the footholds after him. At the top there was no cover except for the expressway rail. Crouching on its other side, they were invisible from the motel but exposed to lights and splashes from the onrushing cars. Alex just hoped nobody chose this place and time to hit the brakes and go into a sudden skid.

He helped Suzanne get her free arm into the proper sleeve, and then zippered the new coat closed around her. It was slowly dawning on him how vulnerable you were when you could use only one hand. He hoped you also felt exposed if you were packing a revolver and wearing a mask when fire engines and cop cars came circling about looking for something wrong. He had already heard the first sirens, and soon he saw a flashing blue light make a long curve off the exit ramp. The cop car disappeared underneath the highway, then reappeared and took a sharp left into the motel lot.

"Five minutes," he told her. "Pick you up here, and we're both gone."

13

WARM MILK

Hurrying back down the hill, Alex fixed his attention on fitting his boots into the snow steps. He tried to hurry forward, yet to balance his weight on his heels. He wanted to get down to the motel without being noticed and without falling on his face. In spite of himself, and despite a dash of guilt, he was impressed at the commotion he had caused.

The emergency door he and Suzanne had used remained open, and so did another one at the end of the building, which he hadn't seen before. Guests wrapped in yellow motel blankets or their own coats milled busily but randomly about each door. In the emergency spotlights, the fat drops of snow fell faster and thicker out of the dark. The guests' heads, mostly unprotected, were turning brilliant white.

As he drew closer to the nearest group, Alex could see that some people wore bathrobes underneath the coats and blankets,

some wore street clothes, and a few seemed to be wearing nothing at all. Everyone had stopped for shoes or slippers or boots,
though, except perhaps for some children being carried by
adults. It was hard to tell about the children's feet, because the
grown-ups had wrapped their coats protectively around the children's legs.

An excited babble rose as the guests milled and stamped
their feet, waiting for flames to leap out of the roof or for someone to tell them they could go back inside. Most of them looked
toward the building, not the highway, but Alex knew he had
been spotted by a big man at the edge of the crowd. The man's
meaty hand was wrapped around the hand of the girl who had
stared at Alex in the hall. His white legs were ghostly between
blanket and boots. His face seemed puffed up by fear or anger
or cold. "Excuse me," Alex said, hurrying straight into the
crowd. The girl stared again, but this time an injured expression
came across her lips, which seemed to Alex to be blue with cold.
Her lips started to make words, so Alex said, "I smelled smoke,"
as he brushed past. He said, "Excuse me," again and again, trying to project an air of authority, pushing his way farther into the
crowd and then at last out the other side. He hoped there would
be no security men or zealous guests blocking reentry to the
building. His plan wouldn't turn out very well if it left Suzanne
crouching in the breakdown lane of Route 128 while he got
lynched down below.

Nobody blocked the door, however, and others besides him
were going in. He merged with the flow of guests scampering
through the crossway and stepping in triumph into the busier
scene on the parking-lot side. Across the snow, in the lot itself,
the crowd was bigger but more spread out. Like others wearing
boots, Alex tromped around the slow-moving column of guests
clogging the plowed path. Some who preceded him were slam-
ming car doors and starting engines, while others were gathering
around the two police cruisers or scattering to stay out of the way
of the first hook-and-ladder truck, just roaring in. Now he could
see that the car that had been blocking his was gone. He made
himself walk, not run, and then quickly brushed the snow from
the new windshields and drove, slowly, out of the lot. A-plus for
imagination, he told himself. Luckily, no one seemed to have
gotten trampled in the stampede. Did the Constitution protect
you if, to protect a guest, you yelled fire in a crowded motel?

A-plus, but the two pursuers could still be close by. Alex turned left, away from the highway, onto the busy commercial Middlesex Turnpike. He decided not to risk a fender bent into his wheel—or worse—by cutting suddenly across traffic here. Instead, he turned right into a Burger King, circled it, and looked carefully in all directions for the green Cutlass. When he didn't spot it, he headed back the other way, toward the highway, crossing under it and then taking the curve of the cloverleaf as fast as he dared. It had been more than five minutes, of course. He kept to the breakdown lane, at thirty, and then slowed as he came opposite the motel. Suzanne materialized in his headlights, a small figure waving one arm, running toward him through swirling snow.

He stopped, swung open the passenger door, gave her a hand, and then pulled the door shut. Her teeth literally chattered. Alex put both hands on the wheel, accelerating and fighting his way onto the road. "Heat'll be up in a minute," he reassured her. "I'm getting off at the first exit. I'm gonna wander around north and east until we hit I-93. If anybody's following, we ought to know it. You don't know anybody with a green Oldsmobile, maybe five years old?"

His eyes were busy, so he couldn't watch her response. "Uh-uh," was all she said.

"Oh. You get any sleep, before all this?"

"A little. Not much. I was worried."

"That I wouldn't come back?"

"That you'd decide you ought to turn me in."

Alex slowed coming up to the exit, and then he could take a minute to sneak a glance. Her legs, soaked and shivering, were drawn up on the seat, against her chest. Her hair was wet, face streaked and dripping too. She looked like a wet cat, like his landlady's cat Antoine, who usually had a proud, independent, inquisitive air, but sometimes would get stuck outside in a storm.

"There's a tape recorder in the pocket here," Suzanne said. It was half complaint, half challenge. "What am I supposed to do now, confess?"

The dashboard lights made her face a little bit green. He couldn't see her eyes. That somebody had come looking for him at his shop was not surprising. That they had reappeared at the motel, after he was sure he'd lost them, troubled his sense of order. Bernie knew where she was. Tommy knew. Nobody else knew, unless she'd been followed from the mall—or had called somebody, anybody, once she got to the motel. Alex wasn't going to put her out into the storm, but he wasn't going to break out the warm milk or dry towels yet. He said, "It's for Bernie to hear the rest of your story, whatever the rest is. We're going to New Hampshire, we won't see him again."

Taking the exit, he felt a flow of warm air, which meant that the Saab's engine had heated up enough to share its heat with the coolant, and the coolant with the fins of the heater core. That was comforting to him, just as the warm air had to be comforting to Suzanne, whatever burden of misery and fear and defiance she might be carrying. She slid her legs down to take advantage of the heat. She buckled her seat belt and unzipped the parka. After a minute she reached under her sweater. There was a sound of Velcro being separated. Alex could tell she was freeing her injured arm from the sling. He crossed under the highway and headed north. In a minute he came to an intersection with a small commercial district, closed now. He saw there was some kind of clinic, a hair-cutting place, and a shop that advertised scuba gear.

"New Hampshire," Suzanne said. "If you go right, it'll take you over to 93."

"Thanks," said Alex. "Did you grow up around here?"

"Here? Not me. Saugus. That's why I asked Professor Phillips to meet me at the Typhoon. From there I thought...but then Scat disappeared. I was out looking for him. That's why I sent, why Natalie went instead. But Tommy and some guys rent an apartment, so I drive around here some. I'm not making too much sense, am I?"

Alex turned where she said. He didn't know his own way, and the road had a route number and a sign promising Woburn and Burlington. As he followed twists and turns through darkened buildings and dark scrubby woods, he shot a glance at his passenger struggling with her arm, maybe trying to get its circulation restored. He relented about the warm milk. "Wait a minute," he said, signaling and braking to a stop. "Wait a minute, let me help." He waited a minute himself to be sure no big car materialized behind. Suzanne said, "I've got to get this sweater off," raising her free arm over her head.

Alex lifted the hem and began to pull the sweater slowly and gently over her head. It was the same way he'd stripped Maria so many times when she was too tired to get herself undressed. But the difference pointed as much as anything to the problem he now had with Suzanne. It might be that she needed help with her arm. And it might be that she was trying one more way of leading him where she wanted to go. And it might be that she was confused about the difference. The question was, was he?

With the heater on, the air in the car was clammy and steamy at once. They were parked on a dark, slippery roadside where ghostly lights roared up and past. There was no locking of glances, because of the dark and because Suzanne's eyes were hidden by the black wool that he'd now pulled up over her head. But she wouldn't need sight to know that his eyes, close in the semidarkness, would be wandering over her skin, over soft curves, her ribs opened by her lifted arms, her breasts half-risen out of the sheer bra. It didn't matter what he'd thought or said in Trevisone's office. The fact was that he liked women and they tended to like him. He didn't prolong his helpful operation, but there was still a little time to go with the fantasy about what his lips and fingers might do in this territory. There was also a little time to puzzle over whether that might bring him any closer to knowing her, or her to knowing him.

Then the sweater was taken care of and he'd tossed it into the backseat, bringing back buried high school memories. He concentrated on the sling, a modern contraption that hung from one shoulder but also fit around her waist. It used one Velcro strap, already undone, to fasten the injured arm by the wrist. Suzanne undid the second clasp, which buckled the waist strap, and handed the sling to Alex while she slipped her bare and goose-pimpled arms into the parka. She took the sling back and refastened it outside the coat.

"Thank you," she said. "My arm was frozen stiff in there."

"Sure," Alex answered, pulling back onto the road. He thought about women being propositioned by their therapists and gynecologists and the like. It was something about the care-taker/client relationship, and something about social taboos, what pieces of body or mind were supposed to be kept hidden unless you wanted to extend an invitation. It was fucked up, no doubt about it, but there it was.

"So, um, where do you live?" he asked.

"I live in Dorchester, near school. I mean, I can only afford a room, but I found one."

"I tried to call you there. All day Sunday. You live by yourself, that's why nobody answered?"

"Yeah, one room with kitchen privileges, in a lady's house. She only charges seventy-five a month, and I do some shopping and stuff for her. The cops have probably been there, poking through all my stuff. And Mrs. Brady is telling them everything she ever knew or guessed about me, lonely as she is." Alex felt that she was looking at him now, so he briefly did meet her glance. On impulse he said, "If you had any dry pants to change into, you'd need me to help peel your jeans off too."

"I know," Suzanne laughed, cracking up. A big smile split her face, and she kept it toward Alex as she turned around to retrieve the sweater which she used as a damp towel on her face and hair. "I'm kind of stuck with you, and I guess you feel like you're stuck with me. It's not you, it's those detectives going through my room that makes me feel...invaded."

"Why?"

"That was private space, the first I had in a long time. It was like a diary when you're thirteen—maybe like your car is to you, I don't know. What did you feel like when they smashed it? Well, I guess you were more worried about Maria, but still..."

"So, how do you afford that room, and school? Do you have a job or a scholarship or something?"

"Yeah. Both. I did. At this rate I'm gonna lose them both. I have a job at school, clerk, in financial aid. Fill out this form, fill out that, ten copies of each." Lights and big green overhead signs appeared ahead. She added, "I'll tell you and your lawyer the story, but I'd like to get something warm in me, and some caffeine to stay awake. There's a place up here, and I think there's a CVS where I could get a couple T-shirts and stuff to wear."

"Right," Alex said. He still wasn't sure what had just happened, whether anything was settled. But he thought it was better to have happened there and then, not later, in some motel room where the stale air and stale decor reminded them they were strangers together, where the only furniture made for use and comfort was a big, soft bed. He waited while she shopped, and then in the restaurant she disappeared to the ladies' room and he called Meredith to report in. When her answering machine clicked in, he hung up. He tried Kim, who was home, so he told her what had happened today. He asked her to relay this to Meredith and to Rosemarie Sturgeon also. He asked Kim to re-

106

mind Meredith that the invitation to join him in New Hampshire still stood. He asked her to stress that his entanglement with Suzanne was legal and professional and perhaps a certain amount parental, that was all.

Kim said, "Methinks the fellow doth etcetera." She added, "I know you don't feel this way, Alex, but your cancer makes some of us feel you're just back from the brink of death. So we worry about you. I won't speak for Meredith, or lecture about the wonders of monogamy. I just care that you come out of this adventure unhurt. And I trust your judgment best when you've got a clear, uninfatuated head."

14

CALLAHAN

Alex drove north in a single line of cars doing forty behind a snowplow. The snow had gotten drier, the flakes smaller and faster, as he headed into the center of the storm. He asked Suzanne how she knew Caroline Davis's death wasn't an accident.

"Because Scat told me it was arranged for him to run into her."

"Did he tell anybody else, do you think, or only you?"

"I don't know about that. I don't have any evidence except my word for it, if that's what you mean."

Suzanne motioned with the recorder, free hand clasped around it, built-in mike a few inches from her mouth. She added, "I didn't ask him to do anything like this. He wasn't in that kind of shape."

"What did he tell you?" Alex asked.

"Understand, I called him from your place, after I heard about it on the news. I caught the last bus and he picked me up in Plymouth. Scat has—he had—this condo in Pepperell Woods. So that's where we went, but as soon as we got there he changed his mind and said he had to get out. I drove while he did some lines. All the way down he was kind of blubbering to himself. He told me it was set up. He said they told him she'd already be dead, that all he'd be doing was running over a corpse. He said it was just destroying evidence, like burying a body or flushing something down the toilet."

"Did he know who she was going to be, beforehand? If he knew who, then..."

"Then he could have warned her or something, yeah. He said no, he said they wouldn't tell him that—any more than he would tell me who it was that gave him his orders, that set this up. He told me that after he hit her and called the cops and all, finally he had to ask them if they knew who she was."

"Did you believe that?"

"He didn't sound like he believed himself. If he believed himself, maybe I could've let well enough—worse enough—alone."

"Why? Why would that have made it okay to 'leave worse enough alone'?" Alex heard himself putting quotation marks around her apt if ungrammatical phrase. It lent a touch of paternalism that his question didn't need. But Suzanne only answered in the same steady voice, speaking into the tape recorder as if she were confiding to the kind of diary she would keep now that she was no longer thirteen.

"It wouldn't have been okay, but I might've done it, and then I wouldn't be where I am now. I tried to talk to him about facing yourself, taking responsibility for what you've done. Whether he killed her or somebody else did, he was going straight downhill with that on his conscience. I brought him to Natalie's and we both stayed with him. I thought he would come around to the idea of turning himself in. That's why I wanted to meet Professor Phillips. I wanted some help, some advice about that. Somebody objective. Somebody that wouldn't just see me as an ex-junkie still stuck on my ex-dealer and ex-boyfriend, okay?"

"That's what Natalie thought? Natalie thought you should just turn him in?"

"Yeah. Funny, isn't it? Probably Professor Phillips thinks you should just turn *me* in."

Alex didn't rise to the bait. "Look, Suzanne," he said. "Did you kill Scat, or not?" He recognized the tone of voice this time, too. *Look, Maria. Did you brush your teeth, or didn't you?* It wasn't easy to convince somebody she was better off telling the truth, no matter what. It wouldn't get easier, either—assuming he was still among the living, to be in a position to deal. *Look, Maria. Are you trying to steal Elizabeth's boyfriend, or not? Look, Maria, I want to know whether you're doing drugs/having sex.* I don't know, Alex thought. After a certain point, it's no longer *Tell me the truth*; it's *Show me you can handle it right, that's all.*

"No," Suzanne said. "No, Alex, I swear to God. He was keeping his nose full and not thinking too straight, but I really thought he was coming around to turning himself in. And then I guess he woke up and panicked and decided that wasn't the way to go. And then somebody killed him. They did it because of what he knew. They didn't kill him fast. In the time it took, he would have told them that I knew it too. That's why I ran. Then I saw that only made it look like it was me."

I want that part again, slower, Alex thought. But for now he let her go forward. He asked, "Where did you run?"

"I took his bike—the keys were on the kitchen table. He was in the parlor, on the rug—stabbed, blood everywhere. It was— he was still warm—I—I thought he was dead, but I wasn't sure. The knife was next to him on the floor."

"Did you touch it?"

Suzanne shuddered. It was an involuntary shudder, a spasm, her shoulders deciding they felt a cold burden that they could not bear. Alex felt it, shot her a glance, and watched the wipers brush the snow up and down, back and forth. "No," she said. "I didn't touch it. No. But I touched him. He was warm. I've seen a lot of bad shit, even people I was afraid could be dead. I never saw anybody that really was. I never saw blood like that. I could smell it. I had to get out. I took his keys. I got on his bike and got to a pay phone and called the cops. I didn't say who I was, just said they better get an ambulance there. Then I drove his bike up into Arlington. I can tell your lawyer friend where the phone was, where I left the bike, what kind of knife, all of that. Then I hitched a ride out to Tommy's. He hid me somewhere. But that was no good, not forever. Last night I talked to Natalie, she told me about you and Caroline's grandmother, what she hired you to do. If you can find out about Scat and Caroline, maybe that'll lead to who killed Scat too. She thought it would be safe by then for me to come to her place. If I got there, she'd set something up for me to get together with you."

Suzanne stopped then, didn't go on right away. Alex saw she

had laid the recorder in her lap. Her free hand was rubbing the bad shoulder, maybe because of the memory of what had happened to it, maybe just to keep busy. Ahead of him, two drivers got brave and veered out around the plow. Alex just followed the taillights of the car that remained between it and him. He had a lot more story to hear, and he had no need to get brave. He said, "This is today, right?"

"Right." She picked up the recorder, pressed the play button, and continued. "Today I was supposed to end up like that girl Caroline, except today I got lucky again."

No, Alex thought. No, one is enough, not you too. He told himself to keep his two eyes on the road, and the third eye that Terry talked about on the line of parts that made up this story, a thin line of events that should be laid out neatly one at a time. He said, "Tell me what happened today."

"I went to Natalie's, like I said. If I was a killer, who would expect me back at the scene of the crime? I was sitting in the kitchen, waiting, thinking that's Natalie coming up the back steps. Instead it's this guy. He says, 'I'm Detective Callahan. From here on, anything you say can be used against you.' I thought, this isn't real, this isn't happening to me. Next thing I knew he had his arm around my neck and something against my ribs. He said if I didn't want to bleed to death like Scat, I'd cooperate. He tied me up like you saw. He sat there kind of toying with a knife, a long folding knife, a fishing knife I think it was. He said on second thought he was going to arrange it so I died like that nosy bitch instead."

"Caroline?"

"That's what I said. I said, 'You mean the one Scat ran over?' He didn't answer that. He reached in his overcoat and came out with a needle, a syringe. He held it up. He said, 'It'll be painless this way. You come with me, all you'll feel is a pinprick, it'll look like an accident and everything'll be okay.' He kind of smiled and then held up the knife in his other hand. He said, 'You don't, you feel this slide in and out of a warm wet hole you didn't use to have. You'll be screaming, but you still might hear the air bubbling out the wrong side of your lungs.'"

Alex turned from the swish-swish of the wipers and the red taillights of the car ahead. He turned long enough to watch her lips form expressively around her last words. They stayed parted, making a hiss that illustrated the sound of a leak, air from a tire, from a basketball, maybe from a punctured lung. She sounded the way people tended to sound when they were repeating the story of a disaster or narrow escape that had happened to somebody else—with shock but also with relish, as if they believe but at the same time they can't accept that it's real. A bad actress might sound like that, too. But so would somebody who had been terrified—had reason still to be terrified—and was trying to separate herself from her fear in just that way. Alex understood something about that.

"Jesus," he said. "How did you get away?"

"I told him okay, I'd go with him. He went down the steps first, backing down to keep an eye on me. The only thing I could think of was to make a ball and roll down sideways. I went bumpity-bump like a sled or something out of control. I shut my eyes, I couldn't help it. All I know is I hit him and he either missed me or else he didn't use the knife. I got up before he did, and I ran. I was around the house and on the street before I knew I was hurt. I passed a few people who looked at me funny or called out, 'Hey, are you okay?' I couldn't even talk, not yet, but I wanted to get to you instead of the cops if I could. When I got there I tried ringing the bell with my nose. I kicked the goddamn door and banged on the glass with my head. Then I just kind of wore out, gave up, I guess. I figured I wouldn't die, or if I did maybe that was God's way of winding up the whole thing."

"Suzanne..." Alex said, because he didn't like the idea of this gutsy young woman giving up. But he was also thinking that if she'd rolled down a flight of stairs, then besides what happened to her shoulder, there ought to be bruises on her arms or her ribs. He hadn't been looking for bruises when he took her sweater off. Of course, it sometimes took a day to get black and blue. Suzanne read the thought without much trouble. She said, "I've got a hell of a bump on the back of my head."

There was no need to answer. Alex reached out his right hand and felt her thick hair, still damp from the snow. It reminded him of when Meredith had discovered the lump in his neck. She'd put his hand on it, told him she'd first noticed it while they were making love the night before. He'd felt the lump, been unable to deny it, and his first reaction had been anger that she knew something about his body that he hadn't

111

been aware of at all. Now he pressed against Suzanne's scalp too hard and felt her wince. She was right. There was a hell of a bump there.

"This guy that claimed to be the cop, Callahan. You didn't recognize him? He wasn't anybody you ever saw up in New Hampshire or down in Cambridge with Scat?"

"Nobody I can remember clear enough, anyway. A big guy, nobody I remembered, or I wouldn't've believed him, would I?"

Right, Alex thought. You wouldn't've. "So now he's got more reason than ever to come after you again."

"And I owe you again," Suzanne said, "for getting me out of that motel."

"Uh-huh. Now go back and tell me what happened Monday, why you weren't there when Scat got killed."

Suzanne undid the clasp around her forearm and now she held the tape recorder up with both hands and her voice grew matter-of-fact again. "He disappeared. So I went out looking for him. Natalie went off to meet Professor...Meredith and bring her back."

"When did he split?"

"Monday afternoon, late, just past when I talked to you. I went out to get him cigarettes. Natalie was there, but it was like I had some kind of power over him that she didn't. He ran."

"On foot?"

"No, the car, his car, remember? I went out looking for him—I went to his folks' house, to a couple bars, but he wasn't there. I came back to Natalie's, and I saw his bike was parked out front. I went in—and the rest is like I already said."

"Why did he come back on his bike instead of the car?"

"I don't know," Suzanne said. "Now tell the truth. Do you believe me?"

Alex didn't answer. He had asked all the sharp questions he could think of. Between now and Sunday, unless he found a reason not to, there was nothing for it except to believe. After that, what he thought wasn't going to decide where she spent the rest of her life. Probably some parts of her story could be checked. Possibly her performance on a witness stand would matter more than any facts. But it occurred to him to try one more test. "You went to his parents' house?" he asked.

"Yeah, looking for him."

"Who'd you talk to? His mother? Do you think she'll admit

112

that now?" Alex waited for her answer, for hesitation, for Suzanne to decide she'd talked to Scat's mother, even though Graham Johnston had said his wife was in Europe.

"His mother? No. It was just, you know, the maid who opened the door. She didn't speak much English. Or maybe she pretended not to understand." Passed that one, Alex thought. If Suzanne had talked with Josefina the seviche chef, Josefina could testify that the accused had been there, knocking on a Brattle Street door, and not at home during the time Scat might have been killed. But would she? That depended, possibly, on whether Josefina was legal. Most Salvadorans and Guatemalans were not. Kim had been active with a group that got the City Council to declare Cambridge a "sanctuary city," guaranteeing access to municipal services for refugees whether they had immigration papers or not. That wouldn't get Josefina her job back, however, or protect her from the INS if the Johnstons decided to turn her in.

"Yes, I believe you," he said at last. "I still have a couple more questions, though. One is that there's something I don't understand about Scat. He didn't have to do anything but sit on his ass and collect dividends from some great-granddaddy's stock. Why was he mixed up in drug deals and shit, and the people that come with that line of work?"

"To—you know—pull himself up by his own bootstraps, I sometimes thought. Did you ever hear of the Opium Wars?"

"The British beat up on China in the 1850s or sometime, so they could ship Indian opium in—isn't that it?" Alex answered, surprised.

"Scat knew all about the Opium Wars, had read every book about them, though that isn't very many, I guess. He used to say he was just a good Yankee trader, and narcotics traffic was an old and honorable trade."

"Um," Alex said. The car in front pulled out to the left of the plow, and since the interview was nearly over, he followed its red lights around. Beyond the plow, the car left black tracks in the snow. "You know," he said, "you and Caroline were alike in some ways. I mean, different classes, social classes, but you both ran off from your futures to wait tables instead of going to school. I guess you were a few years ahead of her, but your tracks were parallel in a lot of ways. I need to ask you about that, and

113

then we can shut that machine off and forget about confessions, as far as I'm concerned."

"What about it?"

"Caroline got to be friendly with a woman or women up there that were hookers. Expensive ones, I think, catering to the resort trade. I want to know if you ever met anybody that you knew was into that. And I want to know if, while you were an addict, you ever...worked...yourself, up there." Now he'd asked the question, so he could stop talking and wait for her answer. He felt, though, that he ought to keep going, to say somehow that it didn't matter, that any answer was okay with him. "I didn't want to ask in front of Tommy. But I'm looking for anything you know that sheds any light on why Caroline was killed."

"No," Suzanne said. "Sorry. I didn't know Caroline, I don't think she was there when I was. And I've never been in that line of work. It's a way to make a living, I guess, but I'm not so philosophical or I didn't need the money that bad. One or the other. And I'm not starting on you, no matter what I owe you for—if that's what you've been trying to figure out." She laughed, as if she too had said something that might cause offense, and she wanted to soften the blow. "I mean, this has got us a long way from the university, and I'll call her and you by your first names and all that, but you're my professor's sweetheart, for Christsake. If we ever get out of this mess, I *would* like to pass her course."

15

THE WOODS

By pushing the furniture around, Alex was able to make enough space to do his stretches, his balance exercises, and his kicks. He opened the curtains and saw the sun breaking through thin gray clouds above a low mountain covered to its summit with trees. Alex had been to Britain, but not to its first and nearest colony. So he didn't know what Rosemarie Sturgeon Davis or William Butler Yeats had meant, specifically, when they urged the heart to fly to a place where hill was heaped upon hill. Yet he thought it was an apt enough description for the White Mountains.

A Westerner—looking for alpine meadows, glacial lakes, and skyscraping summits—wouldn't regard New Hampshire's heights as mountains at all. The country here was rugged but rounded; the heights were cold and desolate, but low. The roads through the mountains did not rise in grand, sweeping curves past vertical waterfalls to high passes with immense views. Rather, they followed deep, narrow valleys—notches, in local parlance—cut by swift but unspectacular streams. It was old, stern, mossy country. Indeed, it was the sort of place where the brotherhood of sun and moon and river and wood had long since worked out their will. New Hampshire had furnished masts for the Royal Navy, Meredith claimed, when the British had exhausted the forests of Ireland. Later it had furnished pulpwood to float a million books. Now it was Ski Country, so dependent on the winter sports trade that the local chambers of commerce put out glossy pamphlets referring to the highway from Boston as Ski-93.

If the sun was rising over the nearby mountain, the motel window had to face east. For the purposes of the tai chi form, however, you called whatever direction you first faced "north." Alex faced the mountain and planted his bare feet on the synthetic carpet, trying to find in it some connection with the stony, glacial New Hampshire earth. He let his arms float slowly up as if they were being raised by strings attached to his wrists, then brought them in toward his body and let them float down the same way. He relaxed, allowing weight and energy to settle into his legs. He remembered that the most important thing was to breathe. This directive was a variation on the old chemical company ad: Without Breathing, Life Itself Would Be Impossible. Had Scat Johnston actually heard the breath bubbling out of the wrong end of his lungs?

Alex didn't hold on to the thought of Scat Johnston, or of Suzanne Lutrello sleeping off all the things that had happened to her the day before. He let the form, nearly a habit now, come slowly as he concentrated on his breath and on the placement of his weight on one leg, then on the other. When he'd reached the first Cross-Hands he was facing "north" again, ready for the movement known, curiously, as Embrace Tiger. That meant a slow, 135-degree turn, right leg raised from the earth and empty, weight sinking and energy rising through the left. His hands blocked downward and then outward, and as he finally shifted to his right foot he swiveled his hips and let the motion carry into his right hand. The hand slashed across his body, palm down, about where the neck of an uprooted opponent ought to be. Then the left hand pushed the opponent out of the way. Embrace Tiger. Alex like tigers, of course: their unabashed stripes, their grace, the sinuous way they moved.

Rolling back from this stance, he could see Suzanne watching him, both eyes open and intent, though her head hadn't come up from the pillow. The form directed his gaze away from her until he was into the Repulse Monkey, glancing to his side as he stepped back. Now she sat upright, back against the headboard, wearing the baggy, Nike logo T-shirt she'd bought the night before. Even in winter, her neck and crossed arms were several shades darker than the clean new shirt. Conscious of watching and being watched, Alex lost track of how many steps he'd taken. He stopped and swung his arms loosely, like a rag doll's. Repulse Monkey was as far as he knew, anyway. In three months he'd covered thirty-eight positions out of 150, according to Terry's way of counting—though the sifu made a point of discouraging counting at all.

"Tai chi chuan," he said, turning to Suzanne again. "It's a kind of slowed-down Chinese martial art. If you do it every day for ten years, it might begin to pay off in a fight."

"I know," she said. "You do it for your health, right? You take lessons from Terry Newcombe. Maria told me about that too."

Alex passed over Maria's surprising bond with Suzanne this time. The one confidence would have followed the other: he's healthy now, and a thing he does to stay healthy is he studies that tai chi. What hit him was the inflection of familiarity that Suzanne's tongue put on Terry Newcombe's name. "You know Terry?" he asked.

"He used to come once a week to give meditation classes at the program I was in. He's some kind of distant cousin of Natalie's, or their mothers go to the same church, or something." Suzanne slid out of the bed, the T-shirt falling partway down her thighs. Without the tight jeans, her legs looked flabbier and more utilitarian, not so strongly sculpted as they had the day before. Or was that just because she had made the limits of their partnership clear? Suzanne tested the bump behind her head and scratched an itch at the top of her spine. She disappeared into the bathroom. Alex heard the toilet flush, the shower go on and then off. She reappeared dressed in yesterday's black sweater and jeans, fastening her left arm into the sling.

"We should get going," he said. "We can stop for breakfast, and I guess Rosemarie Davis has to buy us both a few more clothes."

The approach to Pepperell Woods followed a branch of the Pemigewasset River. The plows had been out overnight, and the road up the valley ran clear and dry between snowbanks six feet high. The evergreens wore clumps of new snow like fat white mittens on their boughs. The dark green mountains wore white where ski trails had been cut, or where rockslides on steep faces had removed the trees. The valley was narrow and steep and sparsely developed until it abruptly widened, upstream, into a large and flattish bowl.

Alex had never been here before. By reputation, the ski runs were long and well maintained, but the lift lines were long as well. Seeing the size of the development ahead, he understood why. The vanished farms and woodlots of the old Yankee settlers had been replaced by what looked like an architect's model, jigsawed out of balsa wood and pieced together with glue. Block after block of multi-unit condominium buildings sat on the valley floor and the lower surrounding slopes. Construction trailers, new semicircular drives, and empty excavated lots showed that the building boom wasn't over yet. Alex guessed there could be five thousand units either occupied, under construction, or on the drawing boards. If they went for, say, $200,000 apiece, then the Pepperell land and neighboring properties had turned into something like a billion dollars' worth of vacation homes. Plus the hotels, the eating and drinking places, and other recreational facilities on top of these.

The real-estate office stood proudly at the entrance to the complex, a residential-looking place with two stories and old-fashioned shuttered windows and a door painted bright red. Alex imagined it must be sell-sell-sell, build quick and unload quick while the Massachusetts economy boomed for the business and professional class. There would be tax write-offs, most likely, and real estate seemed to be everybody's favorite investment right now—at least to hear the owners of the newer Volvos and Jaguars and BMWs talk.

Sometimes Alex felt guilty working on imports for people like that, when American auto workers were being thrown to the dogs. But he liked these machines, he liked the way they ran, and anyway, Buy American rankled him the same way as My Country Right or Wrong.

"Busy, busy, busy, as Bokonnen would say," he remarked to Suzanne. He didn't expect her to catch the *Cat's Cradle* reference, and she didn't bother to ask who in hell Bokonnen was.

"Too busy," she said. "They put wood stoves and fireplaces in every room, back to nature, you know. The air is great during the day, but at night you could choke on the smoke."

"Plenty of work, though?"

"At peak time, yeah. You can always get work cleaning and booking reservations, cooking for the charter-bus parties, dishing out food and skis, hauling out dirty laundry and trash. I did all that shit, off and on. There's construction, too, whenever the weather's good enough, but mostly just for guys. Take a left up there, I'll show you Scat's place, okay?"

"You sound like a tour guide," Alex said. Her nonchalance was too forced. She might have been offering to point out where John Belushi had lived.

"I guess. It's just that my life depends on giving you the best information I can."

Touché, he thought, and turned left where she said. The condominiums, the heart of the place, bore the names of mountains. They loomed like mountains, too, three- and four-story complexes with wood siding and tall chimneys and lots of picture windows. Alex drove past the namesakes not only of New Hampshire and Vermont peaks (Monadnock and Mansfield) but Wyoming and California (Teton and Shasta) as well. It was midday on a Thursday. The parking lots were nearly empty. Few owners would be in residence, and the weekend rental crowd would not yet have appeared. Anybody who *was* here would be off enjoying the clear crisp day and new snow.

"Did Scat buy his place, or did it used to be his parents', or what?"

118

"They gave it to him, no mortgage, no nothing, when he turned eighteen."

"That's a pretty weird thing—to own a home outright, just when you start to vote, start to be officially responsible for yourself. Of course, I guess to him it was just a fancier version of what anybody gets that's your first space on your own." He thought of Suzanne's room in Dorchester. "I mean, the driver's seat of your first car, or a dormitory room, a bedroom in an apartment with other kids..."

"No, what was weird, if you call it that, was Scat didn't feel that way. He said he needed to own something in this valley, like that place was his log cabin or something."

"What do you mean?" Alex asked.

"Well, he said to me one time, 'Doesn't your mother's family have some valley in Italy? Someplace where some of them are still fuckin' peasants, and you could go back there if you wanted?' He wanted his roots, and to him that's what this place was. Up there, where it says Katahdin, see?"

Alex pulled into the entrance drive for Katahdin Homes. He didn't know whether Graham Johnston had designed Katahdin Homes, but whoever did it hadn't made any effort to cast the buildings in a New England mode. They weren't ugly—they had nice angles, avoided the phony Swiss bric-a-brac common in Ski Country, and were faced with a pleasant gray, weathered-looking wood. But they might just as well have been in Vail or Aspen, or for that matter in suburban Chicago or Philadelphia. There were no gables, no clapboard, no weathervanes, no white picket fences. He searched for Scat Johnston's door, number B-71. It was painted dark, deep blue. So was every third door in the row of nine.

"Funny place to go back to the land, if you ask me."

"He didn't mean actually get his hands dirty—like a fuckin' peasant—he meant to belong somewhere, like a country person does. He kind of felt they—his father—had sold that out from under him."

"What about his mother?" Alex was trying to understand where and when the conversation might have taken place. Behind that blue door, it would have been. Was it late in the night, post-drug-rush and/or post-orgasm? Was it late in the morning, trying to recharge depleted batteries over real or instant coffee?

119

What had Suzanne felt for Scat, and what had he felt for her? "I mean, she was the Pepperell, not Scat's father, right?"

"His mother, more like, had dropped it, or ran away from it. She spent most of her time in Paris. She had a French boyfriend —ran off with her ski instructor, Scat said, but later I found out the guy was from some rich old family, nobility, over there."

"Do you think Scat felt guilty about his class?"

"Maybe." Suzanne nodded. "To tell you the truth, that's something I can think about now, but it wouldn't've meant anything if you'd asked it to me then. When I met Scat, I didn't know anybody knew how to be ashamed of being rich."

"Uh-huh," Alex said. He didn't want to attract attention, lingering too long in front of Katahdin Homes unit number B-71. Yet nothing distinguished it as a place where somebody had tried to set down roots, or as a place whose owner had recently died. Well, what did you expect? Alex asked himself. A state trooper? A For Sale sign? A crepe-paper black letter *D*? He wondered who was inheriting Scat's home, and who if anybody had been inside it since he died. All he could tell by looking was that evidently, owner alive or owner deceased, somebody had the job of shoveling the walk. He asked, "Do you know anybody that would have a key?"

"Better than that," Suzanne said. "Scat kept a key hidden in the ski closet outside. It was there last weekend, I used it to lock up when we left."

16

WITHOUT BREATH...

Alex had tried and failed to reserve a one-bedroom condo after meeting Rosemarie Davis on Tuesday night. The reservation clerk had suggested a hotel room instead, only of course they weren't called hotels, they were called inns. All the inns were named after native New England trees. For seventy-five dollars a night, Alex had gotten the very last room in the Black Pine, which was a grade below the Sugar Maple and two grades below the Silver Birch. The Silver Birch, top of the line, had a fancy restaurant. That was the restaurant where Caroline Davis had worked.

Alex planned to start by talking to Caroline's co-workers, but first he wanted Suzanne out of his way. The question was what Graham Johnston might have told Trevisone, and whether Trevisone would therefore guess that Alex had been headed up here. Would the sergeant have alerted the local police, and would the locals have taken the time and trouble to comb the reservation lists or put out an alert to the front desks? Alex could try re-registering under a different name, but probably there were no more rooms to be had. Possibly, considering the green Oldsmobile and "Detective Callahan," it might be just as well for Suzanne to get caught. She might be better off in the hands of the local police.

The Black Pine Inn at Pepperell Woods looked at lot like the Days Inn in Burlington, only it had decorative wood trim, painted black. Alex parked in the lot, left Suzanne in the car, and signed his forms and collected his key without the receptionist narrowing her eyes or making any furtive calls. He gave Suzanne the key and was glad to have a chance to do Rosemarie Davis's work on his own. He decided to go give Scat's place a quick once-over before he started flashing Rosemarie's letter and drawing attention to himself. He drove slowly back to Katahdin Homes, turning over in his mind that curious conversation between Scat and Suzanne about peasants and roots.

The key was in the outdoor shed as promised. It fit smoothly, and just as smoothly turned the tumblers built into the doorknob. He pushed open the dark blue door and stepped inside. By the time he'd shut the door behind him, he realized that somebody else either had been assigned or had elected to give the place a going-over.

Whoever it had been had not gone wild. They hadn't thrown things around or broken anything. But neither had they taken pains to disguise their visit. In the kitchen, to Alex's right, some cupboard doors were open and some were closed. He passed up the kitchen and headed for the living room, straight ahead, where he could see the couch cushions, pink and bare, removed from their cases.

The couch was brown and beat up—rips mended with tape,

and cigarette burns on the arms. Besides this, the furniture consisted of a deep pile carpet, also burned, a big padded chair, a dark wooden cabinet holding the sound system, and two big speakers encased in the same wood. The wall decorations were framed posters—museum show announcements and female superstars, intermixed. Some of them hung crookedly on the smudged white Sheetrock walls. Alex picked up one of the empty brown cases of the couch pillows. There was nothing inside but lint and grit. He turned his back on all this and headed up the carpeted stairs.

The stairs led to a hallway, also white Sheetrock, whose open doors showed a bathroom, a master bedroom, and a smaller bedroom set up as a sort of office. Alex chose the office, which contained a desk, metal with Formica top, and a safe—not a big safe, maybe one foot square, but authentic-looking, with a big combination dial. There was also a fold-out couch that had been opened to expose the mattress. Alex was more interested in the ladder mounted to the wall. The ladder was wooden, with wide, flat rectangular rungs. It led to a trapdoor.

Alex climbed the ladder. He found that the trapdoor was not locked, and it was hinged in such a way that it stayed open when lifted. He saw bookcases with books and magazines and papers and video and audio tapes, many of them spilled onto the floor, meaning that this loft, too, had been searched. He saw mattresses, another sound system, a TV and VCR. His first impression, standing on the ladder with his upper half through the trapdoor into the loft, was that it was very hot here. He wanted to scramble the rest of the way in and strip off his winter coat. His second impression was the faint smell of sweat.

The loft was big, running the length of the unit, with three vertical walls and a long, sloping roof on the fourth side. Skylights in this roof gave grand views of the mountains. A man was sitting on the floor, his bare back to Alex, doing sit-ups facing the mountains. The man was big and beefy, with reddish brown hair to his shoulders. Before Alex could stop staring, the man had whirled around and launched himself across the room, his big hands reaching for Alex's wrists as Alex tried to retreat down the ladder.

Alex let go and jumped, keeping his feet, but the man landed behind him with a heavy thump. The next thump was Alex hitting the carpet, arms protecting his head. He'd been tackled expertly behind the knees. The big man's weight was on his ass. The big man's hands pinned his shoulders. He told himself that Suzanne would have mentioned it if "Detective Callahan" had sported shoulder-length hair. Wouldn't she? He thought somebody else did have hair like that. He just couldn't remember who.

The man on top of him was breathing hard and loud, like a ventilation system. Alex wished he could do the same. The man leaned forward, shifting weight to his knees. The pressure on Alex's pelvis eased, but now his shoulders were crushed to the floor. Alex concentrated on the few cubic inches between his face, the puffy arm of his coat, and the rug. Without breath, his lungs reminded him, life itself would be impossible. The carpet made what air he got smell of chemical cleaners, carcinogens he was sure. He kicked upward, hoping he could slam his heels into the man's kidneys, but they didn't reach that high.

"I know," the man said. His voice was deep, which was not surprising, but gentle too. It seemed distinct from the speed and power with which he could obviously act. Alex thought of Terry Newcombe. The man said, "I know," again, but sounded unsure, still trying to nail something down—nail it with sure strokes, but hands that could be soft. Being soft until the moment of impact, not closing off the channels but concentrating the energy, then suddenly becoming rock-hard. Terry had said something about that. Alex realized he was getting confused, blamed it on the lack of air. "You were in the church," the man said. The big hands relaxed and Alex forced his chest up with his arms. He breathed and then spoke, wonderingly: "So were you!"

The man stood up, stood over Alex as if he had no question about who would come out on top in another fight. Alex sat up and rested his back against the wall. The man wore jeans, waist maybe forty, forty-two. His belly bulged out of them, a deep navel surrounded by hair that was more reddish and less brown. Despite the sit-ups he was losing that battle with his belly, Alex thought. His face was clean-shaven, pink. He might be twenty-five, maybe thirty, judging by the wrinkles around his blue eyes.

"Why?" the man said. "What was your interest there?"

"Curiosity," Alex said truthfully.

The man shook his head. The corners of his mouth turned down. "That's a hell of thing to say."

"I'm sorry. But don't you read obituaries of people you don't know?"

That was taking a chance. In fact Alex hadn't meant to be so flip. But somehow this man struck Alex as somebody who related to the printed word. A woodsman, old-fashioned, maybe that was it. A throwback to the days when reading was respected, even if the newspaper was all you read. If that was all you had, you read it well.

"You didn't know Caroline?" the man asked.

Pay dirt, Alex thought. This guy was in Scat's house, but he knew Caroline. He was the other mourner whom Rosemarie hadn't known. Alex could tell he cared by the way he said her name. It was like the way Suzanne said Terry's name, only much more so. Like the name had a taste to it. You couldn't fake that. He knew Caroline and he liked her, Alex thought.

"I didn't even know what she looked like. In fact, I still don't. I want to. I want to know what she *was* like."

"Why?"

"I want to know"—Alex shied away from "who killed her"—"I want to know why she died."

"Right answer," the man nodded. He pointed toward the ladder and the trapdoor. "Up," he said. "I'm camping out in the loft there. I can give you a warm beer, that's about all."

Alex stood and climbed. He liked this man. He liked Suzanne, he liked Tommy, he liked Natalie, he liked Rosemarie Sturgeon. He liked too many people in this affair.

17
LANDLORD/TENANT

Alex sipped the warm beer, Miller's, from the golden aluminum can. He flipped through the pages of Scat's photo album, which lay open on his lap. The album was dark blue vinyl, the same color as the front door, but gilded like the can. He knew the man who'd been doing sit-ups in Scat Johnston's loft was studying him. He thought it would be okay to show both puzzlement and surprise.

It had surprised him that Scat kept a photo album at all. Keeping photo albums didn't mix with dealing hard drugs, in Alex's mind. Not that anybody distinguished between hard and soft drugs anymore. Between the ones that bound you to the torturer's wheel and the ones that might expand your options, your mind. Anyway, Scat had sorted and stored his photographs for reminiscence or display. Alex recalled what Suzanne had said about the Opium Wars, what Bernie had said about the John-stons and the slave trade. Those ancestors would have had photo albums, however unsavory their businesses. Well, not photo albums. They would have hired portrait painters.

So surprise had faded as Alex examined things from several angles. He'd flipped through the album, skimming over group shots, party scenes, photos of skiers in action, and nature shots with no people at all. None of it remarkable, nothing to show why the big man whose sit-ups he'd interrupted had chosen this of all Scat's possessions to lay, silently, on Alex's lap. He looked up, puzzled. The big man said, "There's two more inside that flap in the back."

There were—two glossies, thirty-five-millimeter shots, the same as the rest but waiting to be mounted, not yet preserved behind plastic as a piece of picture-book life. Now they never would be. One picture showed an icy surface with a round hole in it. It reminded Alex of *National Geographic* features about seals and polar bears, but otherwise meant nothing to him at all. The second picture caused his face to lift again in surprise. "Now you know what she looks like," the big man said. "Her and him both." Therefore the picture said that Scat and Caroline had been lovers. This was a possibility that had never crossed his mind.

No, he told himself. Slow down. The picture said that Scat and Caroline had sat up in a bed together, arms around each others' shoulders, grinning for the camera, naked from the waist up. Who knew? Maybe naked from the waist up was some kind of rule around here. In fact, the picture itself didn't even say that this happy couple were Caroline and Scat. It merely showed a woman and a man of about the right ages. Surprise faded to skepticism. Alex thought it would be okay if this change, too, showed in his face. He reached for his wallet and pulled out the letter from Rosemarie.

"I guess I have to take your word for that," he said, handing the letter over. "I'm Alex Glauberman, this says why I'm here. Anything you can tell me, I'll be very interested to know."

"I'm Dennis MacDonald." The man looked over the letter and scratched the sole of one bare foot. "Kids used to call me Dennis the Menace and Old MacDonald until I grew enough that they got scared to. 'Course, some people think they've gotta call me Big Mac. I've been waiting here twenty-four hours now for something to happen. I'm tired of going through this guy's shit. That's him, and that's her, and that picture is the only unusual thing in the place."

"The only one?"

"Well, I don't know what's in the safe, but I can guess. When they open it they'll keep the cash and throw the dope away. The guy read westerns and sci-fi and *Playboy* and best-sellers. His music taste was like a top-forty chart. He didn't hide nothing that I could find."

"Weren't the police or his parents or somebody here before you?"

"The police know better than to poke their noses in here, and I guess his folks aren't in a hurry either. He didn't die here, it's just where his possessions are waiting around to be collected, that's all. But I thought maybe somebody would come along that might be worried about something. Or sooner or later I'd get caught, and the cops would charge me with something, and then I could sound off about how they weren't doing their job."

"You've discussed Caroline's death with the police, then?"

Dennis MacDonald drained his can of Miller's as if Alex's question was dumb enough it could be put off until after the more important swallowing of the last drop. Then he said, angrily, "I fucking-A have."

"Tell me," Alex said. "Because I can't."

"Can't you? I wonder why, but we'll get to that, I guess. You know the Woods, the layout here?"

"No."

"Jesus. That letter says what you're doing but not why it's you. We're talking about an isolated stretch of dirt road, no speed limit posted, the motto around here is Live Free or Die. People drive like a bat out of hell on the back roads, and anybody that lives here knows it. There's a ski trail through the woods uphill from the road, going the same way the road does. Parallel.

Going parallel, till it turns down a real gentle slope to the place where you're supposed to cross. Now there's also an old logging road, overgrown, goes straight down the hill. They say she decided to take a shortcut, went bombing down the logging road flat out, didn't think to snowplow, nothing that shows she tried to turn at the bottom. She went over the snowbank like she was going off a jump, right into the path of the car. They showed me the pictures they took of the tracks. And I went out and looked at them myself."

"And?"

"The tracks showed what they said. You can't see 'em, last night's snow would've covered 'em up. But why would she do that? Why would anybody ski flat out like that onto the road?"

"You asked the cops?"

"I asked. They shrug. Tired and in a hurry, maybe, they say. They frown. Wrecked maybe, one guy says. Fucked up. Yeah? Did you do a test, I say. Sure. The driver consented to a urine test and a breathalyzer. He wasn't squeaky clean, but he was under the limits. No, I say: a test of the victim. They look at me like I'm nuts. Not the victim, they say. No law against skiing under the influence. But why would she do that, I say again. They look at the floor and wiggle their tummies, embarrassed. For her, not for their own dumb asses. Kind of a mixed-up kid, they say. Dropped out of a fancy college, waiting tables at the inn instead. Coulda been suicidal."

"So you think—?" Alex asked.

"There's two choices. One is the cops are right, she made the tracks, and nobody'll ever know why. The other is she didn't make the tracks. Somebody else made the tracks, before she got hit, or right after. Somebody else made the tracks while there was a car stopped on the road, so they knew *they* wouldn't get hit."

"What happened when she got hit?"

The big man turned away and looked at the mountains. He looked back at Alex with wet eyes. "The guy, Scat, and the cops say she hit the road kind of spread-eagled, with her skis twisted upside down. He couldn't stop the car, she couldn't get up. Her skull got crushed right away, they guess, and a lot of bones got broke. The car went into a skid and dragged her a ways before the rear wheels went over her too. I wasn't facing all this at first. That's why I didn't know how dumb I sounded, asking about autopsies and drug tests and shit. They didn't take her to the hospital. Straight to the funeral home and shipped her out to the Coast."

"Who was she to you?" Alex asked.

"Tenant. I mean, we shared the house, she paid some rent, did some cooking and cleaning. Old vacation cottage, I winterized it..."

Dennis MacDonald let that linger as if he wanted to say more but couldn't or wouldn't. Alex mentally added, "...when I first moved out here with my ex-wife and kids." Maybe. Or else it was some other plan, some other imagined sequel that had gone wrong.

"And you think maybe she was already dead or unconscious, and the 'accident' destroyed the evidence of how that was done?"

The big man shrugged. His chest expanded and then slumped. The extra meat on it bounced, but not for long. It was mostly muscle. It bounced like a car with nice new shocks.

"That's farfetched. But it makes more sense out of what happened than anything else."

"And so you've been camping out here, trying to find anything that would show why or how or whether Scat Johnston would have been involved in doing something like that..."

Alex stopped and looked back at the photograph, which he'd been trying to avoid. It made him uneasy. He realized he'd been separating the deaths even while he looked for a connection. The separation had gone "bad boy, good girl." But here were bad boy and good girl in bed together.

Scat looked like Alex had thought he might. Not like his father. He was skinny, his ribs showed, his grin was toothy, his head was square, with a hard jaw. But Caroline, Alex had expected, would look kind of subdued. Maybe because her grandmother knew so little about her, maybe because of the seriousness with which she'd grappled with the morality of prostitution. Alex had been seeing her as pretty but introverted, maybe even shy. Here she was smiling, a bright smile in a round face fringed by short, curly blond hair. She looked healthy and comfortable, freckled, unembarrassed. That her breasts were bare did not seem to matter. She neither slumped her shoulders nor arched her back. She was not being shy, or coy, or seductive. Yet she was posing, the two of them were, they obviously knew the camera was there. Alex wondered whether there was somebody behind it, or whether one of them had set the timer and jumped back into bed. Before he asked any more questions, he thought it was only decent to share the fact that there was some evidence to back up what Dennis MacDonald had decided on his own to believe.

"Apparently Scat told somebody that's what happened, before he died," Alex said. "Apparently he was thinking of turning himself in."

Dennis's eyes opened wide. In his wide sockets, under his broad forehead, they looked like frozen-over ponds between pink ridges at dawn. This had all been theory, Alex realized. The big man had been theorizing about a kind of malevolence that was foreign to him. Now he was squeezing and crushing the empty beer can in his hand. Alex looked back down at the photo, turned it over in search of a date, found none.

"You lived with her," he said finally. "Was she, like, a physically modest person, would you say?" That district attorney edge had crept into his voice again. But it seemed he'd done the right thing, maybe by instinct, because he drew a deep laugh out of Dennis MacDonald.

"You mean because of her tits hanging out in the picture like that? No, if you want to put it that way, she was probably the most physically immodest girl I ever met. She'd walk around how she felt like, and she'd walk in a room without knocking too. If it was the wrong time, she'd just say, 'Oh, sorry,' and walk back out."

"Oh," Alex said, interested. "Well, would you say she was asexual, or that her ideas about privacy were just different?"

"A-sexual?" Dennis drew out the word. He didn't seem sure what Alex meant.

"Not interested? So what turned other people on just might not seem that way to her?"

"No, I think it was what you said about the privacy. Uh, about the other, being interested, she said she was . . . healing, that's the word she used. She said she was getting over something, somebody, and maybe she'd be interested again when that healing was really over and done."

"Did she tell you this because you told her you were interested in her?"

Dennis smiled. "Well, I was healing too. The thought did cross my mind that we might heal each other." His smile faded as he looked at the crushed can in his fist and flexed his fingers around it. "I could do this to the guy who drove over her. I can understand why somebody else wanted to cut him up like hamburger." He gave Alex a long, steady look. "I hear that's what somebody did."

"Uh-huh. But, like you said, if she was really killed and it was made to look like an accident, there had to be two people involved. It may have been the second person who killed Scat, to keep him quiet."

"Right. It might've. Probably was. That's who I've been waiting for. Coming back to look for what might tie him in."

"This picture," Alex said again. "You've had lots of time to think about it. Pretend I don't know anything. Tell me who you are, why it surprised you, what you think."

"Who I am? I work construction, I do maintenance, I like to ski, climb, canoe. I been here five years, that makes me a new-comer in the valley, in the towns, but it makes me an old-timer in the ski operation, in the Woods. I knew Scat, sure. He wasn't what you'd call deep. But he had a lot of parties, and there was always something to get off on there. The thing is, I didn't know Caroline knew him. She wasn't shy, but she wasn't all that much of a party person, any more than me. Remember, she only got here this past fall."

"Maybe she had friends that knew him."

"She had a few girls she hung out with, outdoor fiends, hikers, climbers, cross-country skiers. Shit, I don't know...I guess she ran into Scat somewhere, or came here with somebody to one of those parties maybe. Maybe she got it on with him the way it looks. Or maybe this was some kind of party game getting played." He waited, then said what else he had decided to believe. "I don't think they were really involved, though. If it was more than a one-night stand, then I think I would've known."

Alex waited. In the time Big Mac had been brooding over the picture, he would have developed more ideas than this.

"One thing I thought of, though. Maybe whatever she was doing at his place, she saw something she shouldn't've seen."

"Like what?"

Dennis shrugged that good-shock-absorbers shrug again.

"You implied Scat was a dealer."

"Yeah, sure, and everybody knew it. But his name was enough to keep him from harm over that. And he didn't sell to kids, local kids anyway. The cops are locals, from the real towns and the real woods. So that was the rules on the dope trade. Keep to the outsiders, the Pepperell Woods folk, everything'll be okay. Let the locals go down to Manchester or Concord if they're determined to buy."

"Was there serious money in this, for Scat?"

"Lotta money in the state these days. Down south, cities and suburbs, up here in the resorts. I read in the paper that more dough was spent in New Hampshire on cocaine than whiskey last year. And a lot gets spent on whiskey, cold and long as the winter gets. Anyway, Scat kind of had the franchise around here. That's why he had to agree to a test—it wouldn't be cool for people to think he'd been protected from something like that, driving under the influence, running somebody down. 'Cause enough people already knew he was being protected about his business."

"So, if Caroline saw something she got killed over, it wasn't a drug transaction, that's what you're saying. What was it?"

"That's the trouble. Damn if I know."

"Who comes here on the weekends? Families mostly? Families and college kids?"

"Yeah, and friends, you know, a bunch of friends'll get together, rent a place like this, fill it up."

"Couples mostly?"

"I don't know. Some. Or it could be a group of girls, group of guys." He narrowed his brows. "We're still talking about sex, is that it?"

Alex nodded. Dennis thought a minute, then asked, "You ski?"

"Yeah." Alex nodded again, knowing what he meant. Downhill skiing was an exciting sport, but also a social one. It was a show-off sport. You skied in flashy outfits if you could afford them, and you showed off your flashy technique if you had any. You performed in front of a lot of strangers, and they performed in front of you. Between runs, you bunched up in lift lines where there wasn't much to do but look at each other and chat. Flirtation was almost an official part of the sport, certainly a big part of the winding down.

"But what I mean is, people—older men—that come alone, or college guys maybe, that don't want to take the trouble to pick a woman up? Men that might be in the market for buying sex? And if there's a market, is there a supply?"

131

"Economics one-oh-one," Dennis MacDonald winked. "If there's a demand, I thought there was always supposed to be a supply. Yeah, I've heard about that. Again, now I think about it, the cops make the same kind of rules. No local girls, no houses. Girls imported from the city, that come to your condo, your hotel room. Yeah I've heard about that kinda thing."

"But you don't know anybody yourself, in that line of work?"

"No. I don't."

"Caroline's grandmother said Caroline did. She knew one or more prostitutes who worked the Woods."

Dennis shook his head, the long red hair floating out, incongruous. Alex thought suddenly of Meredith, hoped she was thinking about him. "Well," Alex asked, "how would I do that— get a call girl to come to my room?"

"You? Oh, speaking hypothetical, you mean. Talk to the bartender at Larabee's, that's what I've been told."

"Larabee's?"

"That's the drinking lounge in the conference center, the place with all the function rooms. Mostly it's not really conferences, not in the winter. It's ski weekends. Book whole groups into places to stay, bring 'em up in buses or maybe they drive. Feed 'em in batches, like a banquet. More like pigs in a feedlot, quality of the food."

Groups, Alex thought. Bernie's law firm had an annual ski weekend, for lawyers and nonprofessional staff. The student activities board, or whatever it was called, offered one at UMass. A blowout weekend. Lots of singles, or attached men spending the weekend on the loose. You wouldn't want to stand out as the guy who didn't score. The bartender would learn to spot you too: "Hey, friend, you look a little down. How would you like me to find you a nice girl?"

"Dennis," he said. "My girlfriend is coming up tomorrow, I hope, but tonight I'm a single man. Can you take me to Larabee's and point out the right bartender for me to see?"

18

PARKER HOUSE

Dennis MacDonald had been able to give Alex the names of a few of Caroline's friends. He knew where her best friend, Pamela Parker, could be found right now. Pam served out soup and hot drinks from ten to four, at the Parker House lunch cabin, located six kilometers out on the network of cross-country trails. She'd worked there since it was put up two years ago, Dennis said. Somebody had thought it was funny to name it after her.

Alex drove to the ski touring center to rent a pair of skis through Sunday. The man behind the counter offered him new ones, state-of-the-art, crafted of foam and fiberglass, with a computer-designed bottom that would grip all types of snow without wax. Alex asked for the old-fashioned wooden waxable ones, but was told the center did not stock these anymore. Alex liked the waxable skis not just because they were old-fashioned, but because they went with his tinkerer's nature. If the ride wasn't smooth enough, steady enough, he wanted there to be something he could adjust. The color-coded sequence of waxes allowed for this tinkering. You could replace hard waxes with softer ones as the snow warmed up or got worn down. Still, today he took what he could get. He looked forward to an hour's workout, alone, that would get him to Ms. Parker's domain.

Enjoyment came easily. Grooming crews had been out, so Alex found himself gliding quickly along newly set tracks in the fresh, powdery snow. The trail led across an open field, probably a golf course in summer, and then began to wind upward, following a brook through a forest of birch and fir trees. Alex didn't hurry. He concentrated on technique, sinking into a crouch for better purchase on the snow. It was like tai chi, all breath and rhythm and shifting of weight from foot to foot, from heel to toe. And it made the winter an ally for a change. There was no bracing against icy surfaces, nor steeling the skin and muscles against insidious cold. As long as you kept moving, footing was sure and the body generated more than enough heat.

The trail crossed over the brook on a wooden bridge, slabbed the side of a hill, and dropped steeply into another finger of the valley on the other side. Alex crouched even lower, tucked his poles, and let gravity and the tracks and the banked turn take him swiftly down and around. Then he stretched out again, working harder, up the gentle grade through a patch of woods that seemed to be all birch now, or birches interspersed with some darker but also leafless trees.

The ridged plastic ski bottoms, Alex had to admit, bit nicely and glided well. The birches, silvery off-white, slid by like bright moments, uncountable ones. Alex was disturbed only by the thought that this same sensation may have been the last one that Caroline Davis had ever felt. But that notion assumed she'd been peacefully skiing when she was felled by a knockout dart fired at her neck from behind a tree. Hardly likely. If the accident had been staged, her death or immobilization would most likely have happened somewhere else, even indoors. Especially if there was any truth in what Suzanne's assailant "Callahan" had said. Alex concentrated on his motions again, and was sorry to be interrupted by voices ahead. Soon he could see a small thicket of skis planted tips-up and tails-down in the snow, with the cabin behind.

The cabin, built of greenish, rough-sawn boards, still looked raw and new. Smoke rose from a stovepipe that angled out beneath the high end of the prefabricated corrugated plastic roof. Beside the cabin was a map engraved and painted on a large signboard mounted on two poles. Alex studied the map while catching his breath and waiting till he felt ready to go inside.

The map indicated White Mountain National Forest boundaries with grooves painted yellow, trails maintained by Pepperell Woods with grooves painted red, other trails with grooves painted black. Alex saw that he was well into the National Forest already, that the resort corporation must pay some kind of use fee to the feds just as lumber companies would, or cattle and sheep ranchers out West. North of the cabin began the wilderness trails, labeled FOR EXPERIENCED SKIERS IN GOOD PHYSICAL

134

CONDITION. Wilderness was an exaggeration, Alex thought. It just meant the paths were not tracked or patrolled. The Forest Service would furnish a few signs and bridges and occasionally clear out fallen trees. In the other direction, south, the maintained trails circled back into the main valley. One red groove, Alex saw, ran for quite a while parallel to a secondary road. That would be the one from which Caroline's alleged tracks diverged. He pushed open the door of the Parker House, built to succor novice skiers in indifferent physical shape.

Inside the cabin, three picnic tables had been set around a plywood counter that surrounded a wood-burning stove. The place was stuffy and smelled of sap and coffee and something less pleasant, maybe mold. The sudden heat reminded Alex of climbing into Scat's loft, but perhaps this was also because the woman in charge seemed like Dennis MacDonald's female counterpart. Pam Parker was nearly Alex's height, broad-shouldered, broad-hipped, and broad-bosomed. Her blond hair, dry like straw, was plaited into a long braid that hung far down her back. She looked like an ad for vacationing on an authentic Swedish farm, except she was wearing old jeans and a sweatshirt and her expression was surly rather than welcoming. Alex watched her wipe the counter with a cloth and then accept a dollar from a skier who looked like a midget beside her. She served the skier coffee in an enameled aluminum cup and did not give her any change. The skier sat down at the only occupied table, where she rejoined her two companions, college boys by the look of them.

"Excuse me," Alex said quietly when the customer sat down. "Are you Pam? Dennis MacDonald said I could find you here."

"Pamela," she said, not looking up. "You trekked out here to find me?"

"From Boston, actually." He passed Rosemarie's letter across the counter. It was becoming a kind of visa that allowed entrance to otherwise hostile enclaves in Pepperell Woods. "Except for Dennis, none of Caroline's friends came to the service her grandmother held."

"No," Pamela said, still wiping. "A funeral out West. A memorial in Cambridge. It was like people picking over the pieces after the meal is done. Anyway, I don't believe much in relatives." She reached below the counter, got rid of the cloth, and pulled out a sign hand-lettered in Magic Marker. GONE TO OUT-HOUSE OR SOMEWHERE, it said. SELF SERVICE, PLEASE PAY. BACK IN

135

FIFTEEN MINUTES OR SO. She lifted a hinged section of counter and walked to the picnic table farthest from the one where the three college students were. She sat with her back to the counter, leaving it behind.

"I know what Dennis thinks," she said. "I think it's wishful. If I were going to wish..." She formed one hand into a fist, as Dennis had, but didn't crush anything inside. She surrounded the fist with her other hand, twisting and rubbing like a ball-in-socket joint. She switched hands, making the left one the ball and the right one the socket. "I'd wish for her to still be alive." She was clearly upset, but her face showed only a flat Nordic reserve. "I mean, whatever you find out about how she died isn't going to bring her back."

"No. Maybe it's just that her grandmother wants to understand her better. Was Caroline a very secretive person, would you say?"

"Uh-huh. She was." Pamela sat up straight and folded her arms across her chest. Alex decided that Pamela was hurt, even rocked by Caroline's death, yet there was a distinct childish quality to her response. *You can't make me*, she was saying. But make her do what? As if to confirm Alex's thoughts, she added, "And so am I."

"Did you know Scat Johnston?" Alex asked. If she had disliked Scat, he might find more give there. And there was a theory—the crudest but therefore simplest theory—he wanted to check out.

"No."

"I thought everybody knew him. The thing is, I think somebody knew too much. Apparently somebody was blackmailing his father to keep some of his secrets from being revealed. Is it possible that could have been Caroline?"

Pamela uncrossed her arms, went back into the ball-and-socket routine. "Doesn't sound like her," she said grudgingly. "Caroline was idealistic. Not about changing the world. About honesty. That's one reason she was hard to know. It's hard to be honest and also talk much about yourself."

"So she was quiet?"

"No. Like you said. Secretive. Like I said. So am I. I think it was an accident, bad and crazy as that seems. She, I don't know, she thought the snowbank was softer than it was. She thought

136

she'd sink into it and stop. Instead it was icy and speeded her up."

Alex put the picture of Scat and Caroline on the table next to the letter from Rosemarie. If the letter was his visa, this was his gun, his badge. This was what he had to flash that apparently nobody knew to expect. Pamela didn't anyway. She didn't say anything, but somewhat to Alex's surprise what she did was blush. He watched the blush spread like a red tide through her neck and face and ears. Even her hands, red already, seemed to deepen their color. Finally she said, "I guess I didn't know her all that well. I guess some of the things people said about her were true."

"What people?" Alex asked.

Pamela got up, circled past him, and retreated to her station behind the counter. She put the sign away. Alex followed and repeated his question, eyes as sharp as he could make them, palms down flat, uncompromising, on the wood. Pamela shook her head; her face was slowly getting its whiteness back.

"It doesn't matter," she said. "They're both dead. It doesn't matter to me."

19

FLATTERY AND IDLENESS AND MIRTH

Alex skied back more distracted than he'd come. So he got his weight forward on a downhill and then he fell on his face when his right ski hit a bump. One minute there had been beautiful motion, a free ride, and the next minute there was cold snow rubbing his cheek raw and more cold snow up his sleeves. He brushed himself off, embarrassed, and considered whether everybody—Suzanne, Dennis, even maybe Scat himself—could have been wrong. Maybe she'd had something on her mind, maybe also something in her brain, in her blood, and she'd made a bad, a fatal mistake. She'd thought she was in control. When you were nineteen, you relished being in charge of yourself. You didn't like to think that you weren't. When gravity showed her otherwise there hadn't been much time left.

Maybe, but Alex still doubted it. He waited a minute, regaining his balance, and then pushed off again. He needed enough time to shower and change clothes and clean up Scat's condo. He had no illusions about control, but only wanted to stack the deck as favorably as he could. When he reached the cross-country center, he stashed the rented skis in his car and drove back to Katahdin Homes. This time number B-71 was empty. He called Suzanne at the Black Pine and told her he'd be meeting Dennis MacDonald at Larabee's at six. "If I can make a connection, I'm going to bring whoever it is back here," he said. "Just sit tight, and I'll get back to you as soon as I'm done."

"I'm okay," she said. "I'm fine. I don't want to get in your way."

He showered and changed clothes, using the shower that Scat, no doubt Suzanne, and possibly Caroline Davis had used. Two dead, and one alive. It used to be, when people didn't move around so much and made things to last, that it was quite common to sleep in the bed or ride on the saddle or cross the threshold that you knew for a fact had been used by someone now dead. He threw the clothes he'd been wearing into Scat's washing machine. He thought that going through Scat's domestic motions ought to tell him something about the man. It didn't, except that Lowell Townsend Johnston had died down to the bottom of a carton of detergent. While the machine ran, Alex straightened up the place so there'd be no sign of a search. He switched the clothes from washer to dryer, and then he climbed the ladder into the loft where Scat apparently had spent most of his time. He sat watching the mountains not move.

After a while he got up and practiced cleansing the marrow and then he practiced Punch Under Elbow and Repulse Monkey several times. He made his own movement as slow as he possibly could—like the mountains, not like the swiftness of skis or of cars or of human lives. When he climbed down from the loft, his clothes were dry. They had the softness that came from machine drying, and a fresh smell that he associated with the clean air outside. Scat Johnston may not have been much of a human specimen, but he still would have appreciated the feel and the smell of his freshly laundered clothes—assuming he ever did his own laundry, of course.

Alex nursed his drink and rehearsed. His name was George. He was here for the weekend with the Industrial Chemists' Association. The chemists' program was already laid out in interchangeable white letters on a black signboard in the lobby: Friday banquet and band in the Slalom Room, Saturday breakfast in the Traverse, etcetera through Sunday afternoon. Alex thought he could pass for an industrial chemist. George had been able to come up a day early, but wasn't finding much action and was feeling lonely. It had been a long time since he'd last slept with a woman. How long was long? A month? Six months? What was the best way to rehearse that?

Alex made his eyes roam around the mostly empty tables and up and down the bar. He wasn't sure whether George was single or was no longer on intimate terms with his wife. Not that he actually planned to spew out George's tale. It was just that he'd been told having those kind of details down helped an actor relax into a part. He wanted to play the part, for a while. He didn't want to scare the woman, whoever she would be, away. That's what he'd told Dennis MacDonald, before Dennis had pointed out the right room and the right bartender. Then Dennis had wished him good luck and drifted away.

What was funny was that the conversation going on at the bar had been right on the mark. There were two men, one of them older than Alex, the other probably Alex's age. Three women. It was hard to tell who was connected to whom. "You don't even know how the two of us got back here," one of the women said. She had said this before, at least once, but she repeated it as if she had never gotten a satisfactory response. "You left us, but we got a ride over here with this guy in a Jaguar. He offered to take us"—she paused for effect—"*any-place* we wanted to go."

"You came here," the older man said at last. He had gray hair and a red nose. He was clean-shaven, his sweater looked expensive, but his accent revealed that he did not come from the upper class. A self-made man, as they said. Business or professional, it was hard to choose which. The woman had light brown hair, styled short, and a tan in February.

"Yeah," she said in exasperation, real or feigned. "And you

don't even know how. He tried to talk me into coming with him."
This got no rise, so she paused again. "I bet I could have gone
with him and got three hundred bucks for the night."

Like a conductor's baton, that brought a quick, almost audible hush all around. Then everybody laughed, and the second
man followed it up, anxious to demonstrate that the comment
had been a little rough, maybe, but still it was only a joke.
"Right," he said. "We all know Donna has got what it takes. Anyway, Donna, what's a nice girl like you doing in a place like this?"

Donna laughed. "Hey, honey?" she asked the bartender. He
looked young and collegiate. He was dressed in a white turtleneck with the sleeves rolled up. The "hey, honey" was more
motherly than flirtatious, Alex thought. "Is this place going to
liven up? We get a lot better crowd at Happy Hour on Route 1."

"Route 1?" the bartender said. "You mean the Palace? Dia-
mond Head? Platters?" He sounded homesick. They were talking about the same stretch of North Shore that housed the
Typhoon.

"You know Route 1?" the younger man said. "Did you ever
work there? I met my wife in one of those clubs."

"Did you?"

"That's right," one of the other women answered. Alex
thought she was the one who'd been abandoned with Donna on
the slopes and had got the ride back with the guy in the Jaguar.
"He saw me dancing. He came up to me and said, 'Let me take
you away from all this.'"

"And you said," the older man jumped in, "for three
hundred dollars, let's go." By the time he finished, it had become
a chorus, the unwelcome thought banished in jollity. The five of
them had ordered another round, drunk it down, and headed
for dinner. Now Alex held up his empty glass. When the bartender came, he said, "You know what they were all talking
about, before?" He inclined his head in a wistful way toward the
group's stools, which were empty now.

"What?"

"Oh, about the three hundred a night."

The bartender squinted at Alex's glass, then added fresh ice
and refilled it. "I don't think she was worth that much," he said.
"I think there are some girls who are."

"That's what I was wondering about. I don't want to spend
all the time I'm up here alone."

The bartender turned away but inclined his head toward Alex to show that he was listening. There was a crisp part, like a crease from an iron, in his straight blond hair. Alex waited while he wiped the bar and slid some new, clean wineglasses onto a rack where they hung upside down. "There is a kind of escort service," the man told him. "If taking a lady to dinner is what you want."

"That would be great," Alex said. "I'm up here with the Industrial Chemists," he added self-importantly, "but I thought I'd get a head start. I'd like, uh, somebody I could relate to as equals. Maybe a college girl, somebody like that."

"Sure," the bartender said. "There's a finder's fee, head-hunter's fee, a hundred cash to me. Then the rest is up to you and she."

"To me and *her*," Alex corrected. He handed over five crisp bank-machine twenty-dollar bills.

"For another hundred," the bartender added, "I can make sure to find somebody that's free all night."

"I'm not that hard up," Alex smiled. "Let me meet the lady first."

The bartender smiled back, no doubt because the customer was always right. "You're not that hard *on*, you mean. Where do you want the lady to meet you?"

"Tell me a good restaurant. The one upstairs?"

"No." The bartender wrinkled his nose. "Why don't you meet her at the one in the Silver Birch? If you can afford her, you can afford it."

Rosemarie Davis could afford it, Alex hoped.

She looked like a model, Alex would have said. She looked like one of the mannequins at Jordan Marsh. She looked like a Revlon ad. He tried to look as if he already knew her, as if they were already friends. That's what George would do. George would try not to gape or stare.

She had straight dark hair, cut to look spiky and wild. She wore tailored pants and a flared brown suede jacket that buttoned at her slim waist. Under the jacket was a white blouse, maybe silk, with half of its buttons left undone. Her eyelashes were impossibly long and dark, her lips impossibly rounded and an impossible cool dark red. She looked to be the same age as

141

Caroline, nineteen or twenty. Any man with her would be sure to enjoy the covetous glances of the other men passing by.

"Hi," she said. "I guess you must be George." The dialogue was not original, nor was it dressed up with hype. The tone was cool and professional, but friendly. "I'm Lena Hanson."

"Hi, Lena Hanson," Alex said. He thought it was strange that she gave him a last name. It was part of the fiction, he guessed; it meant that the name was a fiction too. He guided her to a table and ordered wine. When the wine came, he led in clinking glasses. "Lena Hanson," he repeated. "Where are you from?"

"Nebraska."

He realized he'd been expecting it. It was something about the name, but he'd had two bourbons and now he was drinking the wine. Lena was like Ilene, of course, the name, this much of a connection swam up at him in a dreamy way. She didn't look like Ilene, who wore big round glasses and a suit when Alex first met her, whose light brown hair fell halfway to her shoulders and then curled up—who had looked just like what she was, the librarian.

"Really," Alex said. "You're not from Nebraska. Tell me where you're really from."

"What are you, George, a mind reader?" Lena Hanson raised her eyebrows, impossibly rounded and dark. She let a doubtful curve break the symmetry of her fashion-model lips.

"You tell me," Alex answered. "Did you really grow up within a thousand miles of where you said?"

"A thousand miles? Yes, within a thousand. The true story is that I grew up in Dubuque."

The way she said it meant that it might be the true story and it might not, but Alex decided to believe that it was. Dubuque, Iowa, he thought. That made some sense, that she could get from there to here, because Dubuque wasn't so far from New Hampshire after all. A poor town, a factory town, farm equipment and animal feed and packing houses. Switch the packing houses for pulp mills and it might be northern New Hampshire, say Grafton or Berlin. That was his impression, anyway, though he'd only driven through Dubuque. Well, stopped to eat lunch and buy groceries, in fact. He'd been driving Laura's car, it would be about a year and a half after that day in the library when he first met Ilene. In Dubuque he'd been driving, with

Laura beside him, as New York as she could be, leaving Grand Island and Hans Heidenfelter and Ilene Paciorek behind. Before he knew it, Alex found himself telling so-called Lena Hanson all this.

"Are you sorry?" she asked.

"No, I guess not. I got a daughter out of it. And I got back here where I probably belong." And I'm staying here, he added to himself. Apparently New England is where I'm going to live this new and perhaps final phase of my life. This is where Maria and I live, it's where Maria and Laura live too. If I move in with Meredith, that will only be confirmation of the fact: Boston, the White Mountains, the Atlantic, Cape Cod. Not the Great Plains or the Rockies or the high sunshine of Cuernavaca or the fog of San Francisco Bay. With Meredith Phillips, not getting married in the eyes of court or church, but planning to be with each other in sickness and in health. Till death do us part, amen? Alex found he was unconsciously feeling for tumors at the base of his neck. He quickly put his hand to the neck of his wineglass instead. There was a certain similarity between Ilene and Meredith, he noted. Unlike Laura, they were both literary sorts. And then he had it. The connection floated up like a bubble and lodged in his head.

"Willa Cather," he said. "That's it, isn't it? Tell me that's not where you got your name."

Lena Hanson smiled back, a real smile, though she got it quickly under control. "I'd like the brook trout, if you don't mind. And a small garden salad. Who is this Willa Cather, by the way?"

"And I'll have the pheasant, or prairie chicken, like we used to go after with our shotguns on the long summer days after we were done fixing cars. Willa Cather wrote stories about people who lived on that prairie, Norwegians and Bohemians and people like that. Ilene taught me about Willa Cather—so many of the stories were about romances, or missed romances, between sophisticated Easterners and yearning but ignorant prairie folk. There's a Lena Hanson in one of the stories, or some of those stories..."

Alex stopped because Lena, or whoever she was, signaled for a waitress and then sat back so that Alex could be the man in charge and order the meal as it was supposed to be done. The waitress was older, in her thirties, Alex thought, and she wore a wedding ring. If she knew Lena Hanson, if she knew Lena came in every weekend or every other weekend with a different man, she did not let on. She took the order, as from two strangers, and went on her way. If this weren't tonight, but say a week ago, Caroline Davis might have taken the order. But then he wouldn't be here, of course.

"'Her name was a reproach through all the Divide country,'" Lena Hanson quoted then. "'She wore a pink wrapper and silk stockings and tiny pink slippers, and she sang accompanying herself on a battered guitar. She had heard great singers in Denver and Salt Lake, and she knew the strange language of flattery and idleness and mirth.' You have a very good memory for literature, George. Now tell me some more about yourself."

"My name is Alex," Alex said, feeling that after her admission somehow he owed her this much. It occurred to him that he could be her father's age, if her father in Dubuque had married as young as they often did. He didn't say any more, or ask any more, directly anyway. While they waited for dinner they talked about the deadness of winter on the plains, about the condition of the ski slopes here in the Woods, about it being late February and mud season not all that far away. Then they ate, sometimes locking glances, and sometimes Lena Hanson's fingers would brush Alex's fingers or the back of his hand.

All in all, Alex was impressed with both her performance and his. It was almost possible to believe that this was just dinner, two attractive people getting acquainted, nothing being bought or sold. While he talked, and looked, he mused on the idea of selling one's body. It was really only certain rights to her body she was selling—her labor power, which Marx would say all proletarians sold, but this type of labor was supposed to be private and to mean more than what it physically was. Which was more offensive, he wondered, having to sell your body or having to sell your blood? Somebody might conceivably pay for his own sexual services, but nobody would want his blood. Though somebody did want one of his lymph nodes for a study, Dr. Wagner had once pointed out—"someday, when it's convenient"—and then she had let the request rest.

If your body was going to disappear, Alex thought, did that make it a more precious commodity, one that would fetch a higher price? Men would pay for Lena Hanson's body because of its youth as well as its beauty. Because youth disappeared. Alex sipped and ate and watched Lena Hanson and enjoyed thinking these morbid but interesting thoughts. He wasn't sorry that he wouldn't really be going to bed with her. Not that he would mind feeling Lena Hanson's warm body, but he didn't want to feel George's empty soul. He was partly sorry, and partly glad, that he *was* going to pry further into Lena's real life.

She brought the charade to an end, delicately, by declining Alex's offer of dessert. "My diet," she said in a disparaging way. She patted her waist, then took Alex's hand in hers and squeezed it. She said "my diet" the way somebody says, by way of excuse, "my job" or "my boss." "A hundred to me now for another hour," she added. "Three hundred if you're going to keep me busy all night."

Alex sighed dramatically. To business, then. When the questioning about Scat and Caroline happened, he wanted it to be in Scat's place, not here. Maybe she'd know something to search for, something Dennis MacDonald had missed. Maybe in that setting it would be harder for her to get up and walk out. Maybe he just wanted to collect some of those covetous looks on the way out of this room.

"Another hundred is all I've got, I'm afraid. I do have a condo. I'm hoping you could come see it now."

To his surprise, Lena's eyes widened with shock. As if some signal had gotten crossed, and he'd made an unexpectedly indecent proposal. His second thought was that he'd let slip out whose condo he was really taking her to. Then he realized she was seeing something over his shoulder, and turned to see it too. He saw Natalie storming—there wasn't any word for it—across the room. She wasn't yelling, but she might as well as have been. Her arms were swinging like clock pendulums and her purse flailed out like a double-bladed ax she planned to take to someone's backside. She flung the purse onto the table and stood over him, glaring. "So," she hissed. "I see you got yourself a date, honey. Mind if I sit down?"

Lena's shock died away, but her former interest did not return. She had pocketed the five twenty-dollar bills. She said to Alex, "I think maybe it would be better if I left."

"Not on your life, honey," Natalie insisted. "You've been paid for your time, and just 'cause he's mine don't mean he hasn't got a right to make use of what he buys. I'm Natalie Cooper," she added, extending her hand. "Alex's wife."

"Lena Hanson," Alex said. He felt that Natalie was one step ahead of him, as always, but whatever she was up to, he ought to play along. "Look, darling," he tried in a placating tone, "do we have to do this in public?"

"No," Natalie said. "Why don't the three of us all go home?"

The face Lena turned to Natalie now was stone. "What he buys, lady?" she said icily. "I've been paid for a dinner date, and now the dinner is done. It's not in my job description to help clean up the mess."

"I'm afraid it is," Natalie said in a less emotional, more commanding tone. The voice, which had been shrill, dropped several tones, and it dropped a notch in volume as well. She pulled up a chair and checked to see that all eyes were carefully averted from the scene she had made. Then she extracted a flat plastic case from her purse. She flipped it open, quickly, in front of the kiss-me, picture-book face of Alex's date. "You've got to answer some questions," she said. "Homicide questions. Police."

20

BLUE LIGHT DISTRICT

Alex closed Scat Johnston's door behind the three of them. He let Natalie lead Lena Hanson into the living room while he turned right, into the kitchen, where he measured coffee and water into the electric pot. A percolator, he noted, not a drip machine; not quite state-of-the-art, Scat. The words Natalie had spoken in the car rumbled in his brain.

"You have the right to have a lawyer present," she had intoned. "Anything you say may be used against you." During the short ride, Lena had neither spoken nor availed herself of her constitutional right. When they had parked in the space closest to the path leading to Katahdin B-71, though, she had tugged her jacket tighter around her. It didn't offer much protection against the New Hampshire night. Alex wondered what reassurance it gave her. "Coffee in a minute," he called across the counter that separated living room from kitchen. "There's sugar, but no cream, and the milk is sour, I'm afraid. There is Coffee-mate, ingredients mono- and diglycerides."

"Yeah, those," Lena Hanson said. "Give me a cup of coffee with that."

"Sugar," Natalie said. She was on the couch with the brown cushions, under a poster showing two animals that might have been cats or horses or dragons. In Italian, it advertised an exhibit of paintings by Paul Klee. She seemed to Alex midway between a cat and a dragon herself: relaxed yet sinewy, like a cat, but this was a dry, confident, completely together one. Possessed of bluff and trickery like a dragon. He noticed the dull silver earrings with blue stones, like the ones street vendors sold in Harvard Square. It *was* possible: Officer Natalie Cooper, young and bright, female and black, and a townie, Cambridge born and bred. Affirmative action and local preference, all wrapped up together. If that ID was real, though, why bother with the outraged-wife act to throw Lena off balance first? And why was Scat killed in her parents' apartment, and why was she off keeping a rendezvous with Meredith and Maria and Alex at the time? Even if she wasn't a cop, many of these questions still held.

Lena sat on the reclining armchair, under a movie poster of Sophia Loren in a white peasant shirt, translucent and clinging because she and it had just come out of the sea. Lena had buttoned up her blouse and she kept pulling the suede jacket tighter. She also kept brushing imaginary crumbs off her pants. If Natalie was the dragon, who was this? The girl hero, hiding her dagger or amulet in one of those pockets of thin brown suede? Could she have killed Scat? And why? Alex lounged against the counter, waiting. He listened to the coffee beginning to perk.

"Alex could testify that you offered him sex for money," Natalie said. "But of course we've got no interest in that. We're investigating a homicide, Lowell Johnston, committed in Cambridge, Massachusetts. That's where my jurisdiction begins and ends. What Johnston was into here may have some bearing. Your date, Alex Glauberman, is a private investigator hired by the family. He's working with me on this."

True in a sense, Alex thought, if not the family Natalie implied. He guessed that "hard cop/soft cop" was the party game. Soft cop was what he wanted, regardless. He asked across the counter, "What was the name of that story, by the way?"

"The title is 'Eric Hermannson's Soul.' Eric gave Lena up when he got saved by a preacher. But later he escaped salvation thanks to a rich bitch from back East." Lena didn't smile as she said any of this, nor did she quote any more of the author's cadenced words. "Was any of that shit about the mechanic and the librarian true?"

"Yes," Alex said. "All if it. The truth always helps to disguise a lie." He didn't look at Natalie, who demanded, "What the hell are you two going on about?"

"American literature," Lena said, turning to her. "I'll talk to you, but that name, Lena Hanson, will have to do. No other name, no ID. When I get out, I don't want you or anybody knowing where I went." She waited, but Natalie neither agreed nor disagreed. Natalie opened her purse again and took a tape recorder out. It was the same kind Alex had bought yesterday. The last time he'd seen that one it had been in his room in the inn, with Suzanne. Lena watched her press the record button. She started to talk without waiting for a question.

"As I told your partner, Alex or Eric or George, I grew up in Dubuque. My parents saved up and sent me east to college. When the hog plant closed, they both lost cold, dirty jobs that you wouldn't want, and I wouldn't want if I could help it. But they were union jobs, steady, they paid good money, they put me where I was. Now all the packing houses are going non-union and moving further west. My folks couldn't support me anymore. If anything, I knew I should be helping them. I told myself I would do this for a year, and then go back to school. I guess none of this sounds very original to you. Every hooker's lament."

Natalie asked, "Do your folks know where you are?"

"Where, not what. They're churchgoers. I used to sing in the Lutheran choir, if you really want to know. They think I'm a cocktail waitress. They think that's bad enough."

Alex held up a hand to Natalie as he poured the brewed coffee into three of Lowell Johnston's white cups, dishwasher bright, and then he set them on a black lucite tray. Natalie pushed the pause button on the recorder and waited for him to come in and serve.

"You know whose place this is?" she asked Lena then.

"Whose it *was*, yeah."

"Was he the pimp?"

"Please, Officer, no one uses words like that in this resort." Lena looked sincere, but it may just have been part of the disguise, part of the more-sophisticated-than-thou attitude, something that went with the way her eyebrows were arched. "Scat was the personnel manager, you might say, but he worked for somebody else. His name is Paul Jakes, he's a local. He's the one who handles the Jericho town cops. I guess you know they've been paid to look the other way."

"Same as with the drugs," Alex put in.

"That's right. Jakes does the buying, I think. Scat does—did —the retailing in that operation, and in the other he does the personnel. Hiring and firing, labor disputes, that kind of thing."

"And do you know anybody he got on the wrong side of?" Natalie asked. "Anybody that would be mad enough at him to kill him?"

"He wasn't a very nice guy, but he wasn't, like, violent or malicious. Somebody that he hooked on dope, that would be the most likely."

"There's been a suggestion," Alex said, "that blackmail was involved. Is it possible he was in that business too? Hidden cameras, blackmailing your dates, threatening to send photos to their wives?"

Natalie smiled, but she only said, "Or whitemail, as the case may be."

"Never when I was involved," Lena shook her head. "The only picture-taking I know about—" She stopped suddenly, and involuntarily looked upstairs. "Well, yes, it was black- or whitemailing of a kind."

"Yes?" Natalie made her voice deep and no-nonsense. Alex thought again of a cat, one that could simultaneously purr and gather itself to spring. A tiger, with that same unstudied, confident beauty, those same strong shoulders and the eyes that could become slits in the wide, easy-to-look-at face. Her boots—low, soft leather ones—tapped noiselessly against the carpet. But Lena stood her ground. She folded her hands, like a girl in Sunday school reciting. In lieu of a desk, she rested them on her knees.

"Scat was the talent scout, that was part of what he did. They wanted, you know, college women if possible, that would make the high-priced crowd happy. That wouldn't stand out, either, as pros. It might seem to the clients and onlookers both like these guys really did just pick us up. Anyway, Scat had friends in Boston, in different colleges, people he went to prep school with. That's how I got here. A guy I knew happened to mention it, kind of as a joke, kidding around."

Kind of, Alex thought, maybe not quite. He remembered the conversation in the bar.

"I said I had a friend, and if my friend was interested, who would she call? He said he didn't know, but he had a friend who might know who to call. It was all so transparent, but we pretended, you know. So I talked to this Lowell Johnston, the friend's friend, on the phone. He said the procedure was to come up here for an audition."

"Audition?"

"That's the word he used, Officer, yes. He was right too. I mean, mostly they just want someplace they know they can shove their dick, or somebody female to be seen with, or both. But you have to be kind of an actress to make it work."

"And the audition was . . . ?"

"The audition turned out to be going to bed with Scat." She kept her hands on her knees but jerked her head upward without trying to conceal the motion. "Up there, in his loft. He had this camera set up, on a stand, with a remote control. He said the picture-taking was to make sure we didn't get flustered, embarrassed, self-conscious. Of course, it was something to hold over us too. He could threaten to send photos to our lovers or parents or whatever we had—in case we ever made noises like we were going to make any trouble for him."

"Did he threaten you with exposure that way?"

Lena studied Natalie, looking for a putdown in her choice of words. She unclasped her hands and leaned forward, the stiff black strands of hair like spikes on a floating mine. It finally occurred to Alex that this was probably not her own hair, but a wig. He tried to picture her without the makeup, without the lipstick, her head close-cropped and fuzzy and blond. "I wasn't in this to make trouble, Officer," she said. "Does that sit okay with you?"

Natalie didn't answer, but only looked at Alex, who finished his coffee and gathered the cups onto his tray. Then he handed

150

Lena the picture of Caroline and Scat. "You mean pictures like that?"

"That would be one of the tamer ones," Lena said. She handed it back, like something hot but not intensely so, something that could burn you only if you handled it too long. Her fingers were steady.

"Do you know who that is with him?" Alex asked.

She shook her head, but for once she didn't seem to trust her voice.

"Ms. Hanson." Natalie put on her own deep tone again. "This *ain't* that big a place. You don't mean to tell me you don't know the other women who work in the same ring?"

"No, I don't mean to. But she didn't work. Some people must flunk the audition." She looked Natalie straight in the eyes, her shoulders squared, the jacket hugging her, the pose a full-color imitation of the young black-and-white Lauren Bacall. "Maybe she burst out laughing. The tricks don't like that at all."

"Well," Natalie said. "Suppose we go back to who might want to kill Lowell Townsend Johnston. Could it have been for some kind of revenge? Did anybody ever get hurt in this operation, that's what I want to know. Did anybody ever contract VD or AIDS, or have a pregnancy, an abortion? Commit suicide, or disappear—anything like that, anything at all?"

Yes, Alex realized, and the same question applied to Caroline's death as well. If Caroline had been killed to keep her silent, what she knew had to be something worth killing over. Which could be money, but it could also be someone else's death. He noticed that Natalie's tone had gone silky soft. Lena stood and took the tray from him and carried it to the counter. Then she walked down the hallway and into the kitchen, where she slowly washed the cups, running the water loud. Finally she shut off the taps and turned to face Alex and Natalie, her fingers drumming on the Formica. They made a sound that indicated rapid thinking, a sound like far-off galloping hooves. She slowed down and just used one index finger and one middle finger, tap-tap, tap-tap, while she made up her mind.

"I *didn't* know her," she said, but her voice was more tired, less defiant. "But I know who she is. Who she *was*. Caroline Davis, the one he hit before he got killed. She came to talk to me once. She was worried about somebody who disappeared."

Natalie crossed the room, not hurrying, and put the tape recorder down where it would be sure to catch Lena's words. Standing paired over the kitchen counter like that, the two women did not seem so much like antagonists. More like they might be neighbors, roommates, or lovers. And Natalie didn't follow with the obvious question: Who? Instead, from the profile Alex could see, she hesitated with half-open lips, the query not quite coming out. As if she'd been fishing, ever so calmly, but hadn't expected the sharp tug or the wriggling thing that now showed itself on her hook.

So Alex said, "Yes, we thought that might be the case. Caroline had a friend who was one of your co-workers, isn't that right?"

"Yeah. Nell. She quit suddenly, left, went on a trip to Europe with her loot. At least she sent a postcard from Spain, from Barcelona, that said so. Scat showed it to me. It wasn't surprising—one day, I could see it coming, I might just get fed up, have to put down the part, try to go back to being just me."

"But Caroline thought differently?"

"Caroline said it was strange she went so suddenly. Caroline got a letter from her, too, but she seemed to think the letter was strange. You know, how people read a forced confession or retraction, from a hostage or political prisoner or somebody that copped some kind of plea? And they say, 'That just doesn't sound like what so-and-so would write'? That's what she said, this Caroline. And now she's dead. Scat hit her. And somebody knifed him. I can see what brings you two here. Until you, though, nobody asked. Now the day I'm leaving is getting closer all the time."

"Tell me about Paul Jakes," Alex said. It was starting to make a certain kind of sense, but not yet enough. He felt separated from the action, so he came to stand next to Natalie, so he could look down at Lena Hanson instead of up.

"He's a builder, a contractor. Scat used to pal around with him when he was a teenager, they say. I've been thinking anyhow that with Scat dead, this operation may be dead too. Paul's probably outgrown it, doesn't need it anymore."

"Why not? What does he build?"

"I don't know, but plenty. Stuff around here. That's some of his trailers, building the new condos, Denali, Blue Ridge, Mount

Hood. What do they say on them? 'Jakes Construction—Jericho, New Hampshire—Boston, Mass.' I guess he does work in Boston too."

"Just like Graham Johnston," Alex pointed out to Natalie. "An interesting connection to be followed up by the Cambridge police."

"Is it?" Natalie asked. Whatever she thought, Alex's question seemed to have helped her find her voice again. She referred the question to Lena. "Is there something between the Johnston family and this Paul Jakes?"

"I don't know. I don't know Paul, except to say hello. I bet he keeps clear of anything you could put your hands on. Listen, I've done you a favor—no lawyer, no delay, that was a favor I didn't have to do. Do you know if, whoever searched this place first, they came across any more photos besides the one?"

"To tell you the truth," Alex said, "we don't know for sure who got here first. I know there are no photos of you in our possession, and none left here for anybody to find. Now this Nell—do you know her name, her whole name, real name, and where she was from?"

"Nell, her name was Nilda, really. Nilda. I didn't know her last name. Caroline told me it; it was something like Martinez, Gonzalez, Fernandez, something like that. She was, I don't know, Puerto Rican or Mexican, she never said, I never asked. She was real light-skinned, though. I think she was a college graduate, she once said she wanted to be an engineer. She was from New York. I heard she had a kid back there, but I don't know if that's right. I didn't hear it from her."

"Just New York?" Natalie asked. "No borough, no neighborhood, just New York?"

"Brooklyn, I think, I'm not sure. Look, I really didn't get involved with her, with any of that. She left, she went to Europe, and except for that one time this Caroline came to me, I never heard anything else. Haven't I told you enough?"

"When Caroline came to you, did she say where *she* thought Nilda might be?"

"No. She asked questions, like you two. She didn't *tell* me anything more than you're telling me now."

"Well, did she ask anything that revealed what she might've thought?"

"Only one thing, maybe—I didn't put any importance on it—you're cops, maybe it would be different for you. She asked me if Scat or Paul was much into ice fishing."

"Ice fishing?" Natalie let her puzzlement show.

"Yeah, you cut a hole in the ice..."

"That's okay," Alex said, seeing again the photo of pond ice, that's what it had to be, pond ice with a hole cut out. "I understand what you're saying. We know what ice fishing is."

"Yes. Well, I didn't understand. I said I really didn't know. And I don't. Now that I've answered your questions, may I please go?"

Natalie shut off the tape recorder and made a small show of removing the tape and taking a step backward, a step of retreat. She put her hands on her hips and said, "I don't have any more questions, Ms. Hanson, but I do have some advice. I heard you say you think it's time to get out. I'm not going to preach to you about your line of work. Some people, some people pretty close to me, even, don't feel too happy about mine. But my job, most of the time, makes me feel comfortable with myself. If yours does that for you, fine. If not, then I think you ought to consider your alternatives. Whichever way you decide about your line of work, my advice is that you draw your money out of the bank and pack your bags—tonight. Before anybody else comes asking you questions or asking questions about you."

"Yes, ma'am," Lena said. "You've been very decent with me, and I appreciate it. Just please, if you could keep any of those photos from finding their way back to Dubuque. And if I think of anything that might be helpful, once I'm gone, how would I be able to get in touch?"

"I'll be moving around for a few days. The best thing would be to contact my boss, Detective Sergeant Trevisone. If he hasn't received my report yet, you might have to repeat some of what's already on this tape."

Lena nodded and headed for the door. "Thank you, too, George," she added with her hand on the knob.

Alex was busy trying to put everything she had said together with what he knew or guessed, but at the same time he was feeling sorry to see her go so soon. *I'll see you someday, passing through Dubuque,* he thought, but he knew how unlikely that would be. More likely that he'd see her if Bernie had to track her down and put her on the stand. "Wait, you'll freeze walking," he said. "Any-

way, I've got to drop Detective Cooper back at her car." If she *was*
Detective Cooper, which by now he doubted very much. So he
got his coat and followed Lena Hanson to the door, and Natalie
got her purse and her coat and shut off the lights and followed
him. Outside, the stars were shining brightly and the moon was
casting a pale glow on the snow. Suddenly the snow lit up like
day. Alex looked toward a pair of headlights, the source of the
brightness, and toward another light, a blue one, rotating above
the car's roof.

21

HOEING AND FISHING

The headlights went off, but as
the policeman approached slowly, on foot, his six-volt flashlight
had a similar effect on Alex's eyes. Alex felt he was back in Somerville, facing the Reagan and Bush masks again. He was just
as much alone, because Lena and Natalie had disappeared into
the condominium behind him. "Let me see some identification,"
the policeman said.

He was small, Alex could see that through the glare. His
voice was young, eager rather than tough. Alex gave him both
driver's license and Rosemarie Davis's letter. The flashlight
pointed down, toward the documents. To Alex, as his eyes ad-
justed, the letter looked sadly dog-eared and wrinkled, folded
and unfolded too many times, like an old map. "I'm looking for a
suspect wanted for questioning," the policeman said.

"What suspect?" Alex asked.

"Suzanne Lutrello." The policeman held up a key, dangled it
so the flashlight beam lit up its holder of white plastic treated to
glow in the dark. "Since this isn't your property, I don't need
your permission to enter and look around." Alex stood aside to
let him use the key. The knob turned, but the door didn't budge.

"Dead bolt." He sounded frustrated, but not surprised. "We
can go sit in my patrol car all night, or you can ask them to open

up." Alex had been trying to gauge the man, but he realized it didn't matter. The point, he decided, was that Suzanne would most likely be safest in jail. While there is a soul in prison, I am not free, Eugene Debs said. But Alex would be freer with Suzanne off his hands. Bernie could work on getting her out, and meanwhile Alex could gather the evidence he would lay under Trevisone's nose. It didn't matter what he thought of the individual to whom he turned her in—just as it hadn't mattered what Tommy Lutrello thought of him.

"She's not in there," he said. "She's in the Black Pine, room thirty-one."

"Uh-huh," the policeman answered. "Well, then, let's go sit in the car."

The car felt warm and smelled of coffee. In the light, the policeman was young and red-faced. He took off his cap to reveal a military-style crewcut. When he took off his gloves, Alex could see a class ring on one finger. The young cop called in and reported what Alex had told him; he gave only his patrol car number—car number three—so Alex did not get to learn his name. The radio went silent, then crackled and a female voice reported back that the room was registered to Alex Glauberman and that "Chet's car" was on its way over. The policeman offered Alex coffee from a thermos, in a Styrofoam cup. Alex took it gratefully. The effect of the wine and bourbon were only a memory, but he felt a lassitude trying to creep in. The coffee steam and the two men's breath fogged the window, which the cop used his gloves to wipe clean. The radio crackled with static. Finally the female voice came back on. "Chet missed her," was all it said. Then, "Better check the Johnston place. See if any of 'em know where she could've went."

"Sorry," Alex said.

The cop answered, "Whoever's there, see if you can talk them into letting us in."

When Natalie opened up, the cop did not betray any special interest, but only asked her and Lena for identification too. Natalie gave him a driver's license, not the black plastic case. Lena said she didn't have ID on her, to which he shrugged and again did not look surprised. He made notes on a pad and returned both Natalie's license and Alex's license and letter. Then he checked every room and closet on the first floor, every room and

156

closet on the second, and then climbed up and opened the trap-door and shone his flashlight all around the loft.

Alex followed, wondering whether Natalie or Lena would still be there when they got back downstairs. Either patrol car number three carried two men, one of whom was out watching in the cold, or else nobody cared about anybody except the suspect. Finally he said to Alex, "Guess you were telling me the truth. Do you have permission to be on these premises?"

"I have a key that Scat gave to Suzanne Lutrello for her use. I don't know whether that constitutes permission or not."

"Not in my book. Do you have any idea where Lutrello could've gone to?"

Alex shook his head. "She didn't have a car, as far as I know." He followed the man back down the stairs. Natalie was again sitting under the Klee poster on the couch, but Lena Hanson was gone.

"The other lady said you knew where to find her," Natalie reported.

The cop only repeated his question: "Do you have any idea where Lutrello could've gone?"

"None," Natalie said with assurance. "Is it true you were paid off to look the other way about the businesses Scat Johnston and Paul Jakes were in?"

"Just get the hell out of here," the young policeman said. "If either of you comes back, you'll be arrested for a B&E." He stayed put, not self-conscious but with his eagerness gone, until they left.

"Where to, Officer Cooper?" Alex asked. He shifted into second and drifted slowly along the Katahdin drive. At the main road Natalie said, "My car's outside that restaurant where you were having your date." Alex turned right, toward the Silver Birch. The steering wheel felt solid through his gloves. The steering was tight, the linkages firm. A smooth mechanism—no parts banging up against each other at every turn. "How did you find me?" he asked.

"Went to that bar where Suzanne said you'd gone to make contact. Played outraged wife. Quietly threatened the bartender to make a big public scene if he didn't tell me where he sent my husband to pick up his lady of the night." She laughed the laugh that belonged to an old woman. "Cross-racial spouse worked so well I decided to use it again. People can only handle so much surprise, then they tend to lose their hold on everything."

"You told me you got to be friends with Suzanne because of the papers you wrote in that class. That was a lie."

"Does it matter?"

"I can't figure that out. You're an addiction counselor, Suzanne says. I don't think you're addicted to making things up for no reason. You didn't want me to know you'd been her counselor, her caretaker, right off? You thought that if I knew that, I'd leave her problems to you?"

"Why all these questions all of a sudden? Didn't we make a good team with your friend Lena, back there?"

"Why these, you mean, why not a hundred others?" Alex blazed back. A good team they might have been, but not on a steady basis. Natalie appeared and disappeared and reappeared at will. Along the way, too many people knew where to find him, and too many people knew where to find Suzanne. He stopped the car, turned to her, and counted out questions on his fingers, close to her face.

"Why did you pretend to work for Trevisone?" he demanded. "Or *do* you? Why was it your house where Scat got killed? Were you surprised? Why was it your house where that other so-called detective, Callahan, caught up with Suzanne? Did she call you from that motel on 128? Or forget all that, and just tell me this: Where did you tell her to go, half an hour ago, when you called to warn her I was in the hands of the local constable and you thought I might be about to turn her in?"

"Why?" Natalie repeated. She folded her arms in a way that meant she was not going to be hurried. "I'm not trying to be unreasonable. But I need reasons that I should give you answers. That woman Lena, she had reasons. We could hurt her, at least if we were who she thought. Plus she was scared. Plus the Lutheran choir girl inside her thought she really *ought* to tell. I don't have any reasons yet. You tried to make some kind of deal with the local cop that involved shopping Suzanne. Didn't you? Tell me if I'm wrong."

"What I can tell you is that right now she's run away, somewhere, and I don't know where that is, though maybe you do. So have it your way. I'm going to call Trevisone, just like I said I would."

"That's an empty threat, Alex, because I'm sure Jericho's finest have already called big brother in Massachusetts. If I don't tell you where she's gone, then there's nothing you can add, and you know it. Listen, it wasn't my idea for Suzanne to try and get poor little Scat out of his jam. It *is* my idea to try and do what I can for her. For a little while more, you and I have each got our own row to hoe."

Alex turned away from her, opened his window, and took a breath of the fresh air. It was smoky from overbuilding. Even on a Thursday, too many woodstoves and fireplaces were going. Without speaking, he drove the rest of the way back to the restaurant. In the lot he saw the battered Honda in which Natalie and Meredith had driven off four days ago.

"I'm doing what I said," he told her. "You call me at the Black Pine when you want to talk." She stepped out gracefully, said good night, and unlocked the door of her own car. He could follow her. In that thing she probably couldn't lose him. But he didn't doubt she'd be willing to lead him all the way to Maine and back. So he took her advice. He would try to make his own efforts bear fruit.

In room 31 of the Black Pine Inn, he felt Suzanne's absence immediately. She'd been lying on this bed; the pillow was still propped up, still dented from her head. She had left no message. Of course, even if she'd wanted to, a message for Alex would really be a message for whoever got here first. Alex took her place on the bed, resting the phone in his lap. He turned on only the bedside lamp, so he'd be able to watch the stars out the picture window. Probably she was with Natalie. He hoped that was as safe as she seemed to think.

His first call was to Trevisone. Just to make sure, he asked for Officer Natalie Cooper first. There was no Officer Cooper, and Trevisone had gone home. Somebody named O'Connor was willing to listen to what Alex had to say.

He went through it slowly and methodically, from the meeting with Rosemarie Sturgeon Davis to the interview with Lena Hanson that had just occurred. He left Tommy Lutrello and Bernie out of the meeting in the Burlington Mall, and he omitted Lena Hanson's real biographical details and her assumed name. Trevisone would have plenty to chew on, and he could share it with Graham Johnston if that was what he had to do.

Alex gave his number and address in case Trevisone wanted to call him back.

The next call was to Laura. It was nine-thirty, which he hoped would be too late for Maria to be answering the phone. He got Carl, Laura's husband, who greeted him cordially as always and gave him Laura. Alex thought Carl was grateful to him for getting Laura's less conventional years out of the way.

"Has Maria been asking about the missing baby-sitter?" Alex asked.

"Not much, no."

"Well, one thing, I promised to call if Suzanne got found, and she did. She turned up at my house with an explanation, finally, on Wednesday." He didn't say that she had disappeared again, thought it was really this second disappearance that had forced him to call—and even though he really didn't believe in the Suzanne-by-Sunday threat, and anyway he'd done his best to turn her in. "And another thing," he added. "I'm in New Hampshire for the weekend, I might as well give you the number. And, um, when are you leaving for the weekend, by the way?"

Laura said they were leaving as soon as they could Friday afternoon, and why?

"It's just I'm a little worried about her being freaked out by all this. Could you pick her up from school tomorrow afternoon? Instead of her coming home on the bus, by herself?"

Laura said she was *planning* to pick her up, and then they were picking up Carl at work so they could get an early start out of town. She sounded puzzled by the request, and on the edge of being annoyed or inquisitive. Alex couldn't blame her, nor could he tell her she'd told him what he wanted to hear. All he could do was cut it short. "Good," he said. "I'm glad you're doing that. Well, that was all. Good-bye."

The third call was to Meredith, but like Trevisone she wasn't sitting by the phone, waiting. Either she wasn't answering or she wasn't home. Alex left phone number and room number on her machine. "I hope I'll see you tomorrow night," he said. "I love you, warts and all." He stopped, pictured the machine obliviously rotating its spools. "What I mean is, I—warts and all—love you. Suzanne says Terry is related to Natalie, that he taught meditation at the drug-treatment program where Suzanne was a client and Natalie was staff. Maybe *he* knows something. Maybe you could go by and look at his player piano and talk to him about all this."

The thought of Meredith helping to make sense of this puzzle made Alex want to get back in the car and drive south. So did the thought of being in her bed instead of this anonymous, rented one. He hoped Meredith would talk to Terry, if only because that would bring her one step closer to him. Studying with the same teacher was like having the same therapist, the same ideal parent—sharing somebody who understood the tasks and difficulties before you, who displayed convincing confidence even while he made you sweat and work. It was Meredith, in the first place, who had copied Terry's name and phone off a flyer on a campus bulleltin board. She'd brought it home to Alex, who had refused various friends' and acquaintances' suggestions about recovery groups, nutrition classes, and all manner of mind-over-cancer techniques. They reminded him more of high school pep rallies than of anything that might be compatible with the person he actually was. But he'd told Meredith about how much he'd liked watching tai chi performers when he lived on the Coast. "Here," she'd said, "it's in the neighborhood. I'll cover Maria if this is something you'd like to do."

For now, however, Alex was on his own. He'd learned a lot from Lena Hanson, and he ought to use it. He picked up the phone book and found the number he wanted in Canaan, pronounced Cannon, one town to the north. He dialed and counted the rings up to six. He almost hung up, but then somebody answered, somebody he couldn't quite identify as male or female, young or old. He asked for Mr. Jakes. "Hey, Dad," the voice shouted, perhaps let down. "Hey, Dad, it's for you."

The house was fairly new, a split-level, with the bedroom, Alex guessed, in the raised section over the two-car garage. The door knocker, on a tight hinge, didn't make much noise. Probably it operated a switch that rang a bell or chimes. The man who answered wore a blue blazer over a yellow shirt and bluish plaid tie. His face was lined and craggy, with sandy brows over deep sockets, and a nose that had maybe been broken once. The only sag in the face was the beginning of a double chin. Paul Jakes, New Hampshire builder, was built like New Hampshire. If a sizable group of citizens knew he was also a drug wholesaler and pimp, that didn't affect the way he carried himself. Alex knew it would be a mistake to push him too far. But he also knew it would be a mistake to try to pull any wool over his eyes.

"I'm Paul Jakes," the man said. "Come on in." He took Alex's coat, hung it in a closet, and led Alex past the living room where two teenage boys, who were watching television, did not look up. "You mind talking in the kitchen?" Jakes asked. "I've got a little office here at home, too, but it's kind of a mess. Anyway, my wife's on the computer. She's always on it since she went back to school. Can I get you coffee, or a drink?"

"Coffee, please." The evening had started with too much alcohol and it would end with too much caffeine. Alex added, "I hope we can speak frankly. Milk and no sugar, please."

"Here you go," Jakes set Alex's cup before him and settled on the opposite chair with a bottle of Heineken, looking the TV image of domestic contentment and ease. Except that, on the way into the kitchen, he'd closed the swinging door. And now he looked at his watch, as if to say he wanted to get this over with before the kids came in for their midnight snack. And what else didn't Jakes need to put into words? Tied as he was into the local police, he would already know that Alex had been poking around in Scat's condo. Alex decided to voice his suspicions straight out, and also to make as clear as possible what he didn't know. The one thing he was sure of was that Scat or Caroline or both had died because somebody had concluded that they knew too much.

"As I said on the phone," Alex began, "I'm trying to find out, for Caroline Davis's grandmother, about Caroline's death. I think it has something to do with Scat Johnston's death, and something to do with the disappearance of a woman, a prostitute, who went by the name of Nilda or Nell. I think you knew all these people, but I don't have any reason to suspect your involvement in their deaths or disappearances. What I do suspect is that somebody, perhaps you, has been blackmailing Graham Johnston. If I knew what somebody had been holding over him, that might shed some light on what I've been trying to see."

Paul Jakes took a long swallow of Dutch beer and then slammed the bottle on the tabletop. He stood up, turned his back to Alex, walked as far as the closed swinging door, and then turned around again. Color rose into his up-country Yankee face. He said, "Let's get one thing clear here. I was more of a father to that kid than his father ever was. I taught him how to throw a curve ball. I taught him how to chase girls. I taught him how to ski."

All the initiation rites. Alex thought of the two boys in the living room. Had their father taught them what he'd probably taught Scat? How to set up a line to sniff, how to mainline into a vein? Maybe he taught them how to talk about their fears and dreams. Maybe he taught Lowell Townsend Johnston that too.

"The Johnstons and Pepperells have thrown a lot of work your way," Alex said. "Here and in Boston too. You may be a very fine builder, but they didn't have to do that. Was it gratitude for standing in for Scat's father in Cambridge and his mother in France? Or did you have to hold up some kind of mirror to their face?"

"I ought to throw you out of my house," Jakes said. "If I don't, it's because I don't like a fight I don't need. I didn't have anything to do with what happened to Scat or that Davis girl. I didn't even know the Davis girl. Now I'll tell you what you asked. After I make sure you're not wired."

Alex stood and raised his hands over his head. Could Scat have stood, maybe turned his back, and left himself open like this? Alex didn't turn his back. Paul Jakes's hands felt thoroughly for hidden microphones and wires. It was invasive, but it was professional, like Dr. Wagner's laying-on of hands. Alex was glad he had nothing to hide. Then both men sat down on either side of the kitchen table and Paul Jakes took a last swallow of his beer. He set the bottle down on the dark synthetic surface flecked with silver, and put his hands over first his own deep eyes, then his long but not fleshy ears, then the wide mouth above his bony jaw. See no evil, hear no evil, speak no evil, that was what he meant. He said, "The name Johnston makes monkeys out of most people around here. I've got pictures of Scat dealing. Telephoto lens. Not many, just enough. I've got copies of some pictures that he took himself, bedroom shots, him and some working girls. I sent prints of these pictures to Graham, at his office, marked 'Very Personal' on the front. Dates, places, merchandise, and occupations noted on the backs. I grew up poor. I didn't see any reason to stay poor. I let him know about jobs I wanted him to send my way, that's all. He never paid me a dime I didn't earn. Now tell me if he's got a reason to complain."

Alex tried to decide how much farther to go.

"You didn't know Caroline. But you knew Scat well. Do you think he ran into her by accident?"

Paul Jakes shrugged. The shrug made the pretend-brass buttons on his blazer jiggle up and down. His rocky face didn't move. "Search me," he said. The tone made it evident that the irony was calculated. He could search Alex, but Alex had better not try to search him.

"Caroline was apparently worried about somebody named Nell. One of those working girls you mentioned. One who left suddenly. One who Caroline felt sort of disappeared."

"I could look into that," Jakes said slowly. "If something showed me I had to. Got a last name?"

Alex shook his head. "Not for sure. Gonzalez, maybe, Martinez, Fernandez. I could get it."

Jakes looked at his watch again. Alex knew it was time for him to go. "Just one more thing," he said. "Dennis MacDonald and I found a picture at Scat's place. It was the only interesting thing there. It was a picture of a hole in the ice. Pond ice. Somebody mentioned that the two of you used to go ice fishing together." He left it as a statement. He also made it clear he wasn't the only one to know.

For the first time he thought he saw a skitter of fear in Paul Jakes's eyes. Ice fishing. Ice fishermen used mechanical red flags that flapped up if a fish struck the line. So they didn't have to hold onto a cold line by an icy hole in the winter wind. So they could sit by a fire, if they had one, and keep their eyes on a dozen lines at once. It might not have been a warning flag that went up in Jakes's eye. It might have been only a blink. Alex heard the door open behind him, and a woman say, "Oh, excuse me." Out of politeness, he had to turn around. But the door had closed, and when Alex looked back at his host the gaze was steady.

"I hope you appreciate what I told you," Paul Jakes said. "I hope you keep it to yourself, and I hope you don't come back here again."

The road was empty, nothing on it except the dotted white line that glowed in Alex's headlights. Rounding a curve, the headlight beams left the road and caught the four sparkling eyes of a pair of deer standing, alert to the engine's noise, on a farmer's field. Alex slowed to the fifteen-mile-per-hour speed limit in Jericho

Center, shut tight for the evening. He took the turn that led up the river to Pepperell Woods. So Paul Jakes's prosperity was built on photographs of Scat Johnston's misdeeds, and judicious exploitation of Graham Johnston's shame. Now Jakes could afford to forget about supplying the vices of the upper middle class. From now on he could concentrate on building their homes and office parks and fitness centers. Unless he had to worry about the fact that he'd organized the "accidental" death of Caroline Davis. Unless he'd had something to do with the disappearance of a friend of Caroline's named Nell. Alex wondered where Suzanne was right now. And he wondered where Lena Hanson was. He hoped she was driving, too—but in the opposite direction, away. He also hoped he hadn't put himself at the top of Paul Jakes's enemies list.

None of this hoping would do him any good. Instead he tried to make sense of the two photographs that Dennis had pointed out to him. Scat had tucked those two particular pictures in the back of the album—as if he wasn't sure whether to include them or not. As if he couldn't decide either to make them part of his personal history or to consign them to the realm of events suppressed. In one picture was a woman now dead. In the other, the place somebody, or a pair of somebodies, could have disposed of another woman. Alex thought about the fact that the word *disappeared* had acquired a particular meaning in Spanish in recent years. If Caroline's friend Nilda was not living it up in Barcelona or Paris, then Alex was afraid she could be found waterlogged and bloated at the bottom of a frozen New Hampshire pond. He pulled into the parking lot of the Black Pine Inn, thinking he was through for the night. It turned out he had a visitor waiting.

It wasn't much of a lobby, this being the low-budget hotel. No half-timbers or ornate wallpaper, just soft chairs, more painted Sheetrock, a front desk, and a TV. The man at the desk cast a furtive look at Alex, the guest who had attracted questions from the police, but Alex let his own attention sweep past. It came to rest on Dennis MacDonald, sunk deeply into one of the soft chairs, a book lying open on his lap. Dennis shut the book and approached slowly, like a tank.

"I want to know what happened," he began. "Whether you got anywhere with the bartender, and what you learned about Caroline if you did—"

"Why don't I fill you in tomorrow?" Alex interrupted, but then he saw determination in Dennis's shoulders and a certain sly, shy expression about his mouth. "Okay," he relented. He didn't like doing this, but he made his summary purposely short and bitter. He realized that, pleased to have made an ally of the big man who tackled him at the foot of Scat's ladder, he had let his guard down more than he ought. "The short version," he said, "is that the guy did fix me up with somebody, though I promised her I wouldn't tell her name. Caroline applied—or went through the motions of applying—for a job as a prostitute. The job required a trial run with Scat. He liked to take pictures of the trial runs."

Scat, in other words, got to be where Dennis MacDonald had wanted to be but never would. Not in an emotional sense, but the physical fact was there. And suppose Dennis had known it all along? A gentle giant was how he'd been seeing Dennis. But a jealous giant could be quite a different thing.

22

COUSINS

Dennis sat down in the nearest chair, a pale blue one whose upholstery showed the dirt. He opened his book—*A Week on the Concord and Merrimack Rivers*—stared at the page, turned to the page before, turned back, and finally shut the volume with a loud smack. Then he shifted his glance to the desk and then returned it to Alex, his shoulder-length hair wafting like a Dutch boy's as it moved. If the pain was real, Alex thought, it had more to do with loss than it did with jealousy or judgment or sex. No, he corrected himself. The pain *was* real. The question was only whether what Alex had just told him had been new. He tried to put a hand on the big man's arm, but Dennis shook it away.

"Forget it," he said. "I don't want to hear the long version, not right now." Then he said, "I almost forgot to tell you where I put Suzanne."

"Where you put who?" Alex swallowed hard, but tried to appear calm. He said, as if reasoning with forced patience with his daughter, "Dennis, you didn't even tell me you knew Suzanne." He saw Suzanne Lutrello as she'd been on his front porch, arms bound and head pressed against the cold painted floor. He saw her inert body slung easily over one of Dennis's shoulders, her black hair dangling in front and brown boots on limp legs behind. He saw the pond with the hole in it again.

"I don't know her," Dennis said. His pink forehead twisted up as if he felt Alex's alarm but couldn't understand its cause. "I mean, I recognized her when I saw her run out, that's all. I was sitting here, killing time, waiting for you."

"Waiting for me?" Alex said sharply. "I didn't tell you I had a room in this place."

"No, but after I left you at Larabee's I was wondering what was happening. You hadn't told me whether you had a place you were planning to take...whoever it would be...to. I didn't have anything better to do, so I called around. Hell, it ain't exactly difficult to find out where you're registered, once anybody knows you're here in the Woods. So then I called your room here, and a woman answered, so I thought, okay, maybe this is the one Caroline knew. So I came over, and I sat down here, and I put my ass in this chair and waited."

"Uh-huh," said Alex. Dennis sank back farther into the cushion in imitation of waiting. His thoughts went somewhere else. "Uh-huh," Alex said again. Dennis nodded at him and went on. This time he told his story with some interest, and didn't stop.

"About eight-thirty, I saw this girl come out, in a hurry. I wondered about that. Then when she saw me looking at her, she kind of ducked down and hurried out even faster. When she ducked down, lowered her chin into her neck, you know, that's when I recognized her. She used to hang her head like that. She used to be Scat's girl. She looks a lot better now than she did then. It was too much of a coincidence, her being here now, same place as you. I followed her out. She was trying to get through the snow, keeping away from the road, so it didn't take me long to catch up. I said, 'Wait, I want to talk to you,' something like that. She didn't stop till I got close enough to grab her arm. Or I

167

tried to, but she spun around and put her hand out like a traffic cop, a crossing guard, you know? She said, 'Hey. Who the fuck are you?' When we got that straight, she said the cops were coming for her. We talked it over. She said she was tired of running, but she needed to hide out just a few more days. I gave her a sleeping bag and some food and put her in the hikers' cabin up by Contocasset Brook. They'll be looking for her here in the Woods, but nobody will ever think to look for her up there."

Hikers' cabin. Alex remembered a cabin shown on the map of wilderness trails beside the Parker House. "You can drive there?" Alex said.

"No, Ski-doo. I dropped her off, then came back looking for you. She wanted me to tell you where she was. It's a safe place. The safest I could think of anyway." He looked at Alex expectantly. His thumb rubbed back and forth along the spine of Henry David Thoreau's book.

And in the meantime, Alex thought, I'd come back and talked on the phone, and then gone off to Paul Jakes's place. It did fit. Anyway, he couldn't come up with a reason Dennis would invent such a long song and dance. "The longer this goes on," he said, "the more I think someplace safe would be the county jail. I guess she told you, somebody besides the cops has been after her too."

"Yeah, she told me that. Somebody who could have set up Caroline for Scat to run over, and then killed Scat to keep him from maybe going to the cops."

"Maybe," Alex said. "Either it's that, or that's what somebody wants me to think. Listen, Dennis, how far is it from that lunch cabin to where Suzanne is, if I want to go out there myself on skis tomorrow?"

"Let's see, from Pamela's place, you mean? That's not how I went, they got that gate to keep any but their own vehicles off the trail network. I went the back way, old road into the woods. Anyway, the bridge is out, but I guess you could get across on foot. Oh, I guess it's about three miles, not too far, something like that." Dennis lifted himself out of the soft blue chair. "Let me know if you want me to run you out there, or anything."

"Thanks," Alex said. "And thanks for helping Suzanne." It was hard not to trust Dennis MacDonald, hard not to settle back into the idea that both cold-blooded violence and vengeance

168

were foreign to him. "One more question, though. Did Caroline have a friend that you know about, who went by the name of Nilda or Nell?"

"Nell. Yeah. Puerto Rican girl. Little, kind of sweet, talked a lot."

"What did she talk about?"

"Oh, I don't know. This and that. Chatter. Some people like to fill up the silence. Other people don't care." Dennis pursed his lips and lapsed into a brooding examination of the space above Alex's head. He sighed and didn't fill up the silence himself.

"Was she a good friend of Caroline's?" Alex asked him. "Did she come visit? Do you know whether she's still around?"

"No, she split, about a month ago, I guess. She didn't come around my place—it was more like Caroline used to go visit her. She lived in town, in Jericho. There's a few apartments there, over the stores. Those are about the only cheap places you can get."

"Did Caroline say anything about her leaving?"

"She said it was too bad, I guess."

"She didn't confide in you about any suspicions..."

Dennis shifted his bulk in the cushioned chair. "We got along," he said. "I didn't claim she was in the habit of confiding things to me. What do you mean, suspicions?"

"Do you know where Nell worked?"

"I think she worked in rentals or something, over at the mountain. Though I don't remember ever seeing her there. You're telling me that's not really what she did? You're telling me she made her living on her back?"

"Yes. She worked for Scat, and for Paul Jakes. And Caroline was suspicious about the way she disappeared."

"She should have told me," Dennis said. "She always thought she could get along without other people's help."

Alex dreamed he was in the pond. It wasn't cold, but it was dark. He swam in scuba gear. The tanks were heavy, but he wore flippers, huge flippers, that waved on his feet like tropical sea fans. The flippers propelled him steadily forward and down. His flashlight, a long one, held four D-cells like the young local cop's. It illuminated a narrow shaft of water ahead. It was like the light sabers carried by the Jedi Knights. He knew this, in the dream, though he hadn't thought of Jedi Knights since Maria outgrew her *Star Wars* fascination long ago. Use the Force, something told him, but he told himself not to be silly. He used the flippers and knew he was getting close to the bottom of the pond. He rolled over, pointing the beam of light up. It drifted away, like a slow harpoon. It must have bounced off the underside of the ice because after a while it came back.

Now the light went past him, downward, and he followed it down. He knew he was wearing a wetsuit because he grew hotter and hotter inside it. He saw his arms outstretched, rubbery and black. He wanted to get to the bottom, where he would be able to take the suit off. Above him he could hear noises—high-pitched noises, like whale calls. He knew they were the echoes of somebody walking on the ice. Now he wasn't swimming in the pond anymore. He was running down the street where Meredith lived. All of a sudden he knew why she hadn't answered her phone. He woke in a sweat and grabbed for the source of the high-pitched noise.

"Alex?"

It was her voice. "Alex?" it said again. He must not have said anything yet. He sat up and pressed the receiver tighter to his ear.

"Oh. Oh. Yeah," he said. "Hi. I was asleep."

"I hope you were. It's three A.M."

"It is? Where are you?"

"Downstairs."

"Downstairs where?"

"Downstairs here. I didn't want to wake the whole place up banging on your door." Pause. "I have to tell you something."

"Yeah. I love you."

"You're getting repetitive. I know, warts and all." Pause. "It's about Natalie." Pause. "I talked to Terry, as you asked. I didn't look at his piano. I phoned him when I got home and got your message, tonight."

"Yeah." Alex's head began to clear. Terry would have had a hard time answering Meredith's questions with questions. Meredith was a teacher. She was a professional at the Zen/Socratic game.

"They are cousins, but he says he had barely spoken to her in years. Also, he never taught anything at the place where she works. But she rang him up Monday to ask him questions about you."

Alex shook his head, remembering the beam of light that glided through the dark water of the pond. He wanted it back. He wanted to point with it, to illuminate Natalie's white lies, minor lies that didn't make any sense. "By the way," Meredith continued, "Sarah Greenwood confirms that they did write those papers. It was her impression they already knew each other, and chose together to write about the same thing. It was easier, and also they enjoyed the stir their family stories produced in the class."

"Wait a minute." Alex gripped the receiver, an awkward device, not like the smooth flippers or the narrow beam of light. "Did Terry remember *when* she called? Did she tell him *why* she wanted to know all about me?"

"I asked him that, of course." Meredith sounded put out. Alex remembered she had just driven up here in the middle of the night and must have canceled the classes she was due to teach a few hours from now. She was standing in the unfriendly lobby downstairs. "Alex," she said, "why are we talking on the phone?"

"I don't know." He laughed. "You called me."

He heard Meredith laugh, too, before she hung up. He was happy he could make her laugh, whatever the hell else was happening. He didn't get dressed, just went to unlock the door.

In the morning they lingered over complimentary coffee and donuts. No one but the two of them and Dennis knew where Suzanne was. Any number of people, from Natalie to Paul Jakes to Trevisone, might try to reach Alex, and if they did they might leave him wiser than before. Also it was warm and cozy in here, while outside there was a gray, overcast sky and a wind that whipped the branches and made them look mean. Later, Alex was sorry to have lingered.

Meredith, though she had left in something of a hurry at midnight, had not forgotten to bring her skis from home. She had come up early, she explained, because she had gotten over being mad and she wanted to tell Alex in person what she had found out: on Monday, the day Scat Johnston died, Natalie had called her cousin Terry, out of the blue, to ask him to tell her everything he knew about Alex. She had not told her reason,

171

only said it was an emergency, and a secret, and he was not to tell Alex, not yet. Family ties had prevailed, though Terry had felt uneasy. He had tried to remember, for Meredith, just what he told Natalie: that Alex was impetuous but logical, he thought. Well-enough coordinated, but more given to play in his mind than in his body.

"Play!" Alex interrupted.

"He began a long speech about discipline and play being two sides of the same coin. I asked whether Natalie hadn't been searching for something more factual. Then he admitted to having recounted what little he knew about your disease, and some boasting you seem to have done about violent deaths and damsels in distress in your past."

"I didn't boast," Alex said. "We were talking about control, being in control of a situation, an opponent, or yourself. I didn't feel I had anything to boast about."

"No," Meredith relented. "My interpretation, withdrawn. In any case, Natalie already seemed to know something about it. I think maybe Maria had been boasting to Suzanne."

"Do you know what time this happened, this phone call?"

"I asked when she had called him, exactly. He couldn't remember, or wouldn't. He was working on his jewelry, at home, and he was getting hungry, he remembers that. So it was before he ate dinner, but his dinner hour isn't regular, I don't suppose."

"In other words, we don't know whether it was before or after Suzanne called to invite you for that drink?"

"Before Natalie appeared in the restaurant, probably, at least. Before she came to your house to explain herself to—supposedly—me. All in all, I have to think it demonstrates that your interest—not mine—was what Natalie wanted. Do you know for a fact that the person who called your shop, and invited me for that drink, was truly Suzanne?"

"I hardly knew her voice. I assumed it was her. You think..."

"I think it would be a good idea to lay everything you know, including this, in front of Suzanne. And tell her you want her to tell you, again, everything that happened from last weekend until you found her on your porch."

"Final exam," Alex said. "Please put forward a theory that is consistent with and provides a context for the following unassailable facts. Come with me, Professor?"

"Yes," Meredith answered. "That's why I'm here. It may be that you were right after all—that you didn't choose this job, it chose you."

After breakfast, the first thing they needed to do was put Alex's skis on Meredith's car. That's what they were doing when Graham Johnston's roly-poly figure emerged from a sleek gray Porsche. The raw wind made his cheeks a chalky red and drew small tears from the ends of his eyes. His head bobbed angrily where it emerged from an overcoat with a deep fur collar.

"You brought a murderer up here," Johnston said in a shaky voice. "Believe me, you'll go to jail for that." He tried to look around Alex, as if to assure himself Suzanne was not crouched somewhere on the floor of the car.

"You've been paying blackmail for years," Alex parried. He wanted to kick in the door of the Porsche, but settled for paying back the verbal assault in kind. "Did you tell that to the police? Did you tell them everything they need to know to find out all about your son's death?" As he spoke, he leaned a little to his left to block the man's view.

"Who told you that?" Johnston demanded. He raised one chubby gloved hand, as if to threaten, and then thought better of it and instead balled both hands in the pockets of his woolen overcoat, waiting.

"I'm sick of your family," Alex heard himself say. "I'm sick of all of you threatening and bullying and covering up. Tell Trevisone we'll have Suzanne back by this afternoon. Tell him he can come get her then. And tell him we'll give him the whole story, not just the part you wanted him to know." He turned his back on Johnston and saw that Meredith had finished with the skis. He got in the passenger seat and slammed the door. As Meredith drove out of the lot, Alex could see in the rearview mirror that Johnston's Porsche was following along behind. In fact, it tailgated them ostentatiously as far as the cross-country center. "Don't provoke him," Meredith said. "Remember, what we want is time to talk with Suzanne."

Once they got out of the car again, Graham Johnston proved easy enough to leave behind. Alex and Meredith put on their skis, longer and sleeker than the Porsche. Meredith set out into the wind, taking long, regular glides the way a practiced swimmer cuts through the water with slow, efficient strokes. Alex watched her forge ahead, her dark red hair streaming from beneath a red knitted cap. He saw her stop and turn to look back, past him, and he turned to see Johnston repeat his earlier pose, hands jammed into overcoat pockets like a football coach stranded on the sidelines.

Was this the way he kept a watchful eye on contractors and construction workers, Alex wondered—with a baleful glance as they fought winter cold or summer heat to turn his drawings and his capital into monuments to commerce or playhouses for the commercial class? He had something in common with those ship captains facing the wind on the quarterdeck, after all. Don't understimate the man, Alex told himself. Wielding power is something he understands better than you.

"Let me talk to Pamela," Meredith said. They were skiing side by side on the straight section of trail going up the second creek. The lunch cabin was in sight, smoke curling from its stovepipe, Pamela Parker obviously at work. They had decided to stop, briefly, to gather a few more unassailable facts. "I think she'll hear it more easily from me."

"What? You're going to tell her you think she was in love with Caroline?"

"I'm going to ask her to consider whether that's why she's tried to shut the book on Caroline so soon."

That did make sense, Alex agreed. He also thought that, sooner or later, Pam and Dennis ought to share with each other the feelings about Caroline that neither of them seemed to have shared with anybody else. Right now it wouldn't do for any conversation to go on too long. It had been stupid and childish, he now saw, to tell Graham Johnston they were going off to collect Suzanne. If Johnston was here already, would Trevisone be far behind? It wouldn't help for Suzanne to get busted before he and Meredith were done.

Gliding to a stop in front of the cabin, Alex felt sweat dripping down his back. The skiing had kept him not just warm but overheated. Lucky to be stopping and resting inside, he thought, rather than letting the sweat turn chilly in the cold wind.

In the cabin it was steamy and a bit dank. There were no customers yet. Pam looked up from a magazine laid flat on the plywood counter. Alex loitered while Meredith took her by the hand and sat her at one of the picnic tables—like mother to daughter, certainly woman to woman. Alex could see only Pamela's broad back and her long thick braid of hair, but he tried to probe through this to Caroline's friend, to an individual with a history, whatever it was. The first time here he'd seen only the brick wall she'd put up, and the Swedish-travel-poster farm girl whom she'd somehow adopted, or fallen into, as a disguise.

Over Pam's shoulder, Meredith's gaze was level, her cheeks and mouth relaxed, easy, not rushing to hammer home a point. She was not impatient to talk when listening was the necessary thing. That was what made her a good teacher, Alex thought. Of course, she was considerably less patient when off duty—which was fine with Alex, because he did not like to be handled. He preferred sparks to lubrication as a way to make the world go round.

Soon Meredith beckoned him over. He sat next to her, facing Pam.

"I've explained," Meredith said, "that you think Caroline may have been into sex for pay, and that she certainly had friends who were. Pam says Caroline told her about the friends, but she doesn't think what Caroline herself did is anybody's business unless it's crucial to understanding her death."

"I respect that," Alex said. "What I want to know is, did Caroline ever tell you she was concerned about the disappearance of a woman named Nilda or Nell?"

"She didn't disappear. She went on vacation. Caroline even got a letter from her, from Spain. It said she was going to Paris next." Pam laughed, softly, the corners of her mouth turning down in a self-deprecating way. "She made money a lot faster than I do tending this kingdom here. Caroline—you have to understand, Caroline could be so obtuse, but she had a very active mind. Caroline said Nell had a kid, but she didn't have custody. Most people around here didn't know that. She said Nell was saving her money so she could get the kid back. She wouldn't go off to Europe like that."

"What did you think?"

"Caroline's logic seemed pretty farfetched to me. Maybe she gave up, decided to live for herself, I said. I mean, first, she had all these men living through her, through her body, like she herself wasn't even there. Then she was trying to live through this kid, who wasn't really there either. Anyway, Caroline found Nell so interesting I thought maybe she was just pining after her, coming up with reasons Nell wouldn't have abandoned *her* the way she did. Then Caroline started getting really crazy ideas." She looked at Meredith, who nodded. "Or that's what I thought, anyway. She decided Nell had been killed."

"Did she have any proof, any evidence?"

"I'm not sure. She told me she did, but just circumstantial. She said there wouldn't be any proof until spring."

"Spring—what did she mean?"

"She didn't say. Caroline could be very private, very secretive, and she set very high standards for herself. If I didn't believe her, she wasn't going to share any half-baked theories with me."

"And did she say who she suspected of doing this?"

"Uh-uh."

"Well," Alex said, "you remember the picture I showed you. It suggests to me that either she was trying to understand what went on inside Nilda's mind, or else she was trying to get some information out of Scat."

Pam hung her head. Alex didn't like that. He watched her, trying to figure her out. How old was she, anyway? She seemed in suspended animation, anywhere between eighteen and twenty-five. She didn't seem to have done the growing up that Natalie and Suzanne and apparently Caroline had done. Because she was in the closet, even to herself perhaps? Or because something about the Parkers made it unnecessary to grow up? Were the Parkers in the same league as the Johnstons and the Pepperells? Alex saw Maria, at her desk in school, safe now, and safe when Laura would pick her up, and pick up Carl, and leave town for Cape Cod. What would be the thing that would make Maria grow up? And where would she get stuck, and who would unstick her, or would she find that she could do it herself? Finally Meredith said, "Since Caroline died, have you given any more thought to her theory?"

"Some." Pam looked up at last, looked toward the door as if a customer might come in.

"And?"

"I'm sorry I didn't listen. I'm sorry I didn't ask what proof she thought she would have in the spring. Where to look. She must have meant that something...was buried under the snow."

176

"I think we're a little closer than that," Meredith said. "Apparently Caroline spoke with someone who saw Scat and Paul Jakes cutting or standing by a hole in lake ice. They claimed to be ice fishing, or the observer leaped to that assumption on his or her own. Caroline doubted it. Do you have any kind of map that will show us how to get to the hikers' cabin on Contocasset Brook?"

23

ACCIDENTS DO HAPPEN

As Dennis MacDonald had warned, there was no longer a bridge across the brook. Only the uprights high on the banks marked the site of the old bridge swept away by floodwaters. In the streambed the snow hung in irregular drifts, each hollow betraying rushing water beneath, each hump a rock or protruding root. Alex searched upstream for a crossing place while Meredith searched the other way. Alex found a spot where enough sun had penetrated to melt the snow dampened by moist air rising from the brook. He carried his skis in one hand. With the other he held both poles as a kind of walking staff, picking his way carefully from rock to rock above the flow. On a day like this, a soaked foot would soon become frozen and numb.

He found Meredith waiting, because she had discovered a route that allowed her to cross on skis. On this side of the brook the trail widened. The treads of one or many snowmobiles had churned and then packed the snow. From here, according to the map, an old wagon road paralleled the brook as far as the cabin, about a mile upstream. Then the wagon track veered off to the west and descended to a maintained Forest Service road. That would be the way Dennis MacDonald had brought Suzanne in.

Alex climbed awkwardly up the bank, sinking to his knees in

snow. Slowed down, he was able to see the beauty here—the cold and small beauty of the Northeast. The woods might be scrubby, cut down and regrown and cut down and regrown. But there was a timeless, formal wonder in the sight and sound of the snow and ice and brook. Only gradually, as he knelt to refasten his bindings, did Alex became aware of the erosion of this cold calm. Buzz saw, he thought first, but the whine seemed to grow steadily louder. Snowmobile.

"Coming closer?" Meredith asked. Alex listened. He thought it was. Then the noise died. Meredith set off, and Alex followed. After a few minutes the whine recurred. It seemed to get much louder, steadied, and then died away again.

Someone at the cabin, Alex thought. By chance, maybe, but probably not. He speeded up to catch Meredith, and the two of them rushed ahead in a race with each other because they couldn't race what they couldn't see. Leg and arm, leg and arm, Alex concentrated on this, though it wasn't enough to banish the speculations, few of them hopeful, about who the visitor could be, and why. He stopped suddenly, lungs heaving for breath, when he came to an unexpected fork in the road. Meredith caught up quickly. The smaller pathway, to the left, did not appear on the map. That meant this fork was not a trail that anyone kept blazed or cleared, but in winter, with the underbrush covered, it was apparently serviceable enough. Since Wednesday's snowfall, snowmobilers had already used both forks. It was impossible to tell, however, whether a vehicle had come by twenty-four hours or ten minutes ago.

Alex tried to make sense of the motor sounds he'd heard, to plot them in terms of north and south, of valley and hill. He gave up. There were two many contours, too many possibilities to hold in his head. There was nothing to do except push on toward the cabin, hoping Suzanne would still be there, hoping she would still be unharmed, alive. But Meredith pointed down the side trail to something, a small dark blue something on the snow. Alex thought it was just a torn square of plastic, a property marker torn by the wind from the place it had been stapled. Yet it lay there more heavily than a scrap of plastic should. He skied closer, found the hood of a parka, padded, 60-40 cloth, navy blue. He felt the padding, loose rather than spongy—goose-down.

"Suzanne's coat," he said. It sounded like Hansel and Gretel. "I mean, I think it might be her hood. Look, you go on to the cabin, and I'll go this way, okay? Whoever doesn't find her, go the way the other one went."

"Right," Meredith said. "Be careful."

"Yes," Alex said. "You too." He didn't watch her this time, but hurried off. He kicked, and reached ahead with arm and pole, and kicked, and pulled. He hoped he wasn't, or Meredith wasn't, rushing down a wrong road they would regret.

His road wobbled first right, then left, through the evergreens. Then it emerged into a thinner forest, of maples and birches all bare of leaves. Here it straightened out, and Alex could see an orange snowmobile, small and round like a bull's-eye, straight ahead. He slowed and caught his breath, approaching noiselessly, scanning all the whiteness between the trunks of all the trees. He saw nothing and no one, but as he got closer to the snowmobile, he saw it had two parts, the machine itself and a trailing sled. He also found deep footprints, legprints, leaving the trail. He followed these tracks into the soft snow, between the bare trees.

The tracks did not go straight into the woods, perpendicular to the trail. Instead they followed a curving path, as if the walker or walkers were intent on making a semicircular tour. The trees were widely enough spaced to allow for skis, but their branches tore at Alex's coat and beard. The branches made brittle scraping sounds, sometimes cracking as he pushed them aside. Still he saw nothing that didn't belong.

Until at last he did: two foreign colors, silver and blue. The silver was metallic, synthetic, not a dull gray or whitish hue of bark. The blue was dark, navy. Alex skied closer, crouched low, feet flat on his skis. He stopped and held the solid trunk of a maple for balance. The two colored figures were about fifty feet ahead. They were stationary, not struggling through the snow anymore.

Suzanne stood facing his way but not seeing him. A scarf was tied around her mouth to make a gag. The other figure, the silver one, had its back turned. It seemed like a robot, an alien, in its high-tech coveralls, silver with orange stripes, topped by a hood with the colors reversed. Dennis had a snowmobile, Alex knew this, but the figure did not seem big enough to be Dennis. Whoever it was turned sideways to place a rifle—no, it was a shotgun—to place a big shotgun stock-down in the snow. The gun was out of Suzanne's reach, but close to the silver figure's hand. Now the robot bent to pick up something else, a gas can, one of those flat-sided, five-gallon gas cans you strap to the back of a jeep. How the hell had they carried it this far, Alex wondered, another thirty-forty pounds along with the gun? Maybe Suzanne had been forced to carry it. That wasn't fair, with her weakened shoulder. Carrying forty pounds through the snow could ruin the shoulder for good.

Alex didn't even have time to snort at the incongruity of his thought. The silvered arms lifted the can and methodically splashed its contents over Suzanne's head and face and clothes. There was nothing for him to do but yell. Maybe a sudden sound, a scream in the forest, could stop the snowmobiler in the act of lighting the match, of snapping the lighter. A stench of burning flesh came to Alex, but it came from inside, from nightmare, not yet from Suzanne Lutrello here in the New Hampshire woods. The sound seemed to take forever to issue from Alex's throat.

Just as the yell was about to come out, Alex strangled it. Because there was no match, and now the snowmobiler was pushing Suzanne down in the snow, rolling her around in the white dampness. And as he did so he turned around and, flushed from his exertions, pulled the hood from his head. Graham Johnston. Suzanne by Sunday, Scat's father had demanded, and here it was Friday and he had what he wanted. But what was he doing? He retrieved the gun and pointed it at Suzanne, who sat up and raised her arms, wrists together, in obedience to a command. He put the gun down again, carefully placed, and began to tie her hands in front of her. When that was done he tied her legs at the ankles too. Then he pushed her flat again, rolled her facedown, and kicked her one, two, three times in the ribs. Again Alex wanted to yell, but he was stopped by the fact of the shotgun, and by the fact that he did not understand what was going on. He watched Johnston pick up the empty gas can and shake out the last drops onto Suzanne's motionless form. Then the father looked around carefully, studying the snow where he'd been doing his work. Apparently satisfied, he turned his back and began walking away.

One minute Johnston's behavior made no sense, and the

next minute it made everything clear. Graham Johnston the architect was putting a design into action. He was building an accidental death, just as he had built one a week ago. What had worked for Caroline might, with boldness and decision, work for Suzanne as well.

It was not the same accident, though. Suzanne's would be a slower and perhaps more terrifying death. The can had been full of water, not gas. Scat's father was staging hypothermia, the accident that every year took the lives of a few unwise or unlucky adventurers in the New England woods.

The plan was diabolical in its thoroughness, Alex saw. There could be only one reason why he'd tied her hands in front rather than in back: he wanted her to succeed in working the rope loose. He counted on her struggle for life, a struggle that would exhaust her but would result in her ending up free of bonds. Then she would stagger, disoriented by lack of oxygen, slowly making her way to nowhere through the clinging deep snow. At last she'd quit, and then she'd lie down and go into a peaceful, endless sleep. If the murderer was lucky, if his victim wasn't found for a few days, winter would send a new blizzard to cover all tracks.

Cover his tracks, that was the design, and it had been the design before as well. Paul and Scat had killed Nilda, apparently, though Alex had no idea why. Caroline had discovered this, but her evidence, so far, had been circumstantial. Scat had run to Dad, and Dad had determined that Caroline had to die. A perfect accidental death, no witnesses, no proof to the contrary, only Scat had not been able to keep it secret. He had talked to Suzanne, and she could testify as to what he had said. That was why Graham Johnston wanted her. And somehow he had found her, surprised her at the cabin, and brought her here, probably trussed up in the sled.

Caroline might have died quickly—a sudden attack, unexpected, when she thought they were just sitting down to talk. But Suzanne would understand everything that was coming. It would all be so clear to her, right now, as she lay chilled and half choked from the gag and the snow. She would understand, and she would know she had no choice but to make the plan work.

Alex crouched on his skis, his knees and ankles cramped, aching to be in motion, to let Suzanne know that she wasn't alone. He wanted her to know that however she'd contrived to leave her hood as a marker, snagging it on a branch or whatever she had done, it could still save her life. He wanted to cut her loose from her bonds, to peel off the soaked and useless coat, to wrap her up in his own so her temperature would not plummet as Johnston had planned. But he didn't move. He knew he would only have one chance. He knew he had to take into account time, and surprise, and his skis, and the snowmobile, and the gun. Those were the parts, the tools at hand. Somehow he had to fashion them into something that would work. He had to do it before Graham Johnston got back to the snowmobile and saw ski tracks, because at that point surprise would be gone.

He held his position, waiting to see which way Johnston would go. The best thing would be to surprise him and get possession of the gun. Then he could get the snowmobile and drive Suzanne to the cabin, which would be warm from the fire she had left. The worst thing, though, would be to try and fail. That would leave Johnston in possession of both weapon and transportation.

To Alex's relief, the man did not retrace his steps the way he and Alex had both come. Instead he continued the semicircle he and Suzanne had begun. Meticulous to the last detail, he wanted anyone traveling the trail before the next snow to see footsteps going into the woods and footsteps coming out. So Alex turned his back to Suzanne and skied toward the snowmobile. Did the damn things have keys, he wanted to know. If they did, the cautious bastard probably had the key in his pocket. That meant extras precious minutes spent hot-wiring the switch. Battery to coil, and battery to starter, too, if Graham Johnston, fearing heart attack, had paid extra for a starter motor instead of a manual cord.

At least Johnston's circling put his back to Alex for now. Alex skied in his own tracks, bending low under branches, letting them scratch him but careful they did not break with a crack. He left his skis at the edge of the woods and plunged through to the far side of the snowmobile. With luck, even if he was still at work, the machine would shield him when Johnston emerged farther down the trail.

As he expected, there was a key-operated starter switch, and no key. However, his heart rose at the sight of a toolbox, locked but no doubt forceable with his penknife, built into the floor. On a hunch, he slashed at the padded vinyl dashboard around the key switch first. The brittle synthetics parted easily under his knife blade. He didn't even need tools or jumper wire now. He ripped out the leads and studied the controls of the machine: a throttle on one handlebar, and a brake lever on the other. Was it in neutral, he needed to know, but he saw no sign of gearshift or clutch. He peeked up through the windscreen and saw Graham Johnston just making his way out of the woods. He did not want to start the engine in gear, noisily, only to have it stall out. Then the shotgun would become more important than this machine. *Varidrive*, a voice shouted from some forgotten corner of his brain.

Varidrive, that's what it would have—a conical drive pulley activated by a centrifugal clutch. Someone had told him about this, sometime, or he'd read a manual when he had nothing better to do. Hans probably had kept one lying around the shop. The snowmobile would be in neutral, automatically, at idle; the pulley would engage, and the gearing would change as the engine picked up speed. With his knife, Alex cut off sections of woolen glove liner, using one for protection as he twisted the ignition and battery leads together. He touched the starter lead to the juice and the engine sputtered, then caught. He tied the cloth around the twisted wires for insulation. He did not want a short to cause the engine to quit while he was in Graham Johnston's sights. He grabbed both handlebars, advanced the throttle with his thumb, and suddenly was roaring down the trail. Johnston, in his silver robot suit, looked up. He tried to duck back into the woods, and fell wallowing in snow in his haste.

Alex bore down, watching Johnston recover and rise to a sitting position, watching the barrel of the shotgun come up. He hung on to the handlebars while dropping to his knees behind the windscreen. The gunpowder boom clashed with the engine's roar. Alex closed his eyes instinctively, and then fought to regain control of the machine. He thought he heard pieces of shot thud off the plastic screen. He opened his eyes, saw Johnston eject the shell, fire again, but blindly, and then suddenly turn and try to run out of the way. Just as suddenly,

Alex felt the snowmobile lurch over a drift and tilt forty-five degrees.

The shotgun reports still echoed in his brain. His movements felt slow-motion, as tree trunks went sideways and whizzed by. He found himself squeezing the brake lever and wrenching the handlebars in an effort to straighten out the steering skis. Then he was lying on his side in the snow. He jumped, panic-stricken, but the shotgun lay two yards in front of him. Graham Johnston was crawling off, a silver armadillo, his fat behind waving in the air. The snowmobile rested sideways, with its treads up against one birch and its skis snapped off against another.

He picked up the gun, which felt heavy in his hand. It was a twelve-gauge with a long barrel and pump action—for ducks or trapshooting, not for carrying long distances through the woods. Alex pumped in a third shell, calling for Johnston to stop running. He aimed toward the treetops and fired. Johnston did not stop. Alex checked the ejected shell. Number-8 shot was not going to do much damage to a human outside of close range. Alex took off after the gun's owner, the weight of the weapon costing him some of his advantage in youth and size and strength. Suzanne would be shivering, straining at her bonds, hearing the gunshots and hoping they meant help. Alex knew he should give up this chase. It only sapped his energy, and cost minutes that Suzanne might not have.

Yet he struggled through the deep snow, he didn't know why, at last tackling the fleeing man from behind. He felt in the pockets of the silver suit until he found the coil of nylon cord. He told Johnston to cooperate if he didn't want to be left with a leg full of birdshot to bleed and freeze. Quickly he tied the legs together and the hands behind the man's back. Then he turned to stare at the wrecked snowmobile, now many yards behind.

One idea came to him, something he'd heard once with half an ear on a radio talk show. The show must have been about survival tips, or blizzards. Some expert had explained that to survive while waiting to be rescued from a stranded car, you should soak one of the seats in engine oil and light it. You'd have a kind of super-candle, a miniature industrial fire, that would keep you warm enough if you kept close.

Only halfway back to the snowmobile did Alex's thoughts

184

settle enough for him to see why this admirable plan wouldn't work. The vehicle ran on a two-cycle engine, like a lawnmower. The oil would be mixed, at a low ratio, with the gas. There wouldn't be any oil reservoir to drain. The combined fuel would burn hot but fast.

Still he kept going and, when he got there, forced the toolbox latch with his knife. He found a hammer and a screwdriver, laid them aside, and stripped all the upholstery from both driver's seat and sled, like a whaler stripping blubber from his kill. Then he pounded the screwdriver into the gas tank. The fuel flowed onto his pile of foam and fabric. At last he stuffed the soaking mess inside his jacket like a great belly. It would take him a long time to flounder through the snow like this, but the stuff ought to stay flammable. When he got there, he would have to gather wood before lighting the mess up. A long time, too long, was going to pass before Suzanne got warm.

"Suzanne," he cried. "Hang on. Fire is on its way."

A voice answered, though not Suzanne's. He had never been happier to hear Meredith call out his name.

24

CONFESSION

When Alex arrived at last with his prisoner, the air smelled of industry and campfire at once. The flames were bright orange and the smoke a deep black. Meredith sat on Alex's jacket, spread as a groundcloth on top of the snow. The sodden goosedown coat from the Burlington Mall lay useless beside it. Meredith cradled Suzanne, wrapped in her own parka, on her lap. Alex could see steam beginning to rise from Suzanne's jeans.

"She's stopped shivering," Meredith said. "We ought to get some hot liquid into her, but I think she's going to be all right.

Here, you take her. I'll gather some more wood, and then I'll go get help."

Alex sat, glad to get close to the warmth himself, and helped Meredith to shift Suzanne onto his lap. He kept his grip on the shotgun, though. "Over there," he told Graham Johnston. He pointed to the opposite side of the fire. Alex wanted Scat's father within conversational distance, but not within a hand's grasp of his gun. None of this would have accomplished anything unless he talked while still at his most vulnerable.

"Dead standing wood is the best," he reminded Meredith. She had told him about vacations spent tramping in Wales years before, but Alex didn't know what kind of wilderness they had in Wales, or how much roughing it the English did when they tramped. Still, the fire she had built was throwing out a lot of heat. In fact, it was melting the snow beneath it like a nuclear reactor out of control. The minor meltdown had formed a white fire pit. Additional branches, nice big ones, would fit easily over the top. If a kettle and leaves miraculously appeared, they could boil up a pot of tea. When she returned with a new load of branches, Alex asked Meredith to tie up Johnston's legs again. She bound them with grim efficiency. Then she knelt by Alex, kissed him quickly on the cheek where his beard ended, and talked quietly into his ear.

"I'll be back with whoever I can find as quickly as I can," she said, "but there's something you should know. Suzanne thought she was imagining me. She might have hoped you would come, or Natalie, or even the police, but she didn't think I was real. That's why she told me now, trusted me with the truth." Suzanne moved her head up and down, in assent. Alex nodded too, but said nothing, because he didn't know what to say.

He had known this—guessed anyway—possibly since Meredith's arrival the night before, and certainly once he saw the identity of the man in the silver suit. But he hadn't wanted to let the knowledge into his consciousness, and he didn't want to now. The woman on his lap had killed, but he wanted to focus on the man across the flames, the man who had fired at him, who had crafted the plan to leave Suzanne to find her own cold and lonely death. He watched Meredith ski off, weaving between the bare tree trunks. When Meredith disappeared, he asked Suzanne whether she was warm enough. He had heard that hypothermia

186

victims tended to slur their words, and he wanted to hear her speak. She nodded once more, that was all. "At this range," he said to Graham Johnston, "the spread of the shot is a pattern about the size of your heart." He leveled the gun at its owner and added, "Tell me how you and Scat killed Caroline Davis— and why."

"A nice girl could have saved him," Graham Johnston declared. His gloved hands seemed to be squeezing something round, like a ball, that wasn't there. "A nice girl could have given him a proper sense of himself."

"Caroline?" Alex started to ask, but Johnston stopped what he'd been doing with his hands and instead picked a broken branch from the snow and pointed through the smoke. Alex felt Suzanne stiffen, and understood whom he was talking about then.

"She let him destroy himself," Johnston said. "She had no strength, no background, no backbone. And then when she saw where he was headed, she ran off like a rat leaving a ship."

In the kitchen on Brattle Street, Alex had noticed a dissociation between Johnston's tone and his words. That break, that lack of connection, was even stronger now. Close your eyes and let him drone on, Alex thought, and we might be in a boardroom. He might be lecturing about plans on an easel, a pointer the only weapon those hands had ever held. Open your eyes and hear the words, though, and the hatred could cut like the fire through snow and frozen ground to the molten core of the earth.

"When she heard about the Davis girl, oh yes, she came running. No, not running. I'd say swimming, cruising toward the scent of blood like a shark. And then she murdered him."

"I asked about Caroline Davis," Alex said coldly. He kept the shotgun barrel level and his finger not far from the trigger. He thought that Johnston truly did not like to be seen as a bloodthirsty bastard. Possibly he was grateful, right now, for a chance to explain. Probably he was telling the truth as he saw it. Alex had no intention of setting off the powder, of propelling birdshot into his heart. He did want Johnston's confession to continue flowing across the crackling fire and the black smoke in these winter woods.

"The Davis girl was a troublemaker, making trouble was in

her blood. Like you, she stuck her nose in something that had nothing to do with her. Why was it her business, the death of a Puerto Rican whore? It was my business because I was trying to save my son."

"How did you know Caroline was investigating Nilda's disappearance? Did Scat come to you when he found that out?"

"*She* came to me, just as you did. She told me Scat and Paul Jakes had murdered this Fernandez woman, one of the string that worked for them. She said she was coming to me before she went to the police. Her attitude was superior, condescending even. She didn't want money, opportunity, the way Paul did. She wanted justice, she did. She meant she wanted us disgraced, shamed. She said she thought I ought to know, I ought to try to persuade Scat to turn state's evidence. The fact is she had no proof, I could see that, she had no proof, not yet. She held out to me the hope that if Scat talked to the police, the crime would turn out really to have been Paul's."

"But you didn't believe it." Suzanne's voice came out clear, if thin. She was going to be okay. "You never had any faith in him, never showed any faith in him at all. You don't even know that he protected you, protected you and your reputation, God knows why, right down till the end. He wouldn't tell me who it was that put the body in the road."

Johnston rocked as if trying to get to his feet, to get at her despite the shotgun and the fire and the cord around his legs. He sank back into the snow, but again made a circle with his hands, and squeezed. Had he strangled Caroline Davis, cut off her air with those soft, fleshy hands? "It was all my doing," he said to Alex. "Not my boy's. I told him Paul was going to meet with an automobile accident. I showed him the pictures Paul had been holding over me. I showed him how Paul had been playing with him, using him all these years. Perhaps I did lack faith. Without a personal motive, hatred, I feared he wouldn't have the strength for what needed to be done."

"And then he found out Caroline was going to be the victim, not Paul?" Alex asked. He was puzzled, and he felt Suzanne shiver, and in his puzzlement and concern he put the stock of the gun into the snow and reached to put more branches across the flames. Johnston answered regardless. Once started, he wasn't going to stop.

"Only when he helped me get her out of my car and lay her

there on the road. She was already dead then, at least I think she was. She was stupid to let me catch her the way I did. The young are always too trusting. Scat turned to me with a wild face, and he said to me, 'Why her?'"

A lost look, an expression of sadness, finally came over Graham Johnston's face—as if the cherub had found himself out past curfew, locked for the night outside of heaven, amid wind and snow and flame. "I said, 'Scatty, she's been spying on you. She has proof you and Paul killed that other girl and dumped her body in the pond. He said—I'll always hear it—he said, 'Oh, Dad, you ultimate fuck-up, Nell killed herself. Paul has the goddamn suicide note, if anybody needs any proof. All we did was bury her, hush it up. We got rid of her body so nobody would know.'

"It was too late then, though, wasn't it?" Graham Johnston went on, and now he spread his hands, palms up in appeal, and there was almost a note of pleading in his voice. "My boy might have argued then, but he didn't, he did what he was told. In spite of everything, I think he appreciated that I had done this, even if mistakenly, for him."

It was all making sense to Alex, a depressingly senseless kind of sense. He reached for another branch, to poke at the fire, to make the mass of half-burned wood more compact so he could lay more branches across the top before the coals at the bottom grew cold. Suddenly Suzanne was off his lap, out of his reach, down on her right knee in the snow. She had the butt of the shotgun up against her right shoulder, her good shoulder, and the barrel in her left hand, propped by the elbow on her upraised left knee. She looked like a painting, a soldier taking aim during a bleak winter's campaign.

Alex stood on one leg and tried to kick at the barrel before her trigger finger could move. The exploding shell thundered as he fell. When the echo died, he heard rather than saw the last shell being pumped into place. He forced himself up out of the clinging snow. "Don't!" he screamed, but he saw that Suzanne was braced in firing position again. He looked for Graham Johnston, slumped toward the firepit, but Johnston wasn't there. He was three yards off, trying to get farther in a half-crawl, half-slither through the white drifts and the gray and black trunks of the trees. Suzanne's first shot must have gone wide. Alex's kick must have done the job. Now he

189

saw her aim and say something, but whatever it was, he couldn't hear it. Her words were drowned under the sound of a snowmobile, maybe two. She dropped the shotgun and put both hands to her mouth.

Alex stood up slowly, walked warily toward her, then let the gun lie where it had fallen, put his arm around her waist, and led her to sit in front of the fire again. Her face was close to his, the flames crackling close to her blanched cheeks, the light of the fire reflected in her dark eyes. "It's like he's this big, bloodthirsty tick, all swelled up," she said. Her voice came out shaky but urgent. "A big tick that I just wanted to reach out and burn it off the dog. You stopped me, I guess I'm glad. Poor Scat, he was such a bastard, but he learned his ways from that man."

"You did kill Scat?" Alex asked softly.

"I did," she admitted finally. "It started out as self-defense. That story Natalie told you, about Scat wanting to show he was the man, the boss, it really happened, only it happened between Scat and me. Like my letting him fuck me would show he was still in control, it wasn't me trying to lead him to some kind of safety, some kind of peace, but him throwing his weight round all over again...I don't know...I wasn't going through that. He picked up the knife, but you saw me just now, I can't tell you it was only self-defense. Once I had the knife, it was...*I* was the knife, a dagger, rage, I was God. I thought I'd never stop stabbing him, ever, and he was never going to stop pleading and moaning. When I snapped out of it..."

She didn't get to finish the sentence. The snowmobiles roared in like cavalry, like whinnying horses charging and trampling all obstacles underfoot. They didn't stop on the trail, but twisted wildly through the trees. Then both black-jacketed drivers turned down their throttles and jumped from their machines, rifles at the ready in their hands. One of them was the young policeman from Jericho's car number 3. The other was Sergeant Trevisone. "It's all right, Sergeant," Alex called. "Nobody's armed anymore."

Leaving their engines running, the two policemen walked in opposite directions through the snow. The local one took possession of Graham Johnston. Trevisone stood over Alex and Suzanne, staring down fixedly. He said, "Time to hand her over to me."

25

COURTS OF LAW

"**J**esus Christ, Glauberman," Trevisone said Monday morning, looking over Alex's statement again before handing it back for Alex to sign. "You study all this oriental martial arts. Don't they teach you to think inside your opponent's head?"

"Too many opponents," Alex said. "Too many heads. And *you* told him I was in touch with Dennis, right? So after I left him behind, he went to Dennis, claimed he had to find me, life-and-death. Dennis told him I was going to the cabin. I'd already made the mistake of telling him I was going to get Suzanne."

Alex admitted that mistake easily. It had been stupid, but it had also forced Graham Johnston to take a chance. Now Alex got to be the lucky kid, the amateur, and Trevisone got to be the gruff grandfather, the one from *Peter and the Wolf*.

However, Alex understood that all this was beside the point. The important thing Trevisone had said was about the oriental arts. Alex had not tried to shield Suzanne, but he'd done his best to skip lightly over what Natalie had done. So he'd left Terry out of his story. Trevisone wanted to indicate that he hadn't been fooled, that he'd done his own homework in the past few days. Therefore Alex had a further admission to make.

"I got led around by the nose a lot," he said. "Those guys in the dime-store masks I told your man O'Connor about, the way they found me at my shop and again at the hotel? I didn't make them up. But one of them could've been Natalie Cooper, the other could've been Tommy Lutrello. They wanted to keep me moving, keep me involved. The same as Suzanne's story about escaping from the guy with the syringe."

"Yeah," Trevisone agreed. "You swallowed all that. Well, it took guts, the one girl rolling the other down the steps so the

191

bruises would be real. Going ahead with it even when her shoulder popped out."

"Did they have any choice?" Alex asked. "I mean, how deep into the Johnston family's affairs would you have dug on your own?"

Not very deep, was the most likely answer. *It wasn't my job to investigate a homicide in New Hampshire*, Trevisone could say now, but he'd be too proud for that. Maybe, if Suzanne had turned herself in right away, he would have looked into what she claimed Scat had done. Maybe he could have persuaded a colleague in New Hampshire to do so. But most likely not. Instead, it would have been up to Suzanne's lawyer to prepare that kind of defense. Only in the wild claims of Suzanne Lutrello, on trial what for what was indisputably murder, would Caroline Davis's death have been anything but an accident in the eyes of the law.

Trevisone didn't answer. He proceeded as if carrying out a conversation with himself. "They wanted to pin the Johnston kid's murder on whoever turned out to be involved with him in running down the Davis girl. But there wasn't going to be any evidence. I don't see how that was going to work."

"No," Alex agreed. "It probably wasn't." If Caroline's killer had not been Scat's father, though, maybe it would have, who could say? "By the way, that hole in my windshield, that note I gave you? That was really Johnston's work, am I right?"

"Uh-huh. He came in and owned up to that the same day. Embarrassed as all hell, or that's how he seemed. But helping us to do our job, that's what he meant. He hasn't owned up to much else, if you're asking me how he's going to plead."

"No," Alex said, and he imagined himself on a New Hampshire witness stand, under cross-examination: *And could you describe for the court the exact circumstances under which this alleged confession was made by my client?* However, that wasn't what he'd come in today to find out. He waited, and then he asked the question that Trevisone might be willing to answer, the one that had brought him here, in person, rather than submitting the statement through the mail. "What do you think is going to happen to Suzanne?"

Trevisone leaned back in his chair and scanned the small, dusty office—its cluttered bulletin board, its insurance-company calendar, its single window and pale green walls. He stroked his mustache just once, then linked his hands and tried to crack his knuckles, which gave off no sounds. "This is the station house," he told Alex, as if Alex might be lost. "The county courthouse was over by Lechmere, last I heard. Over there, the DA decides about charges and prosecution. A jury decides on matters of fact. A judge decides about matters of law. What do you want me to tell you—who I like if it's Saugus High against Andover Academy, if it's North Cambridge against Brattle Street? She stabbed a guy to death. She could stab another guy. She says it was self-defense. That's the part for a jury to decide. Considering what the jury hears about everything that's supposed to have happened up in New Hampshire before and since . . . yeah, I think the jury'll believe her, now. Whether to bother prosecuting, whether it's involuntary manslaughter or second-degree murder or whatever the hell . . . get your downtown lawyer friend to talk to the DA."

"I will," Alex said. He wondered again about the untold hurts and disappointments in Trevisone's life. He stood up. Was he supposed to just leave or to offer, man-to-man, to shake hands?

"One thing." Trevisone held him with a pointing finger. "Tell me, were you glad when the police showed up to cart the guilty and the wounded away?"

"Yeah. I was glad. And the police were glad to have me to be following, and to find Meredith to tell them which way to go."

Alex left the police station and walked five blocks to Petros's. There was hardly any snow or ice left, but the air was just as cold as the week before. He still felt himself bracing against the climate, against the air that kept him alive. But he brought what was, under the circumstances, the best news. He found Natalie waiting for him. He had invited Meredith, too, but Meredith had replied that this was between him and Natalie, that was all. Natalie went to the counter and ordered, then sat down across the table from him.

"Putting together what Bernie and Trevisone said," Alex told her, "it looks pretty good. Probably a plea bargain and probation." Natalie didn't react. Her skin seemed slack, her eyes dull for the first time. Drained, Alex thought. Used up. She can afford to feel that way now. She waited for the coffee to be served.

"Thank you," she told the waitress. She didn't thank Alex, directly. She just said, "If it will make you feel better, this is your chance to sit here and call me names."

"You're buying," Alex answered. "It's not good manners to bite the hand that feeds. Just tell me why you did it the way you did."

"You've got a daughter. In fact, it was your daughter that planted the seed of the idea." Natalie dropped her eyes, took a long swallow of her coffee. She made a face that probably meant she had burned her mouth. Then her jaw straightened and her eyes got their intensity back. "Suppose Maria got... well, suppose she was the one that got the cancer, and you nursed her through it, back to health, and then somebody, your ex-wife, wanted to take her away. I guess that's not exact. 'Strong analogy, but not quite precise,' that's what Meredith would say. I wasn't her mother, or her mammy—and I wasn't any doctor either, just a counselor. But here was somebody in that place that *I* made the difference to, you understand? And so we were friends, but it wasn't just like friends. Maybe I'm not on top of all my reasons. What I know is that she lost control, like she says, for one bad minute. If I was there, I could've stopped her, but I wasn't there. So what do I do? Sit back and watch her future get grabbed away? What was it going to do to her, to be sent up to Framingham, even a couple years, locked up, treated like shit one more time?"

Old debates about punishment and deterrence floated through Alex's mind, but he brushed them away. As Trevisone said, that was for the judge and jury to decide. "Did it occur to you," he asked Natalie, "that she started out trying to do for Scat what you had already done for her? That the feeling she had to go up there, he needed her—that she was trying to pay you back, to pass on the favor to somebody else?"

"Maybe. She should've picked somebody more deserving, is all I can say. I always had a hard time remembering she really used to be in love with the guy." Natalie went back to her coffee, but sipped slowly and meditatively this time. "Whatever," she said finally. "It ended up by her stabbing him and then running away. She called me right away, at work. We had to figure out something to do. The idea was to get you into it. Number one, for you to find out enough to convince the cops that Scat was a murderer or accessory to murder, so they would go easy on Suzanne. And number two, to get them thinking that maybe whoever else killed Caroline then turned on Scat. Somewhere along in there I got the idea of making it look like this double murderer person was still after Suzanne, trying to make her number three. If *you* believed that, the police might believe you."

Alex didn't like it, but he understood exactly what she meant. In a pinch, you had to fashion something that would work out of the parts at hand. "But even then," he said, "You didn't trust me to do it myself. You were afraid I might find out too much, find out the wrong thing?"

"Well, I didn't want to sit back and wait, leave it to the experts. And a lot of shit we had to play by ear, you know. Suzanne didn't always know what I was feeding you, and I didn't always know about her."

"Uh-huh," Alex said. "How much did you already understand about what happened to Caroline? Before we talked to Lena Hanson, I mean?"

"That Caroline lost her life because of something she knew or guessed. Scat told Suzanne that much, but not the who or the what. What do you kill to cover up? Something that will ruin you or land you in jail, something that nobody else knows. The thing was, lots of people already were aware of most of the things Scat had done. So it had to be something worse, something that couldn't be fixed. That was the direction I wanted to push your thoughts."

"You did that," Alex conceded. "But if you hadn't kept me in the dark, I might not have almost gotten Suzanne killed."

"'Almost don't make it better,' is what my grandmother used to tell me. It doesn't make it worse, either."

Alex let it go. She wasn't going to play contrite child to his grandfather, and he knew it.

In June, Graham Johnston went on trial in the Carroll County courthouse in Ossipee, New Hampshire. He was charged with the murder of Caroline Davis and the attempted murder of Suzanne Lutrello. He pled complete innocence of the first charge, and innocence by reason of temporary insanity to the second.

Rosemarie Davis attended every session of the trial, but Alex drove up only on the day he had to testify himself. He looked out at the crowd, spotting Dennis MacDonald and Pamela Parker, each sitting alone. He wondered again where Lena Hanson was, and what her real name might be. After his testimony, during the noon recess, he sat with Rosemarie on a green wooden bench beneath the Civil War monument outside. She recounted Paul

Jakes's testimony that he and Lowell Johnston had disposed of Nilda Fernandez's body because they did not want their "escort service" to be disrupted by the scandal of her suicide. Rosemarie also told him what more she'd been able to learn about Nilda Fernandez, whose family she had hired a Yellow Pages detective to find.

"She was murdered by hypocrisy," Rosemarie said, "as far as my opinion is concerned. She seems to have felt that now, tainted as she would be in the eyes of any court, she would never regain the custody of her son. I think that may be why she argued so vehemently with Caroline—to assure herself that this taint was not real. Her suicide note said that she would prefer for everyone to think she had simply gone away. So those two men were carrying out her wish, at the same time as their business forced the wish upon her."

Alex asked whether she thought the jury would convict Graham Johnston of her granddaughter's murder.

"I really don't know," Rosemarie said. "I sit there each day and watch their faces—shocked, intrigued, excited, bored. I thought they believed you, today. In my heart I root for a conviction, for my team, for compensation, for an eye for an eye. These are deep feelings, very deep. But I *think* about prevention. Does the verdict matter, will any verdict keep all this from happening again? It may be that the jury's decision matters less than the fact that the story is getting told."

When the trial resumed for the afternoon, Alex did not go back inside. He put on a pair of sunglasses, so as not to meet curious onlookers' eyes. In the sunlight he let his muscles relax, his lungs swell and shrink naturally, his abdomen grow full. Slowly he shifted his weight, turned from his hips, allowed the motions of tai chi to flow outward into his arms and hands. The statue of the Civil War soldier was substantial but lifeless. Alex tried to make himself insubstantial but alive.

What Rosemarie had said comforted him. From the beginning, he had flailed about, off balance, never really rooted, never seeing the parts clearly in a straight line. Much of the damage, which had already been done, was beyond repair. Yet Rosemarie had not hired him to fix anything. She had hired him to find out what happened—to find out what she had been told was unknowable, or known only to the fates that combined to bring about the end of her granddaughter's time. Now it was known to

196

her, the cause of that particular untimely death. That was one less monkey on her back.

Alex kept flowing through the form. He'd progressed since the winter—through Wave Hands in Clouds, and High Pat on Horse, and through the long sequence of kicks that followed. He came to the second Cross-Hands, which marked the halfway point of the tai chi form. Then he tried to sink into his feet as he let his arms float slowly down. He took a few deep breaths, removed his sunglasses, and crossed the grassy common to the place he'd parked his car. The engine started easily, without the choke, and the tachometer showed a nice, even 850 rpm. With proper maintenance, Alex thought, some machines could function well for a reasonably long time.